MW00422873

"A fire," he repeated. He lowered his gaze to the grate. "Mind if I build one?"

"Go right ahead. I was planning to do that right after my bath."

Matt pictured her shedding her robe and sinking into a tub full of bubbles. Damn Gary for having such a woman! If there was anyone who didn't deserve that kind of luck, it was Gary Villard.

He calmed his breathing and said, "Look, Mrs. Villard, I didn't want to interrupt—I mean, if you want to go back to whatever it was you were doing before I rang the bell..."

She seemed to be wrestling with a laugh. "It isn't Mrs. Villard," she said, "it's Ms."

Great, Matt thought, Gary was married to a gorgeous feminist.

"Or Miss, if you prefer," she continued. "I'm Gary's sister."

Gary's sister. Gary's *single* sister! Suddenly Matt wanted to forget what had brought him all this way in the first place.

Dear Reader,

Four more fabulous WOMEN WHO DARE are heading your way!

In May, you'll thrill to the time-travel tale Lynn Erickson spins in *Paradox*. When loan executive Emily Jacoby is catapulted back in time during a train wreck, she is thoroughly unnerved by the fate that awaits her. In 1893, Colorado is a harsh and rugged land. Women's rights have yet to be invented, and Will Dutcher, Emily's reluctant host, is making her question her desire to return to her own time.

In June, you'll be reminded that courage can strike at any age. Our heroine in Peg Sutherland's *Late Bloomer* discovers unplumbed depths at the age of forty. After a lifetime of living for others, she realizes that she wants something for herself—college, a career, a *life*. But when a mysterious stranger drifts into town, she discovers to her shock that she also wants *him!*

Sharon Brondos introduces us to spunky Allison Ford in our July WOMEN WHO DARE title, *The Marriage Ticket*. Allison stands up for what she believes in. And she believes in playing fair. Unfortunately, some of her community's leaders don't have the same scruples, and going head-to-head with them lands her in serious trouble.

You'll never forget Leah Temple, the heroine of August's *Another Woman*, by Margot Dalton. This riveting tale of a wife with her husband's murder on her mind will hold you spellbound . . . and surprised! Don't miss it!

Some of your favorite Superromance authors have also contributed to our spring and summer lineup. Look for books by Pamela Bauer, Debbi Bedford, Dawn Stewardson, Jane Silverwood, Sally Garrett, Bobby Hutchinson and Judith Arnold . . . to name just a few! Some wonderful Superromance reading awaits you!

Marsha Zinberg
Senior Editor

P.S. Don't forget that you can write to your favorite author

c/o Harlequin Reader Service,
P.O. Box 1297
Buffalo, New York
14240 U.S.A.

Flashfire

Judith Arnold

Harlequin Books

TORONTO • NEW YORK • LONDON
AMSTERDAM • PARIS • SYDNEY • HAMBURG
STOCKHOLM • ATHENS • TOKYO • MILAN
MADRID • WARSAW • BUDAPEST • AUCKLAND

Published August 1993

ISBN 0-373-70559-X

FLASHFIRE

Printed in U.S.A.

ABOUT THE AUTHOR

"I was a writer before I could write," says Judith Arnold. After winning a college playwriting contest and receiving a money prize, "it dawned on me that writing didn't have to be something I did on the side." From that moment on, writing was at the *center* of her life.

Now, with more than forty books to her credit, and her last Superromance, *The Woman Downstairs,* nominated by *Romantic Times* as Best Romantic Novel of 1992, she is enjoying the fruits of her labor. But she freely admits that her husband is her greatest inspiration. "Whenever I'm down, he props me up, and the words start flowing once more."

Judith lives in Massachusetts with her husband and two children.

Books by Judith Arnold

HARLEQUIN SUPERROMANCE
460—RAISING THE STAKES
509—THE WOMAN DOWNSTAIRS

HARLEQUIN AMERICAN ROMANCE
449—OPPOSING CAMPS
467—SWEET LIGHT

PROLOGUE

GARY VILLARD STARED at the reflection in the mirror above the dresser and wondered who the hell was staring back. He recognized the sun-bleached hair and sun-darkened skin, the green eyes and freckles. He recognized each and every line that forty-one years of living had etched into the skin above the eyebrows, around the eyelids, framing the lips. He recognized the mouth, the nose, the bone structure, the crooked front tooth, the earring—a small gold *D*—dangling from his left earlobe.

He knew the face. But he was no longer sure whose it was.

"Gary!" Steve's voice came through the closed door. "You up yet?"

"Yeah." He didn't move from the mirror.

"It's after noon."

"I know, I know. I'm up, man."

"Listen, you're not going to believe this," Steve shouted through the door. "They're predicting a snowstorm tonight."

"Yeah?"

"Bet you're glad you're here, huh?"

A humorless smile stretched Gary's lips at Steve's sarcasm. If Gary hadn't taken the red-eye out of Los Angeles last night he could have been enjoying seventy-degree weather right now, driving with the windows down, filling his lungs with balmy, smoggy air, and dreaming about spending the weekend at the beach.

Gary took his friend's comment straight, however. No, he wasn't glad he was here. He wouldn't have been glad to be in L.A., either. He'd screwed up his life, and about the only place he would gladly be at the moment was maybe on a deserted island somewhere where no one could find him. An island miles from shore, miles from Matt Calloway, where he could burrow down and hide until the storm blew over.

Snowstorm. "It's March," he called toward the door. "They've got spring in Massachusetts, haven't they?"

"In bits and pieces, now and then. I've got some warm clothes you can borrow, if you want."

"Yeah, thanks," Gary said curtly, hoping to end the conversation. His throat was dry; his head ached.

He had to be nice to Steve and Marlene. How many friends would put an unexpected, uninvited visitor up on a moment's notice? Gary had phoned from Logan airport at seven in the morning, and Marlene had said sure, come on over. She would be at work all day, but Steve had recently been laid off. His factory manufactured missiles, but since the country didn't need so many missiles these days, Steve would be able to stay home and entertain Gary.

Not that Gary wanted entertainment. Mostly, he told Marlene, he wanted rest. He had never gotten the hang of sleeping on airplanes, so after an overnight flight through three time zones, he'd crawled off the plane feeling exhausted beyond belief.

He'd arrived at the house in Somerville at around eight, just in time to kiss Marlene's cheek before she headed off for the station and her train into Boston. Steve had made up the guest room bed for Gary and left him to catch up on his sleep.

Gary had lain in bed, eyes closed, brain in overdrive. He was too wired to sleep. Too agitated. Too downright scared.

It was bad enough that he'd blown it. Bad enough that he'd crossed a man no one in his right mind should have crossed. He'd survived that, at least, straightened things out with the guy, made good. But he'd blown it with everyone else, everyone who really mattered.

Debbie—the best thing that had happened to him in as long as he could remember. If she ever found out what he'd done, she would leave him. Even though he'd done it to keep her safe, she would be furious. No question about it. She would walk.

Linda... If he couldn't work something out, she might wind up homeless. It was either sell the house or live the rest of his life crushed beneath a foolish debt of his own making. Yet to take her home away from her would crush him, too.

And Matt Calloway... Well, he had to know the truth by now. He must have figured out what Gary had done.

Gary had lain awake for hours in the guest room of Steve's old row house north of Boston, picturing Matt the way he'd looked in Portland a couple of weeks ago. He was successful, poised, living right. He had his own business, a secretary, a house on a hill, respect. Money.

Then Gary had pictured Matt Calloway the way he'd looked twenty years ago, his hair growing out dark and spiky from the crew cut Uncle Sam had been kind enough to give him before shipping him halfway around the world. His skin had been less weathered, his eyes a bit gentler. He'd been poised then, too, calm and unshakable. Everyone around them had been going crazy, but Matt would sit smiling at the center of the madness, talking in that hick drawl of his, saying, "It's all right, Villard. Don't sweat it. We'll get out of this thing alive."

Gary pictured Matt walking point with him, reaching the edge of an abandoned farm on a hot, muggy morning when the air was pink with mist. He'd pictured himself starting into the field and Matt grabbing his arm, yanking him backward, holding him and grabbing a heavy stone, hurling it into the field and setting off a mine.

Gary Villard had lain in the guest room bed all morning, knowing he had to get some sleep but unable to because he couldn't stop picturing Matt Calloway. The man who'd saved his life.

The man he'd sold out just a couple of weeks ago.

Snowstorm coming, he thought, turning in disgust from the loathsome man in the mirror. Snowstorm. That was the least of it.

CHAPTER ONE

WHAT HAD STARTED as flurries outside Hartford two hours earlier had turned into a substantial snowstorm by the time Matt Calloway reached Braxton. Even if he'd been driving his trusty two-ton pickup instead of the subcompact he'd rented at the airport, the ice-slick, narrow, serpentine roads of rural Massachusetts would have posed a serious challenge.

He had lived in a variety of climates and driven through every kind of storm known to man, but he couldn't escape his Missouri genes, which balked at winter weather. His fingers tingled from the cold. The muscles in his neck were stiff from the way he was hunched over the steering wheel. His nostrils itched from inhaling the dry metallic heat pumping out of the air vents.

Maybe his tension had nothing to do with the nasty weather, the treacherous driving conditions and the marrow-deep weariness spawned by a journey begun that morning in Oregon. Maybe it was simply a result of the bitterness that had been seething inside him like something toxic ever since he'd discovered what Gary Villard had done.

A pair of headlights cut through the swirls of white powder as a car passed Matt going in the opposite direction. Although it was only seven-thirty, the night was dark and thick, the moon and stars obliterated by fat storm clouds. He almost wished there were more cars on the road so he could use their taillights to guide him.

The road twisted to the left, then split at a fork, just as the fellow at the gas station on the southern end of town had described it when Matt had stopped for directions. Downshifting, he steered onto the right fork. The tires whined, and the car fishtailed for one dread-filled moment before realigning itself and carrying him up the steeply sloping road. Snowflakes danced in the beams of his headlights. His windshield wipers swept vigorously back and forth. His neck grew stiffer.

There weren't many people Matt would drive through a blizzard for. There weren't many people who could rile him to such a high level of anger that he'd fly three thousand miles across the continent just to catch up with them. Betrayal was a fact of life, and usually he took it in stride. But this time . . .

This time it cut too damned deep.

His rear tires lost traction again, shimmying on the slippery road. Snow was accumulating faster now; no parallel stripes of black pavement showed through the white surface. He cursed the possibility that Gary Villard wouldn't be at the end of this hellish drive.

Gary's girlfriend in Los Angeles had told him that Gary had gone to Braxton. "He left a couple of days ago," she'd said when Matt had telephoned the number he'd gotten from the directory service. "He said he had to go back for a while. I don't know why."

Matt could guess why. "Braxton," he'd said. "That's in Massachusetts, right?"

"Right."

"Did he say when he'd be coming back?"

"Uh-uh. He just took off. He said there was trouble and he was going to go home for a few days. I'm guessing maybe it's something with his family."

Wrong, Matt had thought. *It's something with me.*

Thirty hours later, he found himself skidding along the icy back roads of western Massachusetts, rustic lanes that twisted away from the interstate and into the rolling hills of the Berkshires. No doubt the scenery would be breathtaking in the daylight, but Matt wasn't in the mood to appreciate scenery. He wouldn't appreciate anything but grabbing Gary Villard by the throat and throwing him through a wall. For starters.

He noticed a light up ahead to his left, the beckoning golden glow of a brightly lit house. As he neared it, the glow took on the shape of two large, rectangular second-story windows. Above them rose a steeply peaked roof; below them spread an overhang that sheltered a porch running the width of the house in front. An expanse of unbroken white snow extended from the porch to the edge of the road, where a metal mailbox stood sentry on a weathered wooden post. Snow topped the mailbox like vanilla frosting, but by the twin beams of his headlights Matt was able to make out most of the black letters adorning the side. He saw *V,* two *L*s and a partially obscured *ARD*.

He pumped the brake pedal cautiously to avoid throwing the car into a spin, and turned onto the driveway. Ruts in the white surface indicated that someone had driven in or out sometime in the not-too-distant past.

He turned off the engine and the headlights, and a dark, silent chill descended around him. He shivered. This wasn't going to be easy.

He didn't like battles; he didn't like the hatred that etched grooves into his soul like acid. He'd had his fill of fighting more than twenty years ago. He'd learned how to survive then; he'd learned how to trust his friends and live up to their trust in him.

Now he didn't know what trust meant anymore. Or friendship. He dreaded the prospect of having to learn everything all over again.

He rubbed sensation into his gloveless fingers, then opened the car door and got out. Snow slopped into his loafers and saturated his socks. Ignoring the clammy sensation, he cut across the yard to the front steps, up onto the sagging plank porch and over to the door. Praying for the willpower not to smash his fist into Gary's face the minute the door swung open, he took a deep breath and pressed the doorbell.

He strained to hear the sound of someone moving around inside. Maybe the muted thump he heard was a footstep on the stairs, or maybe it was a wad of snow falling from a tree branch onto the ground. He took another deep breath and let it out slowly, watching it turn into white vapor at the edge of his lips.

Definitely footsteps. He heard a bolt give way, then a click as the door latch was released. The door swung inward and he found himself staring through the glass storm door at a woman.

The fury burning in his gut suddenly vanished, as if someone had twisted a valve, cutting off the fuel that fed it. There was something about the woman, something in her wide hazel-green eyes that denied him his anger, deprived him of it, sucked it right out of him. Staring into them was like listening to a lullaby, soft and sweet and soothing. Whatever the opposite of spite was, her eyes were luminous with it.

He glanced away long enough for their strange effect on him to wane. Then he turned back to her, deliberately avoiding her eyes as he studied her through the glass pane of the storm door.

He must have gotten her out of bed or a bath; she wore a terry-cloth bathrobe and a pair of fleecy slippers. Her hair was reddish blond and dropped in a lustrous tumble past her shoulders. She had creamy skin augmented by a delicate spray of freckles across the bridge of her nose, and full, rosy lips parted slightly in surprise. Her build was so slight the plush white folds of the robe seemed to consume her.

He swallowed and flexed his icy fingers. The realization that Gary Villard had a beautiful woman living in his house infuriated Matt almost as much as Gary's treachery had. The bastard didn't deserve it. He didn't deserve someone like her.

Especially not when he had a woman in Los Angeles, too.

Matt swallowed again, taking comfort in the return of his resentment. For all he knew, this innocent-looking woman was Villard's accomplice, his partner in crime. For all Matt knew, behind her bewitching eyes lay a witch's soul. For all he knew, she was right this very minute thinking of ways to spend a whole lot of money that had just come her way. Matt's money.

"Yes?" she asked, her voice muffled by the thick glass of the storm door.

"I'm looking for Gary Villard," he said in a deceptively calm voice. No sense tipping the woman off or scaring her. Whether or not she was in cahoots with Gary, she wasn't Matt's real quarry. "Is he here?"

"Gary?" She frowned slightly, perplexed. "Is he here?"

'That's what I just asked you.''

'No,'' she said, her frown intensifying. ''He's in California—at least, as far as I know, he is.''

Her confusion appeared to be genuine. Matt weighed his strategy carefully. If the woman didn't know where Gary was, she might search for him herself, leading Matt to him in the process. ''I got word he was here,'' he said.

''He told you he was coming home?''

''No. A—a friend of his told me.'' Matt tactfully avoided the word ''girlfriend.'' Gary Villard was obviously deceitful in all kinds of ways, living with a different woman on each coast. Perhaps they knew about each other, perhaps they didn't. Matt wasn't about to go public with the news of Villard's infidelity.

''He's coming home? That's wonderful!'' The woman's eyes danced with delight, and Matt steered his gaze away so he wouldn't get trapped by their iridescent beauty.

A freezing gust of wind sliced across the back of his neck, helping to focus his thoughts. ''Do you live here?'' he asked her.

She laughed, but he could barely hear the sound through the thick glass. Just as well, he thought. Her laughter was probably as enchanting as her eyes. ''Who are you?'' she asked pleasantly.

''Matt Calloway. I'm an old friend of Gary's.''

''Matt Calloway,'' she repeated, once again frowning as she mulled over the name. Her nose reminded him of a kitten's, small and pink, twitching in concentration. ''Matt Calloway...''

''We were in Vietnam together.''

"Oh!" Her face brightened, and Matt experienced an irrational joy at the understanding that this time her smile was meant not for Gary but for him. "Oh, my God! Of course! I thought your name sounded familiar. Here, come in. Please." She opened the storm door and waved him inside. "I'm Linda Villard. Please come in and warm up."

Linda Villard. Gary's *wife*. Cripes, Gary had a girlfriend in California and a wife in Massachusetts.

A beautiful, friendly, much-too-trusting wife, letting a total stranger into her house during a late-season snowstorm. A stranger who had every intention of beating her two-timing husband to a pulp.

The anger that continued to burn inside Matt was his only defense against the homey charm of Gary's house and his wife. Planting his feet on the braided oval rug inside the door, Matt felt the warmth wrap around him. Snow melted from his hair and shoulders and dripped inside the collar of his fall-weight leather jacket. It oozed through the seams of his loafers and settled in damp, dark spots on the rug. Straight ahead of him he saw a hallway and a staircase with a polished oak railing. The walls were papered in a quiet pattern; on one wall hung a framed lithograph of a New England village green in winter. Next to the lithograph an arched doorway opened into a parlor. Peeking through the doorway Matt could see old, overstuffed furniture.

His gaze lingered on a huge armchair of faded burgundy damask, with a matching ottoman in front of it. He imagined himself sinking into the dense upholstery and letting all the tightness drain out of his neck and shoulders. He imagined himself resting his head against the thick cushions and allowing jet lag to claim him.

No. He was too angry to rest. It was only that the house was so warm and inviting, and the woman...so warm and inviting.

"Give me your jacket," she demanded with a gentle smile. "You must be freezing. You're really not dressed for the weather."

He almost blurted out that the weather in Portland that morning had been mild, fifty degrees and overcast, appropriate for March. How could he have known winter would still have New England in its grip?

It was too soon for him to tell her he'd flown in from Oregon. Too soon to reveal that much to Gary Villard's apparently naive young wife. "Thanks," he said, sliding off his jacket and handing it to her. "I *am* freezing."

"Take off your shoes, too," she said, gesturing toward the arched doorway. "And then go on in and make yourself comfortable. I'll be back in a few minutes. I'm dying to hear what you know about Gary coming home."

Matt watched her carry his jacket down the hall and away, then shook his head and scowled. She was dying to hear, was she? But she looked so petite, so vulnerable in that big fluffy bathrobe. She didn't look tough enough to bear the truth about her sleazy husband.

Don't be fooled, he cautioned himself. Just because the lady looked pure and ingenuous, just because she had a fragile physique and those cursedly hypnotic eyes and that glorious mane of copper-and-gold hair...

He'd been fooled by Gary, hadn't he? The missus was probably in on it, too. She'd probably invited Matt in with the purpose of swindling him out of something more. Right now, as he stood in her foyer, wiping the melted snow off his brow, she was probably in some other room, rummaging through the pockets of his jacket in search of something of value.

No. He couldn't believe that of her. He wasn't stupid enough to trust her, but he couldn't quite bring himself to distrust her, either.

Linda Villard was irrelevant, he reminded himself. The key was Gary, finding him, settling the score with him. Gary's worst sin hadn't been the actual theft; money was nothing more than money. But Gary had been Matt's *comrade,* his compadre, his blood brother. And he'd stolen Matt's trust. The most precious thing in the world, that was what Gary had stolen.

A ripple of icy discomfort coursed down Matt's spine. He chose to blame it not on Gary's perfidy but on the weather. He ought to take advantage of being indoors and thaw out.

After stepping out of his waterlogged shoes, he padded in his damp socks through the arched doorway. The living room was small and almost unbearably cozy, with plump furnishings and woven rugs, cluttered bookshelves and unmatched lamps standing on tables filmed lightly with dust. His gaze settled on the fireplace. A few charred chunks of wood rested on the grate and a basket of split logs, kindling and newspaper stood beside the hearth, which was occupied by a dozing black cat.

Matt recalled how Linda Villard had reminded him of a kitten when she'd wrinkled her nose. He might have guessed she would own a cat. Yet her husband was definitely not what Matt would consider a cat sort of person.

The cat stirred at Matt's entrance, peered up at him with wary yellow eyes, and flicked its tongue over its triangular mouth. Its tail thumped against the hearth and it yawned, baring small, pointy teeth.

Matt glowered. He wasn't a cat sort of person, either.

A sound startled him; he and the cat both flinched and glanced toward the doorway. Linda stood there, smiling bashfully. "Let me just throw some clothes on, and I'll be right down," she said.

His gaze descended slowly from her appealing face to her slender throat and the wedge of skin exposed above where the flaps of her robe met. No lace showed, no hint of flannel. As far as Matt could tell, she was naked under her bathrobe.

Not that the robe was particularly revealing. The sleeves were long and ended in wide cuffs; the hem fell to midway between her knees and ankles. But her legs were bare, and her wrists, and that sliver of exposed skin tapering from her collarbone to a point on her sternum.

Only a single layer of white terry cloth blocked his view of her body.

He was obviously overtired and strung out. If his full allotment of wits were in functioning order, he wouldn't be staring at the narrow swath of pale porcelain skin between her breasts, at the shadowed hollow of her throat. He wouldn't be trying to picture what was modestly covered by the robe, and the vision he conjured wouldn't be causing his breath to become hot and dry, scorching his lungs.

"A fire," he said, possibly because he felt one igniting inside him. He lowered his gaze to the fireplace. "Mind if I build one?"

"Go right ahead. I was planning to build one right after my bath."

"Your bath." Another blistering rush of air filled his lungs as he pictured her shedding the robe and sinking down into a tub full of bubbles. Damn Gary for having such a woman, he thought. Damn that jackass for having someone like Linda waiting for him in a secluded house in the Berkshires. If there was anyone who didn't deserve such luck, it was Gary Villard.

He regulated his breathing until his chest stopped hurting, then said, "Look, Mrs. Villard, I didn't mean to interrupt anything. I mean...if you want to go back to whatever it was you were doing when I rang your bell..."

Her silence prompted him to lift his gaze back to her. She was wrestling with a laugh. "It isn't Mrs. Villard," she said, explaining her amusement. "It's Ms."

Great, Matt thought. Gary was married to a gorgeous feminist.

"Or Miss, if you prefer," she continued. "I'm Gary's sister."

Gary's sister. Gary's *single* sister.

A torrent of ideas flooded Matt's mind, and he managed to snare a few of them: That given her obvious joy at the news that Gary was coming home, his sister might be more loyal to him than even a wife would be. That she might be even more likely than a wife to turn Matt out once she found out what had brought him to Braxton. That if Matt made a play for

Gary's little sister, Gary might be as homicidally in-
clined toward Matt as Matt was toward him.

That she was single. That she was *Miss*. That he and
she were alone in this house, with no one but a cat to
chaperon them, and that she had nothing on under her
robe.

That somehow, simply being in the same room with
her made Matt want to forget what had brought him
all this way in the first place.

"Go," he said, his voice sounding oddly gruff. "Get
dressed. I'll make a fire."

The smile she gave him before she turned and
pranced up the stairs was so captivating, so utterly
lovely, that he groaned.

MATT CALLOWAY, she thought, pawing through her
sweaters until she found the forest green cowl-neck
that set off her eyes. She wanted to look beautiful for
Matt Calloway.

He had saved Gary's life, after all.

Matt Calloway and Jimmy Green and Darryl
Bourke. Their names came back to her, emerging from
beneath the rubble of over two decades of memories.
Matt and Jimmy and Darryl and Gary.

Her brother had told her all about his platoon
mates. The "fearless foursome" they'd called themselves, even though they'd actually been all but para-
lyzed with fear. They had been so young, so far from
home and family. But under siege in a foreign land
they didn't understand, fighting a battle they understood even less, they had bonded into a brotherhood.
They had stuck by one another, kept one another's
spirits up, pooled their courage and shared it. There
had been a few large acts of heroism among them, and

countless small ones. Matt and Jimmy and Darryl and Gary had seen one another through hell, and miraculously, they'd all come back alive.

And now Matt Calloway was downstairs in Linda's living room.

Groping through her closet for her gray wool slacks, she recalled the letters Gary had written to her. She had saved them all, not to reread—she hadn't even looked at them since he'd returned from Vietnam—but simply because they represented such a significant period of her youth. Ten-and-a-half-years old when Gary had enlisted, she had been frightened for him and even more for herself. She'd been left behind while Gary, her big brother, her protector, went off to conquer the world.

He had written her every week, tissue-thin, army-issue pages full of his nearly indecipherable script, describing his adventures and his friends. Jimmy had been the laid-back surfer dude from San Diego, she remembered. Darryl had been the zany cutup from Atlanta.

Matt...Matt Calloway had been the rock. That was what Gary had written: "He comes from the heart of the country and he's as steady as a rock. Anything goes wrong, anything gets us spooked, we go to Matt and he talks us down. Matt's the kind of guy you can depend on through thick and thin and the Vietcong. I love the man. Just being with him makes me sure I'm going to get out of here in one piece."

Once Gary had sent her a photograph of the fearless foursome, and she hadn't needed the accompanying note to identify the three strangers. She'd known immediately that that one was Jimmy, that one was Darryl, and the tall, black-haired, broad-shouldered fellow with his khaki shirt unbuttoned and his dog tags hanging seductively against his bare chest had to be Matt. She'd known from his dark, steady gaze and his enigmatic smile. She'd known he was the rock.

For an eleven-year-old girl, curious about boys but afraid to get too close to them, Matt had been a safe fantasy. She could stare at the photograph before turning off her bedside lamp at night, and then close her eyes and indulge in all sorts of passionate dreams about the bare-chested, long-legged man with the mesmerizing gaze. She'd been young, and he'd been thousands of miles away, and no creepy, gawky boy in her classes in the Braxton Middle School could compare to him.

But she wasn't young anymore. She was no longer that lonely girl, stranded in Braxton with aging parents who didn't understand her and were too preoccupied with worry about their son. She was no longer a child under assault by the first wave of puberty, missing her brother with a fierceness that was exaggerated by every unexpected surge of hormones.

She was a woman, thirty-three years old. And Matt Calloway in person was even more strikingly handsome than he'd been in that ancient photograph.

Her thoughts veered from the past to the present, to the visitor in the living room. She pictured his thick black hair and his dark, dark eyes, his shoulders as broad as she'd remembered them and his legs as long. She pictured his hawklike nose and the day-old shadow of beard darkening his angular jaw. An uncomfortable heat enveloped her, as if she were that dreamy adolescent once more, assailed by yearnings she couldn't begin to comprehend.

She laughed off the strange sensation. Matt Calloway was a friend of Gary's, one of his oldest, most
significant, most trusted friends.

He was a friend, and he brought news. Gary was
coming home.

It was about time, too. Gary hadn't been back East
since Thanksgiving. Linda had flown to California to
spend Christmas with him and Debbie. She'd liked
Gary's girlfriend a lot, their two-bedroom apartment
had been comfortable, and being able to go swim-
ming in December had almost made missing a white
Christmas worthwhile.

But during her holiday week in Los Angeles, Linda
had suspected that something was wrong with her
brother. He'd seemed troubled, edgy. Over the past
several years he'd been at odds with himself, struggling to figure out where he belonged. His move to
California had been part of his search for stability, and
Linda had wanted to believe that he'd found it in his
relationship with Debbie and his job as a limousine
driver. When he'd come to Braxton for Thanksgiving, and before that for the Memorial Day weekend,
he'd seemed happy, regaling Linda with amusing
stories about the celebrities he shuttled around town
and the mansions he'd been inside. He'd been pulling
himself together, getting his life back on track, and
Linda had been thrilled.

But when she'd seen him over Christmas, she'd
sensed that he was floundering. Debbie had informed
her that Gary sank into blue funks sometimes, with-
drawing, sulking over his thwarted ambitions. When
Linda had questioned him he'd snapped, "Stop being
such a social worker, okay? Back off. I'm fine."

She wanted him to come home. If Los Angeles was part of the problem, she wanted him in Braxton, where he seemed to be more at peace. She wanted to be close to him, to help him the way he had always helped her.

If Matt Calloway was to be believed, Gary was on his way home right now.

She set down her brush, studied her reflection in the mirror above her dresser and cringed. Even in the summer her skin always retained a milky hue. Three months after her Christmas vacation in sunny California, she looked practically ghostly.

Her skin was too pale, and so were her eyelashes. Her forehead was too high, her hair too limp, her fingernails too short. Even wearing her soft green sweater, she looked drab.

It didn't matter, she told herself. She didn't have to make a grand impression on Matt. He had come to see Gary, not her.

And she'd darned well better make him feel welcome, since Gary wasn't around to host this visit himself.

Strapping on her wristwatch, she gave herself one last, mildly dissatisfied inspection, then left her bedroom for the stairs. Halfway down, she paused and contemplated her obligations as a hostess. There they were, isolated on the outskirts of town while a snow squall pelted the house and choked the roads. If Gary's little sister were to offer Matt a drink while they were alone in her house, would he get the wrong idea?

She wished she were more experienced at this, more sophisticated. She knew just about everyone in Braxton, and everyone knew her. She couldn't remember the last time she'd had a stranger in her house.

Particularly a stranger who looked like Matt Calloway.

She descended the remaining stairs and walked into the living room. Matt was kneeling in front of the fireplace, assessing the small but promising blaze he'd constructed, and balancing a split log across his palms.

Beside him, Dinah lounged, grooming her paws and eyeing the flickering orange flames. Neither of them gave any indication that they'd heard her enter.

Apparently Matt had found just the right place for the log. He reached in and propped it across two smaller sticks, then settled back on his haunches and analyzed the result of his labor.

"I've got a set of tongs you can use," she said.

The sound of her voice caused him to start. He turned and shoved himself to his feet. "Forget it," he said, dusting his hands on his jeans and sending her a hesitant smile.

His eyes were like two burning coals, black but glowing with an inner energy, a dangerous heat. For a fleeting instant she felt like that mooning preteen again, overwhelmed by emotions she couldn't name. The room seemed too close, too intimate. Matt Calloway seemed too real.

"Would you like some cocoa?" she asked, then winced inwardly at how childish she must sound, offering him such an innocent, wholesome beverage.

His smile expanded. "Have you got anything stronger?"

"Brandy."

His smile reached his eyes, imbuing them with a deep, burnished radiance. "That sounds good."

"I'll be right back." She pivoted and left the living room, then raced down the hall to the kitchen. She didn't stop until she reached the sink. Curving her fingers over the edge of the porcelain basin, she gulped in a deep breath and berated herself for being such a ninny. For heaven's sake, he was Gary's pal and she was a hospitable, mature woman. Just because Matt had looked a little more at home in her living room than she'd expected, just because Dinah—whose regard of visitors ranged from cool dislike to outright hostility—seemed to have taken to Matt as if he were one of the family, just because the fire had illuminated Matt's harsh, masculine features from below, emphasizing the sharp lines of his jaw and his brow...

Brandy, she thought, gazing through the window above the sink at the snowflakes whirling against an inky backdrop of night. Cocoa was for an eleven-year-old girl weaving legends about the brave, strong soldier friends of her big brother. Brandy was for mature adults.

She pulled the rarely used bottle from the back of a shelf and placed it on a tray along with two of her mother's crystal snifters, also rarely used. Mustering every ounce of her composure, she shaped a confident smile and carried the tray into the living room.

The fire was bigger now; the split log Matt had strategically positioned had caught, sending bright yellow licks of flame upward. Matt stood with his hands in his hip pockets, his feet in their damp socks just inches from the warmth. He turned at her entrance and watched as she set the tray down on the coffee table in front of the sofa.

She felt his eyes on her as she filled the snifters. He seemed to be recording her every movement, taking note of the angle of her head, the rotation of her wrist, the curl of her fingers as she cupped one glass and then the other in her palm. Maybe she was doing this all wrong; maybe she was pouring too much brandy, or too little. Maybe the man was supposed to pour it, even if he was the guest.

She couldn't believe how self-critical she felt. It wasn't as if she were an ignorant rube. She had a master's degree; she'd lived in Boston for years. She knew about men and love—she had the scars to prove it.

Besides, this had nothing to do with men and love. It had to do with Matt Calloway, her brother's friend and therefore her own, a man who would always seem heroic in her mind, no matter who he'd become over the past two decades.

She extended a snifter to him and he reached out to take it. "To Gary," she said, raising her glass in a toast.

A shadow darkened his strong features, something cold and bleak hardening his eyes and tensing his mouth into a grim line. Before Linda could question him about what was wrong—even before the sudden change in his mood could fully register on her—his smile returned.

But it was altered, somehow. There was something ruthless in this new smile, something stark and hard. It no longer expressed his pleasure at being inside, sheltered from the storm, in the company of a woman who considered it an honor just to have him in her house. She felt as if the shadow that had briefly fallen over Matt had stretched across the room and dropped its icy veil over her.

"To Gary," he said, his eyes locking with hers and filling her with an unnamed apprehension. "Of course. To Gary."

Turning back to the fire, he took a long, slow drink.

CHAPTER TWO

"LOOK AT HIM," Marlene said with a chuckle. "He's acting like he's never seen snow before."

"Live in Southern California long enough," Steve joked, "and you forget what real weather is like."

Gary forced himself to smile. He continued to stare out the window at the snow, which erased the outlines of the street and the houses, the light poles and fire hydrants. From somewhere down the street came the irritating whine of a car stuck in the snow, revving its engine and spinning its tires. Closer to Steve's house, a dog barked exuberantly and a couple of kids shouted insults in the course of their snowball fight.

"Everyone's always complaining about the traffic in Los Angeles," Marlene remarked, crossing the living room with a mug of coffee for Gary. "I'll tell you, gridlock and loonies shooting each other on the freeway are nothing compared to rush-hour in a Boston snowstorm."

"It almost makes me happy to be unemployed," Steve remarked.

"Temporarily," Marlene emphasized. "They're going to rehire you as soon as orders go back up."

"Sweetheart, the only way orders are going to go back up is if the country goes to war again. We need another war."

"We most certainly do not," Marlene argued.

"You'd rather I stay unemployed?"

"I'd rather we don't have any more wars."

Gary took a sip of coffee and tried to think of a way to change the subject. He didn't want to talk about wars. He felt too embattled as it was, at war with himself, his own stupidity.

How do these things get started? he wondered. Nursing his coffee, he nodded at the right times so Marlene and Steve would think he was paying attention to their conversation. How does something like this happen? You make a tiny mistake, that's how. You reach a little higher, want a little more. You look around and see everyone else getting theirs, and you've been waiting for your turn for so long you get impatient, and you take a chance.

And the next thing you know, the whole world is coming down around you, burying you like the thick snowflakes burying the street.

"Did you talk to your sister?" Marlene asked.

He lowered his coffee and shrugged. "Not yet."

"Feel free to use the phone, if—"

"I'll call her tomorrow," he said. "If I call her tonight, she might want me driving out to Braxton now."

"In this storm?" Steve shook his head in disbelief.

The real reason Gary hadn't called Linda was that he didn't know what to say to her. Cripes, what a mess. Debbie thought he was in Braxton with Linda, Linda thought he was in Los Angeles with Debbie, and here he was in Somerville with Steve and Marlene, wishing he knew how to live the rest of his life without earning the hatred of everyone who mattered to him.

He couldn't hide in Somerville forever. He couldn't avoid his sister or Debbie. He didn't really want to. But he needed a little more time to figure out what to say to the women in his life, how to explain it all, how to make them understand.

He needed even more time to figure out how to elude Matt Calloway, at least until he could work out a way to make things right between them. Calloway was a good man. Gary had done what he'd had to do, but it anguished him to know that his old pal had had to be sacrificed along the way.

Seeing Matt a couple of weeks ago had been a shock, not because Matt had changed, but because he hadn't. He had looked pretty much as Gary had remembered. Despite the passage of time, he'd developed no paunch, no fleshiness around the chin, no bald spot or vision problems. He seemed a bit more reserved than he'd been as a kid, but still solid and sure of himself, still a rock. When Gary had followed Matt's secretary into her boss's office, Matt had greeted him with a true smile, a confident handshake, a spontaneous embrace.

Matt acted genuinely happy to see Gary. "Jimmy Green told me you were around," he said once he'd released Gary and slapped him on the shoulder for good measure. "He told me he'd seen you a few times down in L.A. I never thought you'd make it this far north, though."

"Hey, I'm a northerner by birth, you know?"

"Yeah, you still sound like a Hah-vahd boy."

"And you're still thinking like a hayseed hillbilly from the Ozarks."

Instead of correcting Gary about the location of the Ozark Mountains in relation to his hometown, as he so often had in the past, Matt only laughed. "Look at you. You're still built like a broom handle."

"Give me a break. I weigh at least ten pounds more than I did in 'Nam."

"It's all in your earring. What is that, a *D*?"

"Yeah. For Debbie. The love of my life. I offered to get her name tattooed on my arm, but she said she didn't want me to mutilate myself."

"So instead you poked a hole through your ear. You're still a wild man, Villard, aren't you."

"Always was, always will be."

"Listen," Matt said, moving around his desk and shuffling the papers on his blotter. "We've got a lot of catching up to do. Let me sign a few things, and then we'll clear out of here and go somewhere for a drink. Okay?"

"Sure, sign a few things, be my guest," Gary said, his heart pounding. Maybe he could forge Matt's signature. Maybe he could ask to see one of the papers Matt was going to sign. Maybe the blotter liner would hold a lingering impression of Matt's signature. Maybe Matt would look up from his desk, read Gary's mind, give him one of his patent smiles and say, "Don't sweat it, Villard. You know the way I am. I'll do whatever I can to get you through this mess alive."

Standing in the unadorned inner office at the Calloway Construction Company headquarters, Gary had prayed for a way to emerge from his reunion with Matt with what he needed to get through this mess alive: money. Lots of money.

God must have heard Gary's prayers, because what Matt was signing were checks. It gave Gary an opening. "I guess you do a lot of that when you own your own business," he remarked.

"Signing checks? Yeah."

"How do you keep it all straight?"

"Hmm?"

"I mean...man, you're right. I haven't changed much since you last saw me. I can still talk my way out of anything, but money management... It just boggles my mind."

"Well, I don't make many mistakes," Matt told him. "But when I do, the bank covers it. The company has one of those all-together accounts, where the bank will shift money from the savings portion into the checking portion to cover my checks if for some reason I botch the arithmetic."

"I see." *Thank you, God!*

It was amazing to Gary, even now, that all he'd thought about while standing in Matt's office was that his jaunt to Portland was going to be a success, that Matt had inadvertently revealed enough information to enable Gary to solve his problem. Gary hadn't considered the morals of what he was planning, the ramifications, the repercussions. All he'd thought was that he was going to be able to pay off his debt and live the rest of his life with all his body parts intact, and with Debbie safe and sound.

He didn't think about morals until later. Until he'd executed his swindle and fled from Oregon. Until he'd remembered the way Matt had welcomed him, the way he'd lowered his guard and opened up, told Gary about his life, his marriage, his ups and downs, triumphs and disappointments, his grief at learning of Darryl's death a few years ago. "It wasn't like any of us kept in close touch," he'd said over his beer, "but when he died it was like losing a brother."

"We *were* brothers," Gary had said.

"We still are. I've got enough siblings to know that a brother is a brother for life."

"Through thick and thin."

"All for one and one for all."

"Now and forevermore, in the stinkhole of Da Nang or the sands of Waikiki."

"Or the rainy hills of Portland," Matt had concluded, raising his glass in Gary's direction before drinking.

Gary had tuned it all out. He'd had to in order to do what he had to do. He'd needed the money, and it didn't matter if he and Matt were brothers in the rainy hills of Portland. All that mattered was getting what he needed.

Until later. Until now. Until he discovered that there was more than one way to lose a piece of yourself.

"Why don't we go outside?" Gary said to Steve and Marlene, turning back to the window. "I haven't walked through a snowstorm in ages."

"Great idea," Steve concurred. "In fact, we could strap on the cross-country skis and do a tour of the neighborhood."

"You guys are nuts!" Marlene hooted.

"Yeah, so what's new? Go put on some warmer slacks, Marlene. I'll dig up my old boots for Gary."

"They're in the cellar," Marlene said as she started up the stairs. "This is really nuts, you know."

"Mother Nature was nuts to give us snow in March. We're only going with the flow."

Gary's smile was almost natural. Outside, wrapped in the freezing wind, he would be able to forget for a while that he had a life somewhere else, a job, a woman he loved, an apartment. Outside in the cold,

cold night, he would be able to forget for a while that he had betrayed a true friend.

"Now," LINDA SAID, lowering her glass to the coffee table in front of her and giving Matt an eager smile, "tell me everything."

He was sprawled in front of the fireplace, using the ottoman as a backrest and positioning his legs in front of the hearth so the fire would dry his jeans and socks. Her couch looked more comfortable than the hardwood floor, but he sensed that sitting beside her would be a fatal error.

Sitting across the room from her, gazing at the golden firelight dancing over her face and illuminating its delicate contours, was almost as dangerous. He took another swallow of brandy and reminded himself that her last name was Villard.

"Everything?" he repeated noncommittally.

"About your coming here to see Gary. Did you just fly in today, or have you been in New England for a while?"

He eyed her speculatively. How would she know he'd have to fly to get here? Unless Gary had told her... "What makes you think I don't live in the area?"

She laughed. "If you did, you'd know enough to wear boots and gloves on a night like this."

Her laughter was soft and warm, threatening to melt his defenses as the warmth of the fire melted the chill from his fingers and toes. He deliberately directed his gaze away from Linda and focused on the potent amber fluid in the bowl-shaped glass cupped between his hands. Half of him wanted badly to trust her; the other half knew he mustn't.

"Most people fly in to Boston," she went on when he failed to answer her question. "I think Hartford's airport is a little closer to Braxton, though."

"I flew into Hartford," he told her.

Even without looking, he could picture her nod of approval. It had been purely by chance that he'd picked the right airport; trying to get a last-minute ticket, he'd grabbed whatever was available. Still, it made him feel much too good to know he'd flown to the airport she would have chosen for him. It made him feel closer to her, somehow.

Risky, he cautioned himself. He didn't need her approval, her closeness or her dazzling smile. What he needed was detachment, objectivity, the ability to maintain a firm barrier between himself and his enemy's next of kin.

He lifted the glass to his lips and sipped, letting the brandy glide in a smooth path down his throat to his chest. It was high quality, mellow and soothing. Like Linda, he thought, then quickly shoved the notion away.

To avoid thinking of her, he directed his attention to her cat. After pacing for a while in front of the fire, it retreated a few steps and curled up next to his feet, arching its back against his heel to scratch an itch. "That proves you're a good guy," Linda said, her tone underlined with amusement. "Dinah doesn't usually take to strangers so quickly."

"We made friends while you were upstairs," he told her, rubbing his foot over the beast's fur and feeling the vibrations in its chest as it purred. "I'm not really into cats, but she's all right."

"She's the best."

"Her name is Dinah?"

"I named her after the cat in *Alice in Wonderland*."

He peered up at Linda and frowned. "I thought that was the Cheshire Cat."

Her eyes met his. Alive with sparks of silver and emerald, they warmed him more than the fire and the liquor. For one fleeting, crazy instant he wished that Gary would never show up, that Matt and Linda would remain forever in this snug house on the side of a snowy country road, that Dinah the cat would lead them into their own Wonderland where money and IOUs, false handshakes and broken promises dwindled into insignificance and two loners could conquer a magical new world together.

Turning from Linda, he shook his head at his stupidity. Why should he assume that she was a loner? For all he knew, it was merely chance that she'd been home alone tonight. A woman with her obvious attributes must have a calendar jam-packed with social engagements. Braxton's bachelors probably had to take a number and wait their turn for the pleasure of her company. Perhaps the only reason Matt had found her at home tonight was that her date had been called off due to the weather.

"You're from the Midwest, aren't you," she said.

She was trying so valiantly to get a conversation going, he felt obligated to contribute to the effort. Steeling himself against the impact of her beauty, he raised his eyes to her once more. "Portland, Oregon," he told her. "What made you think I was from the Midwest?"

Her smile grew shy, and she traced the rim of her snifter with her gracefully tapered index finger. "Gary wrote me from Vietnam. He said you were from the heart of the country.''

Matt gave a short, derisive laugh. The dreary, muggy one-horse town where he'd grown up didn't resemble the heart of anything. "I spent my childhood in southern Missouri," he said, pronouncing it "Missoura" like the native he was. "After 'Nam I moved around a bit—Michigan, Colorado, Texas. Eventually I wound up in the Pacific Northwest, and I liked it. So I stayed."

"I see." She continued to scrutinize him. Her gaze appeared benign, curious and utterly enchanting. He steeled himself against it. "What brings you to Braxton?" she asked.

Your brother, he wanted to shout. *Your two-faced, stinking, con-artist brother.*

In fact, he hadn't worked out a cover story for his trip east. Based on his phone call to Gary's girlfriend, he'd assumed he would find Gary in Braxton and not have to justify his presence in Massachusetts to anyone else.

Turning to the fire once more, he hurriedly concocted a story. "I have a friend down in Connecticut," he said. "A business associate. He wanted my input on a project he had lined up down there, and he offered to fly me in. And...uh...I'd called Gary about some other stuff and his girlfriend told me he was here, so I figured, what the hell, I'd drive up and visit."

"What sort of business are you in?"

He tamped down his uneasiness about the fact that she was asking all the questions and decided to let her have her turn. Once she came to trust him, perhaps she would answer all his questions about Gary.

"Construction," he said.

"Your friend's lucky he's got a project in Connect-icut," she commented. "Nobody's building anything these days. The whole region is in a recession."

Damn. Matt had never been a good liar. "Well . . . you're right," he mumbled. "He's lucky. So when do you think Gary's going to show up?"

"You're the one who told me he's coming," she pointed out. "I didn't know anything about it. But you know what? I'll give Debbie a call and find out." She started to rise, then glanced at her watch and lowered herself back into the plush cushions of the sofa. "I'll call her in a little while. She probably won't be home from work yet. I always get so confused with the time differences."

He nodded in sympathy.

"Have you met her?"

"Debbie?" For a panic-stricken moment he tried to recall who Debbie was. Linda's cat? No, that was Di-nah. Debbie must be Gary's girlfriend. "No," he said, acting as if he'd known all along who Debbie was, as if he and Gary were as close as a belt and its buckle. "We've talked, but we've never met face-to-face. Gary's been up to see me in Portland, though."

"That's so nice, that you're both on the West Coast. How about the other men, Jimmy and Darryl? Do you see them, too? Oh—one of them passed away, didn't he."

"Darryl," he said, surprised by her knowledge of his army buddies. "How do you know so much about us?"

That smile lit her face again, all softness and kind-ness, transfixing him. "Gary told me. He tells me everything. He and I have always been very close. Maybe he's told you that himself."

Don't be sure of anything when it comes to him, Matt wanted to warn her.

"I was just a child when he enlisted," she continued, "but once he left for Southeast Asia I lived for his letters. He sent me at least one a week. He told me all about you and the others in them. You were all a part of Gary's life when he was overseas, and that made you all a part of my life, too. By the time his tour of duty was up, I felt as if you were members of the family. I can't believe one of you is actually sitting here in my living room right now."

He felt a stab of emotion—part guilt, part ego gratification. There was something almost worshipful in the way she regarded him. He didn't deserve it, especially not when he'd come here with the intention of tearing her brother limb from limb, but he liked it. He liked having this appealing slip of a woman gazing at him with something akin to awe. What man wouldn't?

"I guess Gary never talked much about me, did he?" She grinned bashfully. "You seemed so surprised to discover Gary had a sister."

"It was a long time ago," he pointed out. "He probably talked about you all the time. I just don't remember."

She laughed and shook her head. "He probably didn't talk about me at all. I was just his annoying kid sister. I used to write him two and three times a week until my parents started rationing the postage stamps because I was using too many. I used to write him all this garbage—I'm sure it bored him to tears. Self-righteous stuff about how the teachers weren't fair and the war wasn't fair—in my mind the two things were on a par. I hated Ho Chi Minh and Richard Nixon and my science teacher with equal passion."

"I've known some pretty bad science teachers," Matt assured her.

Her smile nourished the warmth inside him, a friendly, comfortable kind of warmth. "I missed Gary so much when he was over there," she said. "I used to pour out my heart to him in my letters. He was probably embarrassed by it."

"He probably loved it." Matt recalled how Ellie's letters had kept him sane. Any heartfelt correspondence from home gave the soldiers courage and hope. "I think he did talk about you, Linda. It's just that you were a youngster. I mean, when I try to remember what he told us about you... You were a little girl. His baby sister." For a moment his bitterness vanished in the sweet haze of nostalgia. "He bought you a china doll when he had a weekend pass to Saigon, didn't he?"

"Yeah." She laughed. "I gave him hell over that. I told him dolls were for babies and I was a woman." Her eyes met Matt's and her laughter increased. "I was staring down my twelfth birthday when he got back, but I was convinced I was a woman. I told him he should have brought me black stockings."

The image of Linda in black stockings caused something to twist tight in Matt's abdomen. He deflected the sensation by turning back to the cat, who was grooming her paws, her small pink tongue working them over in steady, businesslike laps. When the tension in his groin eased, he returned his gaze to Linda. "What did Gary tell you about me?"

She lifted her glass from the table and leaned back against the burgundy upholstery, curling her legs under her and looking at him with undisguised elation, as if having him in her living room was the fulfillment of all her dreams. "He told me you were the rock. The stable one. Everyone depended on you."

Matt threw back his head and guffawed. His memory of himself at eighteen and nineteen years of age was that he was anything but stable. He'd been a middle child in an impoverished family, overlooked and underfoot, desperate to get out of his parents' crowded, ramshackle house even if enlisting in the armed forces was the only escape he could find. He'd endured his time in Vietnam by clinging to the knowledge that the government would pay his way through college once he got home. Once he had a college degree he would never have to be a hardscrabble farmer like his father and his two brothers—one of whom had served in 'Nam before Matt, but like a fool hadn't used his GI education benefits when he'd gotten home. Most of all, Matt had endured because he knew that Ellie was back in America, waiting for him.

The closest he'd ever gotten to stability during his tour of duty was the realization, each morning when he woke up, that by some quirk of fate he was still alive. That was as stable as it ever got.

"I didn't know any of them were depending on me. I was so dependent on them," he confessed with a grin. "Jimmy Green was the coolest of the cool. We'd be scared, and he'd say, 'Be cool, man, everything's cool.' And Darryl Bourke would always come up with a joke when we needed one. Some of those jokes were pretty sick, but they got us through the day."

He drifted off, reminiscing. Just talking about the guys made them come alive for him. More than a few times over the years he'd seen Jimmy, who was currently a West Coast sales rep for a sporting goods company based in his hometown of San Diego. Whenever his sales trips took him to Portland he'd give Matt a call and they'd meet for dinner. It was through Jimmy that Matt had learned about Darryl's death in a motorcycle accident a few years back. It was also through Jimmy that Matt had learned, about six months ago, that Gary Villard had gone west, too, that he was living somewhere in Los Angeles.

Matt had been pleased. "Sure," he'd said to Jimmy, "give him my address. If he's ever up this way I'd love to see him."

He sensed that Linda was waiting for him to say something about her beloved brother, something about how much Matt had depended on Gary during their time in-country. He *had* depended on Gary, he was sure of it. He had depended on that wiry fair-haired Yankee with his flat accent and his dry wit. He'd depended on "Gah-ry Vill-ahd" to turn their rations into something edible with the addition of mysteriously obtained spices, to rig wire hangers to his radio in such a way that on clear nights he could pull in a radio station out of Manila. He'd depended on Gary to find out their platoon's orders before anyone else found out theirs, to get their mail before anyone else got theirs, to smuggle into their quarters the occasional illegal intoxicant that helped them to endure the deadly terror they'd lived with day after day after day.

He'd depended on Gary Villard enough that, more than two decades later, he could greet Gary's reappearance in his life with unfettered joy.

And with a single act Gary had negated all that good will and gratitude, all those memories.

How was Matt supposed to explain anything to the beguiling woman on the couch? He stared at her, her slim, lithe body curled up gracefully, reminding him a bit of her cat's body curled up in the shelter of his ankles. He stared at Linda's clear, hopeful eyes, her expectant smile, and felt a weary desolation in the pit of his stomach. *Your brother is slime,* he imagined himself telling her. *Your brother is scum.*

He couldn't do it.

"Gary was a good friend," he forced himself to say. "Your brother got me through a lot of bad stuff over there."

"He's the best, isn't he," she agreed. "I think I'll go give Debbie a call now and see what she knows about his coming east. Please—" She cut him off as he started to rise. "You stay right where you are and enjoy the fire. Are you hungry? I could fix some sandwiches or something—"

"No, I'm fine."

He watched her set down her glass and uncoil her body. An unwanted vision of black stockings leaped into his mind, followed by an equally unwanted one of her in her bathrobe, the way she'd looked just a short while ago, tilting her head up to view him and revealing the silky underside of her chin.

It took every ounce of willpower in him to cling to the fact that she was the sister of a man who had ripped him off both financially and emotionally. No matter how long her legs were, how slender her waist, how glossy her hair, no matter how brightly her eyes glowed as they reflected the green of her sweater and the gold of the blaze in the hearth, she was Gary's sister, and Matt couldn't, shouldn't, wouldn't desire her.

"WHAT DO YOU MEAN, he's not with you?" Debbie gasped.

Leaning against the counter, staring out at the dusty white snow squalls beyond the window, Linda wondered why she didn't feel as alarmed as Debbie sounded about Gary's disappearance. Maybe it was the unaccustomed infusion of brandy into her bloodstream, dulling her reflexes and fuzzing the edges of her perception.

Or maybe it was the man in the other room.

"He told me he had to go back east for a while," Debbie said. "He was going to try to get a ticket on a red-eye Sunday night. His boss didn't call, so he must have arranged for a few days off. Where the hell could he be?"

"Oh, he's probably on his way here, just like he told you," Linda assured Debbie. "If he booked at the last minute, maybe he couldn't get a direct flight."

"So, what are you saying? You think he's been laid over in Dallas for two days?"

"I think..." A feather of concern tickled Linda's brain, making her just a bit uncomfortable. "Maybe he's avoiding Braxton. Maybe he didn't want to see me." She sighed. "Is he angry with me for some reason? Has he said anything to you?"

"Nothing at all."

"When I visited you in December, I think I got on his nerves a little."

"Oh, Linda, he's crazy about you. You're his precious little sister, you know that."

Linda rolled her eyes. Sometimes Gary treated her that way, as if she were precious...and very little. She forgave him only because she knew his big-brother protectiveness was a natural outgrowth of his love for her.

"He yelled at me," Linda reminded Debbie. "He told me I was acting like a social worker."

"You are a social worker. What does he expect?"

"I guess he expects me not to make comments about his moods."

Debbie groaned. "His moods. I don't know what it is, Linda, they come and go. He's been kind of hyper lately. He took a few days off and headed north a couple of weeks ago, said he wanted to look up an old friend."

Matt, Linda thought, her lips curving into a smile at the thought of the handsome man in her living room.

"When he came back, he was kind of antsy. I couldn't get a straight answer from him on anything."

"It's been a tough time for him," Linda said, defending her brother. "You know what he went through during the Gulf War—all those flashbacks, lots of troubling memories. It happened to a lot of Vietnam veterans, Debbie. I saw it in some of my clients here."

"Sure. But that was so long ago. Shouldn't he have gotten over it by now?

"Well, sometimes it takes a while. Maybe it's more than that. Maybe he's going through a mid-life crisis. Turning forty and all... A little moodiness is normal."

"Fine. It's normal. I haven't walked out on him, have I?"

"Are you planning to?" Linda asked, her concern building. Gary didn't seem strong enough at the moment to handle losing his girlfriend.

"Hey, look, call me an idiot, but I love the guy. I wish he'd ask me to marry him, already."

Linda smiled sadly. She wished Gary would ask Debbie to marry him, too. Debbie was good for him, and Linda would be thrilled to have her as a sister-in-law. "Well, if you hear from him, tell him to call me, okay?" she requested. "I'll bet he's just visiting with his friends in Somerville, and he'll be showing up here in a day or so."

"I hope you're right," Debbie muttered. "Call me if you hear from him, okay?"

"I will," Linda promised, then said goodbye and lowered the receiver into its cradle. Turning from the window, she found Matt hovering in the doorway.

He was big. Bigger than she'd realized when he'd stood wet and shivering inside her front door. He appeared to be at least six feet tall, and from the way his sweater outlined his torso she could see that he had broad, bony shoulders and a body of lean, masculine strength.

Her stomach sucked in on itself and her heart thudded in her ears. It was one thing to be seated politely in her living room with him, engaging in cordial hostess chitchat, and another to find him looming before her, filling the kitchen doorway, permeating the room with his presence. In the living room she could think of him as Gary's wartime buddy, but here...

Here he was a man, and she was all alone with him.

"Any luck?" he asked, angling his head toward the phone.

She coughed to clear her throat. "I'm not sure how much you overheard," she began, "but—"

A sheepish smile crossed his lips. "I didn't mean to eavesdrop."

"But you just couldn't help yourself," she countered, feeling not so much indignant as relieved. His smile and his flimsy apology made him more human, a little less like some idealized warrior-god from her brother's past. "Debbie said he left Los Angeles Sunday night. I'm sure he's somewhere around here."

"In Braxton, you mean?"

"Oh, no. If he were in Braxton he'd be right in this room, cleaning out the refrigerator. My guess is he's in the Boston area. He has some friends who live in Somerville, just outside the city. He likes to visit them when he comes east. Probably he went there first, and he'll be heading out here when they've had enough of him."

"So, you think he's just a drive away?" Matt asked. "I could hop into the car right now and drive to Somerville."

She contemplated Matt in the bright light of the kitchen's ceiling fixture. His face gave nothing away, but his words struck her as odd. Why would he want to drive one hundred and twenty miles through a snowstorm at night just to see Gary, when he'd seen Gary only a couple of weeks ago and would probably be able to see him tomorrow, or the next day, or back on the West Coast in the not-too-distant future? What could be so very important that he had to see Gary this instant?

"You could hop into your car," she said dubiously, "but driving anywhere through this storm would be insane. If you'd like, though, I can call up the folks in Somerville, and if Gary is there you can make a plan with him for tomorrow."

"No," Matt said quickly. "No, don't call. I . . . I'd like to surprise him. That's why I didn't call before coming here."

She tilted her head slightly, searching for a different angle, a different perspective, one she hoped would give her a clearer concept of what he was up to. He was up to *something,* that much was certain. Whether that something was truly as innocuous as surprising Gary she didn't know, but he definitely had an agenda. She wished she could fathom what it was.

"I'd suggest that you drive back to your friend down in Hartford for the night," she said, "but that would be as crazy as trying to drive to Somerville in this weather."

His face remained impassive, his eyes opaque and his lips neither smiling nor frowning. "I'd like to stay in Braxton tonight." His voice emerged calmly and evenly, yet she sensed a strain in him, something turbulent just beneath the surface. "Is there a motel in town?"

"There's the Braxton Motor Inn, but it's a real dive."

"That's all right. I can stand it for a night."

"I'm not going to let you go anywhere as long as it's still snowing. Once the storm lets up, the snowplows will be through and the roads will be a lot safer. In the meantime, you may as well stay here."

His eyes seemed to grow darker. Linda attributed it to the shadow as he lowered his head, but a less rational part of her was certain the darkness was emotional. Either he was disappointed about having to spend more time with her, or else . . .

Or else he found the prospect tantalizing.

No. He couldn't be tantalized by her, any more than she could be by him. All Matt knew about her was that she was Gary's baby sister—those were his words. And she could fit all she knew about him into a teaspoon without spilling a drop.

They'd been brought together by Gary and by chance. That was all.

"Look," she said with artificial brightness, "since you're stranded here for a while, you may as well make the best of it and let me fix you something to eat." She pushed herself away from the counter and started toward the refrigerator.

He caught her arm. His long, blunt fingers closed easily around her slim wrist. She saw the calluses on his fingertips, the mark of a man who was accustomed to manual labor. He'd said he was in construction. The hard strength of his hands proved it.

The quiet force of his grip inspired visions of him hoisting timber, swinging a hammer, lifting heavy sheets of glass, drilling into metal. Building things. Standing shirtless on a girder with sweat running in rivulets down his broad, muscular back. A faint shudder passed through her as her gaze rose from his hand circling her arm to his face just inches from hers.

His face carried scars—not obvious signs of injury, but scars left by time and fatigue, by struggle and strife. The skin at the outer edges of his eyes was creased with tiny lines; grooves at the corners of his mouth indicated that scowling came too easily to him. The stubble of beard along his square jaw reminded her of how far he'd journeyed that day, how weary he must be, how keenly disappointed he must be, having come all this way and not found the man he was looking for.

She wondered what the bristly growth would feel like against her fingertips.

That she could even think such a thing shocked her. She was used to being logical and polite, sympathetic and demure. She was *not* used to gazing into the smoky eyes of a man, inhaling the scent of him—an intoxicating blend of brandy, burning wood, leather and musk—and fantasizing about touching him.

"I'm ruining your evening," he said, his voice a low rumble.

"What?"

"You're the one who's hungry, aren't you?"

"Who, me?" For a moment she was unsure of what sort of hunger he meant. She felt her cheeks grow hot.

"I barged in on you, interrupted your bath, and instead of getting yourself some supper you've been entertaining me. You don't have to be so nice, okay?"

"I'm not so nice," she argued, then laughed when she heard what she'd said.

Matt only smiled. The lines at the outer edges of his eyes deepened and the intensity of his gaze diminished. He loosened his hold on her wrist so it felt more like a friendly clasp. "I'm sure I can make it downtown to the motel if you give me directions. I don't want to spoil any more of your evening."

She might have told him that this had been the most exciting evening she'd had in a long time. If she said that, though, his eyes might darken again, and his fingers might close around her wrist once more, his skin rough and warm against hers, his body too close.

He might think she was desperately lonely. He might take advantage of her. Just because he hadn't so far didn't mean he wasn't capable of it.

"You haven't spoiled my evening," she said slowly, carefully. "What would spoil my evening is if you left for the Braxton Motor Inn and wound up skidding off the road where it goes downhill at the fork. Trust me—you wouldn't be the first person that happened to. It's an awful stretch of road—folks wipe out there all the time. You'd survive, but your car would be in bad shape, and you'd be furious with yourself for driving in this weather when you could have been safe and warm and eating a hot turkey sandwich on rye."

"Hot turkey?" His eyes glinted with interest.

"I have some leftovers. Also some mushroom gravy."

"Mushroom gravy?" he repeated with a smile.

"Forgive me if I say *you're* the one who looks hungry."

"I'm not," he insisted, the grooves at the corners of his mouth resembling dimples more than scowl lines. "But I've never been able to resist a hot turkey sandwich on rye."

"With mushroom gravy?"

"Especially with mushroom gravy." He released her arm and stepped discreetly back. "Let me help."

If she were smart, Linda thought, she would send him back to the living room to have another brandy while she reheated the meat and gravy. Not because that would be proper etiquette but because she was too acutely conscious of him in her kitchen, too responsive to his nearness, too aware of the imprint of his hand on her arm. He hadn't held her that tightly, yet she felt his grip not just where he'd touched her but elsewhere, everywhere. She felt it in places she'd all but forgotten, deep inside her.

It would be much, much wiser to get him out of the kitchen until her nervous system cooled off. But he seemed to need to help her even more than she needed to put some distance between them.

He thought she was nice, and she had to concede that he was right. At that moment the nicest thing she could do would be to let him slice the bread.

She handed him the loaf, a cutting board and a knife. "Here," she said with a hesitant smile. "Help."

He took what she'd given him and smiled back, a dark, confident grin that made her feel as if something had passed between them, some emotion he understood far better than she did. Standing beside him at the counter as the night grew blacker and colder around them and the snow heaped higher on the ledge outside her window, she heard the echo of that single syllable, which defined her need far more than his.

Help.

She was out of her depth. She didn't know what was going on. She didn't know what existed between him and her brother, or what might come to exist between him and herself. She hated not knowing. It frightened her.

But she didn't give voice to her anxiety. Instead, she pulled the plate of meat and a container full of gravy from the refrigerator, arranged everything in a pan and turned up the heat, all the while listening to the whisper of the knife moving through the bread and the rattle of sleet blowing against the window.

Listening to the presence of the man in her home.

CHAPTER THREE

DEBBIE KNEW who all those authors must have had in mind when they wrote their books about women falling in love with the wrong man, or loving too much, or loving men who couldn't make commitments. "Here I am," she muttered, surveying the shelves inside her half-empty refrigerator. "Queen of the women who love messed-up men."

Unable to decide on a suitable supper, she closed the refrigerator. Her gaze fell on the calendar hanging from a magnetic hook on the refrigerator door. The top half of the March page showed a picturesque scene of budding flowers in a botanical garden somewhere in New England.

Gary was always buying New Englandy things and leaving them around the apartment: a framed painting of a covered bridge in the living room, pine-scented air fresheners in the bathroom and linen closet, a goofy penlight shaped like a Maine lighthouse, a subscription to *Boston* magazine, the kitchen calendar with its scenes of the changing seasons in western Connecticut, the Green Mountains of Vermont, seafaring Gloucester, opulent Newport. She studied the photograph occupying the upper half of the March page, all those azaleas and rhododendrons and blossoming apple trees screaming that it was springtime. Southern California didn't really have seasons at all.

Her gaze traveled to the lower half of the calendar. Gary had kissed her goodbye Sunday. Now it was Tuesday evening.

Where the hell was he?

Sighing, she left the tiny kitchen, trudged barefoot through the living room's dense shag carpeting to the television set, and clicked it on. She needed noise, distraction, something to keep her mind off the fact that she'd fallen in love with the wrong man.

The air in the room was stuffy. She considered opening a window, then decided against it and turned on the air-conditioning, instead. She had changed from her dress into a pair of shorts and one of Gary's T-shirts when she'd gotten home from the store a half hour ago. In a while she might build up an appetite. There was a container of leftover sweet-and-sour chicken in the refrigerator, or she could throw a sandwich together. For now, a diet soda and some TV was all she could handle.

On the screen a talking head was describing a drive-by shooting in Inglewood. She shoved her thick, dark hair back from her face, refastened the barrette that held it in a ponytail, and took a sip of her soda.

Why Gary, of all the men in the world? What was it about him? He was good-looking, sure, and magic in bed, but that was hardly enough.

Maybe it was his energy that drew her to him. He always had something going on. His mind was always stretching, exploring, experimenting with new ideas. Maybe it was his imagination, his willingness to think big, to dream.

Or maybe what made her love him was the sorrow she sensed in his deep-set green eyes. He'd been through so much in his life. The same year she'd made the varsity cheerleading squad at her high school in Bakersfield, he had been lugging an M16 through the jungles of Southeast Asia. When she'd been attending junior college, he'd been struggling to readjust to life in the United States. While she'd been traveling around the West and supporting herself with temporary secretarial work, he'd been burying his father, and then his mother, and then his sister's fiancé.

He had seen so much death, and he was so full of life. So what if he was moody? He'd earned the right.

She loved him in spite of the moods, and because of them. She loved him because only a heartless jerk wouldn't be torn apart by what Gary had gone through. She loved him because he knew so much of life's dark side, and yet he could make her laugh in a way no one else ever could.

She loved him because one day, back in October, he'd driven up in front of the shop where she worked in Beverly Hills, cruised to the curb in the white limo as if he owned it and waltzed into the shop. He'd lifted a Hermès silk scarf and said, "Excuse me, miss, I'd like to buy this for the woman I love."

Debbie had said, "The woman you love must be worth a lot of money."

He'd looked at the price tag, snorted and put down the scarf. "The woman I love is worth more than money," he'd declared, gazing into her eyes and giving her a dazzling smile. "I'd give my life for the woman I love. I'd give my skin. I've been thinking of getting a tattoo for the woman I love."

Debbie had played along. "What's it going to say? 'Mom'?"

"It's going to say 'Debbie.'"

"Debbie!" She had wrinkled her nose. "What an icky name."

He'd reached his arms across the counter, cupped her face and given her a loud kiss, one that brought a scowl from her boss, who'd been spying on her from behind the counter with the Paloma Picasso purse display. "If I got your name tattooed on my belly, would you be flattered?"

"I'd be nauseated. I don't want you to do that to yourself."

"I want the world to know I love you."

"Then rent a billboard on Sunset Boulevard."

"Tattoos are cheaper."

"Cheaper than a Hermès scarf, too," she'd pointed out. They'd kissed again. Her boss had cleared her throat loudly, and Debbie had pulled back. "Don't get a tattoo, Gary," she'd murmured. "There are other ways to let the world know you love me."

She'd been thinking of a wedding. An engagement, at least. An announcement. A diamond ring. An acknowledgment of some sort that Gary Villard was ready to settle down and claim Debbie Montoya as his partner in life.

He'd come home from work that evening wearing a pierced earring shaped like a *D*, in fourteen-karat gold. Which wasn't the same as a marriage proposal, but was so funny and whimsical and true to form that she had to love Gary for it.

So why hadn't he called her? Why had he run off to Portland a couple of weeks ago, and then come home acting like a man with too many secrets? Why had he looked up from the sports section of the paper Sunday morning, shoved back his chair, pulled her out of hers and carried her to bed? He had made the sweetest, gentlest love to her, then whispered, "I've got to go home for a while, but whatever happens, don't forget I love you." Then he'd packed a bag and vanished.

Where the hell was he?

WHERE WAS HE?

After hearing the phone on the other end ring ten times unanswered, Linda hung up. Despite the wretched weather, Gary's friends in Somerville—and Gary, if he was with them—had evidently gone out.

She wasn't sure how worried she ought to be about Gary's mysterious disappearance. He was forty-one years old, after all. He was a big boy, entitled to come and go without explaining himself to her or Debbie or anyone else. If he wanted to travel to Massachusetts and not stop in Braxton, Linda wouldn't take it personally.

On the other hand... He'd been so restless lately, so difficult to read. Debbie had confirmed that he was still experiencing bouts of moodiness.

And now, out of the blue, Gary's old army buddy had flown across the country right around the same time as Gary's alleged trip east, rented a car and driven from Connecticut through a snowstorm to surprise Gary. Matt Calloway was a big boy, too; he owed Linda no explanations. But even so, there was something peculiar about the whole thing.

Matt hadn't behaved at all strangely over supper. He'd acted hungry and tired, but friendly and willing to answer her questions. He'd told her a little about his construction company, about how he worked almost exclusively with two architects who valued his craftsmanship and the superior training of his crews. Even in the Pacific Northwest, where the economy was stronger than in New England, the construction business wasn't exactly booming. But the Calloway Construction Company—or "Three-C," as he called it—was doing well.

Linda didn't know how good "well" was. Obviously Matt was prosperous; he jetted around the country, rented cars and owned a fashionable leather jacket, even if it wasn't the appropriate outerwear for a late-season snowstorm. His wristwatch, a thin disk on a leather strap, was elegant in its simplicity. That he'd wound up wolfing down two whole sandwiches was a relection on the quality of the airline food he'd been served, not an indication that he didn't know where his next meal was coming from.

She surveyed the kitchen one last time to make sure everything was put away and the counters were clean. Switching off the light, she returned to the living room, where she'd sent Matt after promising him that if Gary turned up in Somerville she wouldn't let on that Matt was in Braxton.

He stood at one of the front windows, gazing out. Dinah was a dozing pile of fur in the center of the armchair. The fire had burned down; the orange coals brightened and dimmed, flickering with an inner life but shedding little heat.

"Is it still coming down?"

He let the curtain drop and turned from the window. "There must be at least a foot of snow on the ground so far."

"More like four inches," she corrected him with an indulgent smile. "Just yesterday, I thought I saw some hints of green peeking through the dead thatch of my lawn. Today, we're back to winter."

He nodded. His eyes searched her face, probing. "Well? Was Gary there?"

She shook her head. "No one answered the phone."

He took a moment to digest the news. "If they can go out, I suppose I can, too."

"If they went out, they put on boots and hats and walked where they were going," she explained. "I really don't think you should drive anywhere right now, Matt."

He turned back to the window and lifted the white drape again. "I've taken too much of your time."

But what would she have done with that time if he hadn't taken it? She would have relaxed for a while in a bath, soaking out the kinks left by a long day at her desk, listening to her clients' tales of woe. Then she would have slapped together a sandwich—unheated, no gravy—and carried it into the living room, where she would have built a fire, curled up in the easy chair with Dinah, eaten her snack and read another couple of chapters of the saga about immigrants from the Lower East Side that she'd borrowed from the library last week. When the fire had finally died down, she would have climbed the stairs and gone to bed.

The fire was dying down. Matt was still taking her time, and she was still willing to give it.

"You can spend the night here," she said. "I've got lots of room."

He rotated to face her. His eyes sought hers, held them, communicated an unfathomable message. "That isn't necessary," he said.

He had misinterpreted her generosity, and she couldn't blame him. She had taken him in, plied him first with brandy and then with food, and now she was inviting him to spend the night. What must he think of her?

Feeling her cheeks burn, she said, "I've got three big bedrooms upstairs. Well, two big bedrooms and a small one, but you'd have your own room. I mean..." Embarrassed, she dropped her gaze to his hands. She noted once more the discreet watch on his left wrist, and then his ringless fingers. The lack of a wedding band didn't mean much, though. "You would have your own room," she repeated.

"Linda—"

Her nervousness made her talk faster. "I don't see why you should go out in this weather, skid all the way into town if you're lucky enough not to wipe out at the fork, and then pay for the dubious privilege of spending a night in a shabby motel. The Braxton Motor Inn isn't the Ritz."

"Linda . . ."

"And, I mean, you're Gary's friend, and any friend of Gary's is welcome here, especially one of the fearless foursome. And you can use the phone to call your wife—"

"I haven't got a wife," he said quietly, making her cringe at how much she was babbling. "Linda, I'm not going to take your invitation the wrong way. You're being nice, that's all."

Why did he keep telling her she was nice? Nice was such a bland, bloodless word. She wasn't sure she liked it. She wasn't even sure he meant it as a compliment.

"Well," she said when the room's silence began to gnaw at her, "if you'd prefer that I not be nice, then go ahead, skid into town. I think the Braxton Motor Inn accepts most major credit cards."

He chuckled, a low, pleasant sound rising from his chest. Risking a glance at him, she saw that the squint lines framing his eyes had deepened, giving him an appealingly weathered look. "I've got a bag in the car," he told her.

A minute later, having wedged his feet back into his still-damp shoes, shrugged into his jacket which had dried stiff, and thanked Linda for the loan of an umbrella, he ventured out into the storm, cutting fresh footprints into her snowy front yard as he hurried to his car in the driveway. She watched him through the storm door, wondering why she had been so insistent on his spending the night under her roof—and what she was going to do, now that he'd accepted her invitation. If only he were older, or much, much younger, if only he were married, if only he were obnoxious or uncouth... If only he were rude enough for her to feel no compunction about sending him down the icy hill to the motel, or else avuncular and sexless enough for her to feel totally safe with him...

She stopped herself. She *was* totally safe. Matt had done nothing to indicate he had any romantic interest in her. Besides, he was one of Gary's closest friends, from one of the most stressful times in Gary's life. Matt would never take advantage of this situation.

She saw the interior light go off as he shut the car door and turned back to the house, a small suitcase clutched in his right hand. He trudged back across the snow to the porch, and she shaped what she hoped was a placid smile. Whether or not she was attracted to him didn't matter. All that mattered was that Gary's dear friend would have a warm, dry place to spend the night.

BEFORE HEADING UPSTAIRS with his bag, Matt asked
Linda if he could use her phone. "I'll bill the call to
my charge account," he said.

"Help yourself," she told him, gesturing toward the
kitchen. "I'll go and get the guest room ready."

He watched her climb the stairs. When she turned
on the second-floor hall light her hair seemed to come
alive, shining with tawny color beneath the ceiling
lamp.

He wondered why she lived alone in such a large old
farmhouse in a down-at-the-heels town on the edge of
nowhere. Most single women he knew lived in apartments or condos, the kind of places they would happily abandon the instant Mr. Right came along and
carried them off.

Maybe Linda wasn't alone—although he saw no
evidence of a male presence in her house. He'd noticed that the coats in the mudroom, where she'd left
his jacket to dry, were all styled for a woman. The
novels lining the shelves in the living room were de-
cidedly feminine in appeal—no techno-thrillers, no
adventure stories, nothing Matt would care to read.
The barn she used as a garage had room for only one
car, and her front porch was in need of repair.

Granted, some men wouldn't be the least bit in-
clined to fix a sagging porch. And there was nothing
to say a woman couldn't fix her own porch if she chose
to. But given how slim and dainty Linda looked, Matt
couldn't help but think that if she had a man in her
life, he would willingly do all the handiwork around
the place for her. If Matt were in her life, he certainly
would.

It was a peculiar thought, and he quickly shoved it
from his mind. Lifting the phone receiver, he placed a

call to the answering machine in his office, leaving his secretary a message regarding his whereabouts. Jean was the only person who knew why he'd come east in search of Gary Villard. As it was, she held herself partly responsible for the swindle.

Matt didn't blame her. She'd made an innocent mistake; it wasn't her fault. But she'd felt terrible about it, and he'd consoled her by telling her he was going to get the SOB and make him pay, in every sense of the word.

After recording his message, he lifted his suitcase, left the kitchen and started up the stairs. The walls of the second floor, like the first, were papered in a pattern of wide cream-colored stripes and tiny flowers. The runner rug covering the hardwood floor was dark red, with faded yellow-and-white flowers scattered across it. He smiled at the homey sound of a crisp sheet being snapped and then lowered onto a bed.

It was all so domestic, he thought. He wasn't used to cozy decor and fresh linens. He didn't deserve to have a pretty woman making up a bed for him in her own home, with her own clean sheets. He should have gone to the motel in town.

The hell with should-haves. He couldn't imagine any place he'd rather be than right here, in this comfortable old house with Linda.

Tracing the sounds to an open doorway at the end of the hall, he entered to find her smoothing a quilted comforter over a narrow bed. A bath towel and washcloth lay folded neatly on a maple dresser near the window. The lamp on the bed stand was on.

She straightened up and turned. "I hope this is all right," she said modestly.

For a moment he ignored the room. He looked only at her, her wide green-and-gold eyes, her sunset-colored hair, her arching cheekbones and soft lips. "It's fine," he assured her.

"The bathroom is right across the hall."

"Okay. Thanks."

Her gaze merged with his for a moment. Then, her cheeks flushing with color, she circled around him to the door. "If you need anything—"

"I'll be fine."

"Well. Good night, then."

"Good night."

Again her gaze locked with his for an immeasurable moment. "Don't worry about Gary," she murmured. "We'll find him." Then she pivoted and vanished down the hall.

He stared at the empty doorway until he heard the distant click of a door closing at the other end of the house. Exhaling, he set his suitcase on the bed and crossed to the window. The lamp created a glare against the glass, and he shut it off so he could see outside. It was still snowing.

We'll find him, she'd said, as if she were prepared to assist Matt in his search, to shoulder the burden with him.

Would she be so eager to help if she knew why he wanted to find Gary? Would she gleefully sign on if she knew Matt wanted to wring every stolen cent out of Gary, and then every blasted lie, every ounce of hypocrisy... Would she take arms against her own brother?

If she had known the truth, would she have even let Matt spend the night in her home?

Not a chance.

Gazing out at the wintry blackness on the other side of the windowpane, he wanted to empty his mind of thoughts of treachery and revenge. He wanted to think only about Linda—about her clear, honest eyes and her defiant chin, about the way she'd blushed under his scrutiny, as if standing alone in a bedroom with him had been a sexual act.

Frustration surged through him. Instead of contemplating the odds that he'd track down Linda Villard's brother tomorrow, he was standing beneath her snow-covered roof and contemplating the even slimmer odds that she might return to his room and press her sweet, full lips to his.

He had no right to want that.

But Matt had learned long ago that right and wrong were irrelevant. Twelve months in the jungles of 'Nam taught him that vital lesson. You figured out what you needed, you went after it, you stayed alive, and if luck was with you you got what you wanted.

Sometimes, luck put something totally different in your path. Sometimes you discovered you'd actually wanted something else all along. And sometimes luck just passed you by.

Right and wrong had nothing to do with it at all.

IN THE MORNING, she was gone.

He knew it the instant he opened his eyes and saw the cat just inches from his face, sitting on the bed stand and glowering at him, its tail switching back and forth. If Linda were home, he doubted the beast would have bothered with him.

He sat up and groaned. His watch lay on the table next to the cat, who courteously refrained from clawing him when he reached for it. No matter that he and

Dinah had made friends last night beside the fireplace; he still didn't think much of cats.

Ten-thirty. In Portland it would be only seven-thirty, so he didn't feel too guilty about sleeping so late. Shoving his hair back from his brow, he stood, stalked barefoot over to the window and raised the shade.

The world outside looked like something out of a dream. Diaphanous white fog rose directly off the snow, giving the earth an ethereal soft-focus. His window overlooked the garage barn and beyond it a hilly meadow bordered by an evergreen forest and the remnants of a stone wall. Far away, past the wall and through the trees, he detected smoke curling from the chimney of a house. Whoever Linda's neighbors were, they weren't within shouting distance.

Again he was struck by how strange it was that a beautiful, apparently unattached woman would isolate herself by living in a rambling farmhouse on a back road in the mountains. That thought was superseded by the more immediate thought that if she wasn't at home, he was all by himself. He had to get dressed. Gary might show up at any minute.

Wrapping the bath towel around his waist, he carried a fresh set of clothes across the hall to the bathroom. Ten minutes later, showered, shaved and dressed in a pair of blessedly dry jeans, a shirt and a wool sweater, he repacked his bag, made the bed and went downstairs, his footsteps echoing in the empty house.

He considered giving Linda a stern lecture about home security. How could she abandon him in her house, surrounded by her belongings, when she didn't know him from Adam? For that matter, how could she have let him spend the night alone with her, snowed in? How could she have trusted him so easily?

Morning sunlight filtered through the eerie white mist to illuminate the living room. He peered out a window and discovered that the road had been plowed and the driveway was shoveled clear. His rental car sat where he'd parked it last night, but the snow had been brushed from the windows.

He frowned. If her car had been inside the garage, she would have had to move his car to get hers out. She must have crept into his room, helped herself to the key, driven his car out into the road, freed her car, returned his to the driveway, crept back into his bedroom and left the key for him on the dresser.

He wondered if she'd tried to wake him up. He pictured her gliding into his room, cupping her hands over his bare shoulders, giving him a shake and whispering, "Move your car, Matt."

But if she'd touched him, if her hands had come in contact with his skin, he would have pulled her onto the bed with him. He would have gathered her into his arms and held her slender body tight against his, and pressed his mouth to her lips. He would have lived every fantasy that had haunted him throughout his restless night, every unreasonable dream he'd had of consuming the sweetness of her mouth and basking in the warmth of her eyes, caressing her silky skin and molding his hands to the curves of her breasts, her hips... Half-asleep, his defenses down, he would have acted on instinct.

She had probably suspected as much. She had probably figured she would be safer shuttling the cars

back and forth in the driveway by herself than asking
him for help.

He wandered into the kitchen. The note propped up
against the saltshaker on the table caught his eye:

Dear Matt,
I hope you got a good rest. I know what jet lag
can be like. There's cereal in the cabinet by the
sink, bread and fresh oranges in the refrigerator,
and coffee in the pot.
  I'll be at my office in the Braxton Public Health
Center on Second Street, just off Main. Drop by
if you need anything. If you see Gary before I do,
give him hell for me.

                                     Linda

He reread the note, trying not to respond to the
femininity of her handwriting with its arching lines
and opulent curls, and the girlish charm of her pink
scallop-bordered stationery. The words were what
counted, not the style. The words—her generosity, her
naiveté in trusting him, her inexplicable kindness.

If you see Gary before I do, give him hell for me.

How could he resist a woman who wrote a sentence
like that?

As he peeled an orange and pried it into wedges, he
tried to guess what sort of job she had. If she worked
at a public health center, she could be a doctor or a
nurse. He tried to picture her dressed for work in a
medical coat, with a stethoscope draped around her
neck. Maybe she wore eyeglasses, or white stockings
and rubber-soled oxfords. Maybe she worked in a
laboratory, shaking test tubes and studying slides and
dispensing good news: ''Yes, you're pregnant.'' ''No,

it's benign." Maybe she inoculated children, and then hugged away their sobs and gave them lollipops.

He was amazed at how easy it was to forget that she was the sister of a lowlife, how easy to think only positive things about her. Wasn't it just as likely that she was a small-minded bureaucrat, telling poor single mothers that their benefits had run out and they could no longer obtain publicly financed health care?

He didn't want to believe that, but anything was possible. Linda could be a heartless bureaucrat, and she could be an accomplice in her brother's criminal activity.

Don't trust her, he told himself, even though every ounce of sentiment inside him argued that he ought to. He'd let his sentiments run the show with Gary, and look what had happened. He mustn't make the same mistake with Linda.

After popping the last wedge of orange into his mouth, Matt filled a mug with coffee, turned off the machine and scanned the tidy counters of Linda's kitchen. He wasn't sure what he was looking for, but a personal telephone book with the address of Gary's friends in Somerville would make a good start.

He pulled open a drawer filled with silverware, one filled with cooking utensils, and finally one with assorted papers and non-cooking items. Near the front of the drawer he found a stack of opened bills held together with a rubber band. Stifling a fleeting pang of conscience, he flipped through the envelopes. Her telephone bill showed two calls to Los Angeles but none to Somerville.

Returning it to the stack, he pulled out her charge-card bill and scanned her purchases. Her entire bill for the month came to under two hundred dollars; the most expensive purchase was eighty-seven dollars and change at a women's clothing shop. A few small purchases at a discount drug store, two gasoline bills and several store names he couldn't identify accounted for the rest of the charges.

Well, he supposed, if she were in cahoots with Gary, she wouldn't be relying on credit cards for her most recent purchases. She would be flush with ill-gotten cash. Even if she'd deposited her share of the loot in her local savings bank, any charge-card extravagance on her part wouldn't show up until the following month's bill.

Sighing, he slid the bill back inside the rubber band and closed the drawer. Rummaging through her bills made him feel like a trespasser. The woman had had enough faith in him to leave him alone in her house; the least he could do was live up to her high opinion of him.

He drained his mug of coffee in several long swallows, then rinsed it out and left it beside the sink. Snatching the sheet of pink stationery from the table, he headed back upstairs to get his bag.

At the top of the stairs he hesitated.

It wasn't really trespassing, he told himself, moving down the hall to her bedroom at the front of the house. It wasn't really snooping. All he wanted was a glance through her personal phone book to find the name and address of her brother's friends in Somerville. And maybe a quick search for unseemly wads of cash.

He hesitated again at the threshold of her bedroom. Morning sunlight filtered through the lacy curtains and dappled the starburst quilt spread across her brass bed. The walls were ivory, the floor covered with a thick rug of moss green edged in white and scattered with small white stars. An embroidered linen runner adorned the oak dresser; a scarf had been tossed over the oval oak frame of a freestanding mirror. A rocking chair constructed of the same pale oak sat in a corner.

His gaze returned to her bed, to the two fluffy pillows leaning against the brass bars of the headboard. He imagined her hair splayed across one of those pillows—and his head on the other, his legs entwined with hers beneath that marvelous quilt. He imagined her lips parted in pleasure as he touched her, and her eyes closed, and her body, her tight, lush body rising onto him and then sinking down, all around him...

A groan tore itself from his throat. Linda had done nothing to inspire such erotic thoughts—nothing but gaze at him with those magnificent eyes of hers, and smile at him with those velvet-soft lips, and invite him to spend the night.

He took several deep breaths and willed his blood to cool off. A phone book or cash, he told himself, venturing into the room. A phone book to get him out of her house and free of her spell, or cash to give him a reason to hate her.

He yanked open the drawer in her night table and poked through its contents: a county telephone directory, a sewing kit, a message pad and pencil, a flashlight. An unopened package of condoms.

"Oh, God." It was half a moan, half a laugh. He tossed the box back into the drawer and sank down onto the bed, shaking his head in disgust at the voyeuristic curiosity that had him wondering whether she'd just bought the box a few days ago or whether it had sat there, sealed in cellophane, for months. Shoving the drawer shut, he stormed out of the room.

It didn't mean anything, he told himself, grabbing his suitcase and hurrying down the stairs. Linda Villard was a smart woman, and smart women in these times kept certain items on hand.

But the box was sealed, a voice rattled inside his skull. If she had a steady boyfriend, she'd have torn the plastic wrapper off before storing it in her drawer. Who would want to have to take time out in the middle of foreplay to wrestle with a shrink-wrapped package?

Thinking about Linda and foreplay caused his blood to grow hot again, flowing swiftly and directly to one part of his anatomy. He leaned against the newel post at the bottom of the stairs, closed his eyes and ordered the muscles in his lower body to relax. Why did she have this effect on him? Why did she make him feel less like a jaded forty-one-year-old man than an inexperienced kid with hyperactive glands?

It wasn't simply because she was generous or intelligent or beautiful. It wasn't merely because from the moment his gaze met hers he had felt, utterly without reason, as if he'd been searching not for her shifty brother but for her, only her.

He hadn't felt that at all, he swore to himself. He wasn't looking for a copper-haired, hazel-eyed beauty with a box of condoms—

Forget it, he cautioned himself. *Forget you ever saw the damned thing.*

Tightening his grip on his suitcase, he walked through the kitchen to the mudroom, where his jacket looked far too natural hanging on a peg next to her down parka. He donned it and then his shoes, which she had asked him to leave in the small back room to dry overnight. Then he retraced his steps, bypassing the stairs for the front door and stepping outside.

The morning, while chilly, was milder than he'd expected. Fog continued to waft lazily up from the blanket of snow covering the yard. The dense white vapor deflected the sun's light, illuminating the air with a diffuse glow.

He followed the cleared front path to the driveway, tossed his bag into the back seat and settled himself behind the wheel. Opening the glove compartment, he pulled out the road map of New England the rental agent had provided, unfolded it and searched for Somerville. It was just north of Cambridge, outside of Boston. Assuming that was where Gary had gone, Matt could make the trip in under two hours—if only he knew where he was going once he got there.

Linda would know. She would know where Gary's friends lived, and she would know whether he'd checked in there yet. If he hadn't, she might have some other ideas about where her prodigal brother had gone.

As troublesome as she was to his libido, Matt had to see her. She was his only chance to find Gary.

CHAPTER FOUR

THE DOOR to Linda's cramped office opened a crack and Kay peeked in.

Linda held up her finger to silence Jack Weyburn, who was seated on the chair across the desk from her. He had been describing for her the dismal week he'd had—three job interviews, no offers, his twelve-year-old son sent home from school again for fighting, his mother complaining that she simply couldn't handle the younger grandchildren anymore. It had been two years since Jack's wife had walked out, and he was doing the best he could. But ever since he'd gotten pink-slipped during the most recent round of layoffs at Braxton Gravel and Asphalt, his best didn't seem to be nearly good enough. He was stretched to the limit, both financially and emotionally. Fortunately, he'd had the sense to seek help before he snapped.

He nodded, and Linda turned toward the door. "There's a man asking for you out in the waiting room," Kay reported.

"Who?"

"Someone named Matt Calloway," the young receptionist told her. "He's not a client."

Matt's visit to the clinic didn't surprise Linda, but it delighted her. She had assumed that he would show up sooner or later. She had dressed with that assumption in mind, pinning her long hair up into what she hoped was a sophisticated twist, dressing in a pastel turtleneck and matching cardigan that complemented her delicate coloring, wearing a flattering skirt, nylons and low-heeled leather pumps rather than the slacks and boots everyone else on the health center staff had worn in deference to the messy weather. She'd even put on a touch of makeup, although in the three hours since she'd left the house most of it had worn off.

"Tell him I'll be taking a break after Mr. Weyburn and I are finished," she informed Kay. "If he'd like, we can have lunch together."

Kay's eyes sparkled with interest. "A lunch date," she singsonged.

"He's a friend of my brother's," Linda clarified, although she allowed herself to share Kay's smile. Matt *was* a friend of Gary's, and nothing more, but Linda's social life was generally such a bore, she didn't object to a bit of good-natured needling from Kay.

As soon as Kay left, closing the door behind her, Linda dismissed Matt from her mind and devoted the next twenty minutes to Jack Weyburn and his problems. She suggested booking his son for a session with her on Monday so they could discuss strategies for controlling his temper before he hurt someone and got himself permanently expelled from school. She promised to arrange for the county's home-care service to send a day worker to his home once a week to give Mrs. Weyburn some time off from the younger children. She helped review his budget, and reassured him that accepting food stamps didn't mean he was a failure.

"It's like welfare," Jack muttered, running a hand through his thinning hair. "I don't feel right about it."

"Everyone has debts," she reminded him. "Sometimes we can handle them, and sometimes they get to be too much for us. Accepting food stamps isn't a crime."

"It ain't exactly an honor, either," he retorted.

"Think of it this way—you've paid taxes over the years, and those taxes have helped other people in need. Now it's your turn to accept help."

"I'm helpless, right? I'm a loser."

"Don't think of it that way. Think of it as a sign of strength, that you're not afraid to accept help. Times are tough, Mr. Weyburn. Lots of people have been laid off. They're struggling to make ends meet, just like you are. They aren't bad people. They've just run into some bad luck."

"You ever have this kind of bad luck?"

She measured her response. As a social worker for the city, Linda would never be rich, but she had never been poor, either. She exercised thrift, but she'd never known real hunger. The fear of crushing debt was something she could only imagine.

Yet it was her job to imagine that fear, and to empathize with those who had to live with it. Sorrow came in all different shapes and colors, but pain was universal. She knew enough about pain to understand what people like Jack Weyburn were going through, and to want to do whatever she could to alleviate their sorrow.

"I've had other kinds of bad luck," she told him. "When I was at my lowest, someone offered to help me. I accepted that help, Mr. Weyburn, and it enabled me to heal. We all need a little help sometimes. There's no shame in it."

"If you say so." He sighed and stood, signaling that he was ready to leave. She ushered him to the door, shook his hand, wished him well and closed the door behind him.

She simultaneously closed a door inside herself. No more grief right now, no more sadness. She was going to have lunch with Matt Calloway.

She jotted her notes into Jack Weyburn's folder and slid it into place in her file cabinet. Returning to her desk, she lifted her purse from the bottom drawer, pulled out her compact and examined her reflection in the small round mirror. A few tendrils of hair had unraveled from the twist and fell softly around her face. Her lipstick had faded into a muted pink.

She touched the puff to her nose, conceded that no amount of powder could erase her freckles, and returned the compact to her purse. Then she stood and left the office.

Seated among the assorted woebegone clients of the social services department, Matt looked sorely out of place. When he rose from the folding metal chair and smiled at her, he looked even more out of place. Gone was the stubble of beard, the weariness and wariness that had shadowed his eyes last night. His apparel was clean and dry, his hair neatly combed.

He looked gorgeous.

A shy smile tweaked her lips. "Hi," she said.

"Lunch?"

"If you'd like."

"Do you have a coat?"

"We won't be outside for long."

Smiling, he cupped his hand around her elbow in a gesture that should have seemed quite ordinary. She recalled the way his hand had felt on her wrist last night. He'd been holding her then, stopping her, commanding her attention. This touch was merely a matter of routine chivalry, yet it had just as wild an effect on her nervous system, magnifying her awareness of him in ways she couldn't begin to comprehend.

Doing her best to ignore the curious stares of the clients—to say nothing of Kay, who gawked at her from behind her reception counter by the door—Linda led Matt out of the waiting room and down a hall to the building's main entrance. "What exactly do you do here?" he asked.

"I'm a social worker."

"I thought maybe you were a nurse or something."

She smiled pensively. She'd been a nurse once, an amateur one, and after losing her patient she'd sworn she would never do that again. "I guess you could say I'm a nurse for people's psyches," she said. "I help them straighten out their lives." She stepped through the heavy glass door when he opened it for her, then waited for him to join her on the broad concrete step. "There's a coffee shop right across the street."

"I was hoping to take you somewhere a little nicer," he said.

It wasn't a date, she told herself. If he wanted to take her somewhere nicer, it was only to repay her hospitality. "I'd love that," she said with a grin, "but I get only a half hour for lunch. We'd probably have to drive a half hour just to find a decent restaurant."

"The coffee shop it is," he agreed, ushering her to the crosswalk at the corner.

In spite of the wintry bite in the air, the sun had done a fine job melting most of the snow. It lay in slushy piles along the curb, but the sidewalks were clear and the normal sounds of downtown traffic were punctuated by a constant undertone of drip-drip-drip as snow and ice melted from the roofs and awnings of the buildings lining the street.

The sun invigorated Linda. Matt's presence invigorated her even more.

That morning, between two clients, she'd squeezed in a call to Somerville and discovered that Gary was, indeed, with his friends there. "Why didn't you call me?" she'd scolded, although she did nothing to hide her happiness at his unexpected jaunt east. "When did you get in? Are you going to come and visit me?"

"Yeah, sure," Gary had said. "I got in Tuesday morning. I'd wanted to arrive in Monday, but I couldn't get a flight, so I wound up working most of Monday and then heading back to the airport straight from work. I was figuring I'd visit a few days with Steve and Marlene and then maybe come out to Braxton sometime over the weekend. Is that okay with you?"

"It's fine," she'd told him. "Have you talked to Debbie yet? I called her last night and—"

"Yeah, I talked to her."

"Is everything all right between you two?"

Gary had muttered something unintelligible under his breath. Aloud, he said, "Don't be a social worker, Linda."

"If you're asking me to stop caring about you, you're asking the impossible."

"I know." A reluctant laugh had escaped him. "So, maybe I'll show up in a couple of days. By the weekend, for sure. Okay?"

She'd considered telling him that Matt Calloway was in Braxton, and that perhaps he ought to con-

sider showing up earlier. But Matt wanted to surprise
Gary, and she saw no reason to spoil the surprise.
"The weekend," she'd said. "Friday night? Saturday
morning?"

"Yeah, whatever."

"Thanks for being so specific," she'd grumbled,
then laughed. Whenever he arrived, she would welcome him with joy. "I'll see you soon," she'd said
before bidding him goodbye.

After she'd hung up, she wondered whether Matt
would be able to remain in town until the weekend. In
all likelihood, he would prefer to go back to Hartford
to stay with his business associate until Gary made his
appearance in Braxton. That would be the sensible
move. Unless, of course, he had to return to Oregon
before he had a chance to meet up with Gary.

She swore to herself that she wouldn't be disappointed if he left Braxton. For Gary's sake alone, she
hoped Matt could stay through the weekend.

The coffee shop was bustling, but they were seated
without delay. Matt gave the place a quick inspection
and apparently found nothing too objectionable about
the vinyl booths, the Formica-topped tables, the laminated menus and syrupy background music. At least
the food was wholesome and cheap.

"Why didn't you wake me up this morning?" he
asked.

Linda peered over her menu at him and grinned. "I
tried."

His smile faded slightly, and his gaze intensified.
She lifted her menu to shield herself from his scrutiny, aware that her cheeks were flushed the same
shade as her pink sweater.

She had felt like an intruder entering his room that morning, wanting to rouse him only so he could move his car. When she'd seen him sprawled out in bed, though, his naked upper torso revealed by the loose drape of the blanket, she had almost run for her life. But the sight of him had been too magnificent to pass up.

The rich tan of his skin had contrasted sharply with the white linens. His black hair had been mussed, thick waves tumbling around his face. His shoulders had spread in rugged shelves on either side of his strong neck, and the one arm slung over the blanket had revealed athletic contours of muscle and sinew. The hint of hair across the upper portion of his chest had tantalized her. If she weren't the sort of woman she was, she would have stripped off the covers and feasted her eyes. She'd had no doubt it would have been a feast.

But she *was* the sort of woman she was, so she'd nervously tapped his shoulder with one finger, whispered, "Matt?" and then retreated at a gallop, snatching his keys as she dashed out of the room.

Something in Matt's piercing gaze told her he could guess what had gone through her mind when she'd seen him sleeping in the guest room that morning. And being the sort of woman she was, that embarrassed her even more.

Fortunately, a waitress approached their table and offered Linda a desperately needed distraction. She ordered a cup of clam chowder and a salad. Matt requested a hamburger. When the waitress removed their menus Linda felt perilously exposed.

His gaze was gentler now. He leaned back against the banquette, studying her with a combination of

amusement and bemusement. "I can't believe you just
left me alone in your house like that," he said.

She shrugged. "You weren't alone. Dinah was
there."

"Ah, yes, the killer cat. Seriously, Linda—letting
me stay for the night in your house, snowed in... How
could you trust me? You don't even know me."

"You're Matt Calloway," she said, as if that explained everything. In her mind it did.

He seemed less amused, more bemused. She wanted
to change the subject, to tell him about her call to
Somerville. Before she could broach the subject of
Gary's whereabouts, the waitress was back with a
pitcher of ice water and a line of patter about the
freaky weather. "Think we'll get any daffodils this
year?" she asked. "I thought I saw a few tips breaking through the soil in my yard just a couple of days
ago, but after all this snow..."

"They'll survive," said Linda. "They're hardy."

"Did you say you wanted some coffee, too?" the
waitress asked Matt. At his nod, she flipped over the
upside-down cup in his saucer. "You new in town?"

"He's just visiting," Linda said, strangely protective of him.

"Oh, yeah? Stay awhile, why don't you." The
waitress gave Matt a saucy wink, then waltzed away to
get the coffeepot.

Matt chuckled. "Kind of forward, isn't she?"

Linda shrugged again. When her gaze intersected
with Matt's she shared his grin.

"How about you?" he asked calmly. "Do you have
a boyfriend?"

Her grin waned as caution overtook her. The question wasn't out of line, but she preferred to keep her private affairs private. "Why do you ask?"

"I spent last night at your house. I'd like to know if someone's going to come after me with a shotgun."

His humor put her at ease. Surely if she could trust Matt to spend the night in her house—and he'd proven himself wholly worthy of her trust—she could trust him with her personal life. "No," she said. "I don't have a boyfriend."

He took a moment to digest that. "Why not?"

"Why should I?" she countered, keeping her voice low and reasonable. "Do I lose points for not having one?"

The waitress returned with the coffee, but Matt deliberately ignored her, staring at Linda with unwavering concentration until the waitress departed. "You're a beautiful, kindhearted woman," he said. "I don't know why you don't have millions of guys banging down your door."

"Braxton hasn't got millions of guys," she pointed out bashfully, refusing to let his flattery overwhelm her.

"So why do you live in Braxton?"

"It's my home," she said, running her fingers back and forth over the paper napkin she'd spread across her lap. She waited to feel nervous or put-upon; she waited for resentment to fill her. But it didn't. She honestly didn't mind talking to him about herself. "Gary and I grew up here," she explained. "In the house where I'm living now. When my parents died they left the house to him."

"I didn't realize your parents were gone," Matt said sympathetically.

"They were on in years. They were already in their thirties when Gary was born, and well into their forties when I arrived. I was an afterthought—or an accident, I guess. When my father died, my mother moved down to Florida and let Gary stay on in the house. She died a few years later and left it to him in her will."

"And you just decided to stay on, too?" Matt asked.

She shook her head. His gaze was so steadfast and sincere, the words flowed easily out of her. "I was living in Boston at the time. I met a man, and we fell in love. We were going to get married as soon as we both finished our graduate work."

Once again the waitress interrupted, this time with their food. Linda smiled her thanks, but Matt gave the woman an impatient nod and she stalked away.

"What happened?" he asked. "Did you get married?"

"No. It was discovered..." She sighed. Remembering no longer brought her blinding, stabbing pain, but there was still an ache, a tender region in her soul. "It was discovered that he had a brain tumor."

"I'm sorry," he murmured, neglecting his burger and reaching across the table. She pulled one of her hands from her lap and slipped it into his. He needed to comfort her; she wanted to be comforted.

"Of all the cancers, that's one of the cruelest. When he was diagnosed, I moved in with him and took care of him. His parents supported us financially. I think they were too traumatized to give him the kind of personal care he required. They couldn't bear to see him having seizures, being unable to talk, to eat..." She smiled sadly. "I couldn't bear it, either, but I

loved him, so I did it anyway. We were together like
that for three years—and he died in his own bed. I was
able to give him that.''

Matt's fingers tightened around hers. ''Last night I
thought you were the nicest woman I'd ever met,'' he
said. ''Now...'nice' doesn't cut it. You're incredible.''

''Oh, I'm not incredible,'' she scoffed. ''I loved
him. When you love someone, you want to do whatever you can for him. Besides...'' She grinned sheep-
ishly. ''Once he was gone I completely fell apart. I
could be strong when I had to be strong, but the moment I didn't have to be strong anymore, I became a
total wreck.'' She tasted her chowder. It was hot and
creamy, soothing going down.

''I can't picture you as a wreck.''

''Oh, I was. The basket case to end all basket cases.
I don't know what would have become of me if Gary
hadn't saved me.''

Matt withdrew his hand and sat straighter. At first
Linda thought she'd said something wrong, although
she had no idea what. Then she realized that he'd released her so he could prepare his hamburger. ''How
did Gary save you?'' he asked as he shook ketchup
from a bottle onto the patty.

''He came to Boston, scraped me off the floor and
carted me to Braxton. He brought me home. He was
working for a trucking company in town then, earning enough to support me as well as himself. He said,
'You've spent three years taking care of Andrew. Now
you're going to take care of yourself.' He saw to everything else so I could see to myself. He gave me time,
peace, brotherly love—everything I needed to heal.''

''And then he gave you his house?''

"It's still in his name. Now that I'm living there alone, I pay the taxes and utilities. But technically, he owns it. He lost his job here a few years ago—the trucking company he worked for went belly-up. So he decided to head out west for a while. I was working at the public health center by then, and it was his turn to take a little time off. He fell in love with southern California—and with Debbie, too. So he stayed. And I stayed here."

Matt ate, his eyes never leaving her.

"Gary and I have always been close. It's kind of funny when you think about how he's eight years older than me. But even when I was a little kid, he never resented me. He always took care of me. And now... he's all I've got as far as family. Even with three thousand miles between us, we still try to take care of each other."

Matt said nothing.

"I'm so glad he found you after all these years," she continued. "You aren't just a friend, Matt. You and Gary have special ties to each other. I bet you feel almost like family, too."

Matt set down his burger and reached for his coffee. "I don't know," he said slowly. "We've both changed a lot since 'Nam."

"Do you think he's changed?" she asked, then smiled and shook her head. "Of course you would. You haven't seen him for two decades." She stirred her soup, gathering her thoughts. Maybe Matt could explain what Gary was going through. He was Gary's age, and he'd lived through so many of the same things Gary had lived through. "I worry about him, Matt. As much as he's always worried about me, now

I worry about him. He's been having a bit of a rough time lately.''

"Oh?"

"He seems to have taken his fortieth birthday kind of hard. He's still unsettled in his life. I think he used to imagine himself married by the time he turned forty, with kids and a solid, secure job. And it just hasn't worked out that way for him." She sighed. "And then there was the whole war thing."

"What whole war thing?"

"A lot of veterans underwent kind of an emotional meltdown during the Gulf War a couple of years ago. It destabilized them. I've seen it in my practice. All those scenes of high-tech warfare on television, all the glory and the parades those soldiers got that you guys never got when you came home. Didn't it bother you?"

He shook his head, but his gaze never shifted from her. "No."

"It was even hard for me to watch, and I'm not a veteran. It broke my heart to think another whole generation of kids was going to go through the hell you and my brother went through."

"We went through it," Matt said sharply. "But we came out the other side. We survived. If all these years later Gary suddenly discovered he couldn't handle it, that's his problem."

Matt's unsympathetic attitude surprised her. She groped for an explanation. Maybe he had no patience for the weakness in others because he recognized the same weakness in himself. Maybe the news that one of his war friends could have been shaken up more than two decades after he'd left Vietnam undermined his sense of stability. Or maybe he simply couldn't accept everyone in the world wasn't as rock-solid as he was.

"Gary *could* handle it," she said in her brother's defense. "I'm sure he's going to shake off his moodiness soon. He's such a wonderful man. He deserves only good things."

Matt took a long, deep breath. His eyes were cold and black, like two dead stars. "He deserves nothing," he said.

She flinched, as if Matt had reached across the table and slapped her. "What?"

"Your brother is a thief, Linda. He's a bum. He's a two-bit thug. And he doesn't deserve a goddamn thing."

WHAT HAD HE DONE? Why? How could he have hurt her like that?

She sat across the table from him, very still, very pale, her lips pressed together and her eyes wide and bright with shock. She gripped the edge of the table with hands so tense the bones pressed against her skin. If he had to choose one word to describe her expression, it would be loathing.

He didn't blame her. Here she'd been, swearing that she trusted him with a faith so pure it seemed like something almost sacred, while less than an hour ago he'd been prowling through her house, snooping through her drawers, contemplating her condoms, for God's sake. She had trusted him enough to enter his room as he slept, little knowing that his sleep had been filled with dreams of how many different ways he could take her.

And now, when she'd proved the depth of her trust by sharing with him the crippling grief she'd suffered

over her lover's illness and death, when she'd peeled
back her protective shell and let him glimpse her vulnerable soul, what had he done?

He'd told her the truth.

He could have done it differently. He should have.
He should have softened it, led slowly up to it, prepared her for it—or else he shouldn't have told her at
all. Yet he'd let fly with the truth like a bullet to her
heart, with every intention of hurting her.

Why?

If he was going to force her to confront the truth,
he'd have to confront the truth about himself, and
right now the truth looked an awful lot like jealousy.
It agonized him to hear her speak so lovingly of the
man who had betrayed him. Nobody had ever spoken
of Matt that way. For all he knew, nobody had ever
loved him so unconditionally, so blindly.

It made no sense for him to be jealous of Gary. The
man was her brother, her flesh and blood. But
still...Matt wanted Linda to believe in him the way she
believed in Gary. He wanted her to say she thought he
deserved good things, and he wanted those good
things to include her admiration, her respect, and
more.

If he could take back what he'd said about Gary, if
he could turn back the clock to a second before he'd
spoken ... But he couldn't. The truth was out. The
damage was done.

He reached for her hand again, but before he could
touch her she recoiled and hid it in her lap. "Linda,"
he said, a plea filtering through his tone.

She opened her mouth but apparently lacked the
ability to speak. Instead, she pressed her lips together

once more and turned to stare at the tabletop jukebox
built into the wall.

"Linda," he repeated, "I'm sorry."

"I can't believe you could say such cruel things,
such vicious lies—"

"They aren't lies." He meant to sound gentle, but
he sounded only defeated. No matter what he said,
he'd lost any affection she might have felt toward him.
Still, he couldn't stop himself from explaining, trying
to justify his accusation. "I'm sure your brother's
been good to you. Not to me, though. I didn't come
here to hurt you, Linda. I came here to find Gary, because of what he did to me."

"My brother is incapable of doing anything so terrible." Her voice came out strained and gritty, as if she
were forcing the words past pebbles in her throat.
"He's no angel, but he's not a—God, a *bum,* a
thug. . . . How could you say such things?"

He exhaled. "I wish there was an easy way to tell
you."

"Tell me what? Lies about my brother?"

"They aren't lies. He robbed me."

"Oh, he robbed you." Her attempt at sarcasm
failed; she came across more desperate than incredu-
lous. "What did he do, swipe a pen from your desk?"

"No. He swiped eighteen thousand dollars from my
bank account."

Once again she flinched. A ghastly image arose in
Matt's mind, a recollection of a guy in his squadron
who'd gone berserk after a particularly brutal skir-
mish shortly before he'd shipped off for home. They'd
come upon a Vietcong lying dead by the side of the
road, and Matt's buddy started firing bullets at the
corpse, making it jump and bounce, until finally Matt

and Gary wrestled his gun out of his hand and dragged him away.

Now Matt was firing ugly little bullets of truth at Linda. The first one had already destroyed her, but he kept shooting, and the impact of his accusations made her jump. Like a crazed soldier on a bad day, he couldn't seem to stop blasting away.

"Gary took twenty thousand dollars in all. Two thousand I knew about. It was supposed to be a loan. He told me he was having some money problems, and—"

"No," she cut him off.

"Listen to me, Linda—"

"No. My brother isn't having any money problems. He earns a good living."

"I'm telling you what happened. He told me he needed some money, and I offered to lend him two thousand dollars."

She gazed around the restaurant, avoiding his eyes, probably searching for the nearest exit. He suspected she would rather flee than listen to him say another word.

If he insisted on telling her the truth, she would despise him. If he didn't tell her the truth, he would despise himself. Resigning himself to her hatred, he plowed on. "I wrote Gary a check for two thousand dollars, and he doctored it. He added an extra zero, and he turned the *o* in the 'two' into an *e* and squeezed in an *nty*."

"You can't expect me to believe this," she said, the pebbles in her throat coagulating into solid stone, giving her voice a hard, heavy quality.

"I don't expect anything," he conceded with a bitter sigh. "But that's what he did, and that's why I'm here."

"That's the most ridiculous thing I've ever heard. I mean—even assuming you *were* telling the truth, what could my brother possibly do with a doctored check? Unless you make a habit of keeping twenty thousand dollars in your checking account, the check would have bounced if he tried to cash it."

"I have one of those combination accounts," Matt explained. "Part savings, part checking. I don't remember how Gary got me to mention it to him, but he did. We were talking about running a company, meeting a payroll, financial services, the way I did business... I don't know. But it came out that I had a combined savings-checking account. Somehow he learned that if I accidentally overdrew a check, the bank would transfer the money from the savings to the checking to cover the check."

"Right," she scoffed. "Your bank automatically transferred twenty thousand dollars and they didn't even bother to confirm it with you."

"They did call to confirm it," he said. "I was out of the office, and my secretary took the call. She was doing a dozen other things at the time, and she flipped through the register and saw the record on that check—a two and a bunch of zeroes after it—and she okayed the transfer."

Linda placed her hands flat on the table, as if ready to push herself to her feet. "This is ridiculous. I don't believe a word of it."

"I don't give a damn whether you believe me or not," Matt argued, his patience waning, replaced by anger. It wasn't fair that Linda would jump to Gary's defense. It made sense, but it wasn't fair. "Believe whatever the hell you want."

Without thinking, he grabbed her hand and pulled her back down. He *did* give a damn. He wanted her to believe him more than he'd ever wanted anything in his life. "Your brother is a thief, Linda," he said, his voice hushed but fierce. "I know you don't want to face the facts—"

"The facts are that when I hit bottom my brother rescued me. When I was in pain, when I was falling apart, he brought me home and gave me the chance to heal. He took care of me, he supported me, he did anything and everything he could for me. He's the most generous man I know. He's not a thief."

"He's the worst kind there is," Matt retorted. "He didn't just steal my money. He stole my history, my memories. We were brothers, Linda, as close as two guys could be without having the same last name." He heard the building fury in his voice, the barely tempered rage, and he didn't try to quell it. "I know exactly how generous Gary can be, lady. He and I went through hell together. We saved each other's lives in more ways than you can count. And he stole that from me, Linda. He stole that trust, that history. He ripped it out of my gut."

She fidgeted with her napkin. He observed the jerky motions of her hands in her lap, heard the whisper of paper tearing and then saw her deposit a shred of white onto her place mat. "You're the one who stole my trust," she muttered tautly. "I opened my house to you, I fed you, I—" She seemed to rethink what she'd been about to say, and altered course. "And now you've got the gall to accuse my brother of being a thief."

"That's what he is."

"You're crazy."

Her refusal to believe him hurt as much as Gary's betrayal had. Not because she had stolen something from him, but because she'd stolen the promise of something.

He wanted her. If he'd kept his mouth shut, if he'd strung her along and waged his fight with Gary out of her view . . . If he'd been as dishonest as her goddamn brother, he might have had a chance with her.

But he'd been honest, and he had no chance, none at all.

She tossed what was left of her tattered napkin onto the table, next to her barely touched soup. "Stay away from me," she warned, her voice trembling with barely suppressed hostility. "Just stay away from me and my brother." Shoving herself to her feet, she grabbed her purse and stalked out of the coffee shop.

He watched her storm away, then sank back in his seat and closed his eyes. Defeated, he let out a long breath. If only there had been another way to deal with this, if only he were as much of a liar as she'd accused him of being . . .

But he wasn't. He'd told her the truth. She would never forgive him.

And he still wanted her.

RACING THROUGH the waiting room at the clinic, she tuned out Kay's coy question about her lunch date and hurried down the hall to her office. She slammed the door behind her, collapsed into her chair and waited for the quaking in her bones to stop.

She didn't believe it, not a word. Matt Calloway was a liar. He was despicable, detestable, evil and possibly deranged.

A groan escaped her. She couldn't believe such terrible things about him any more than she could believe the terrible things he'd said about her brother.

Gary had had his problems lately, but they weren't money problems. The limousine company paid him a decent wage, and he usually received extravagant tips from his passengers. Debbie's job selling overpriced apparel at a Beverly Hills boutique brought in good money, as well. Gary had no reason to rob anyone. And he would never, ever do anything to hurt one of the fearless foursome.

So why did one tiny spark of doubt inside Linda refuse to gutter and die? Why couldn't she dismiss Matt's absurd charges? Why couldn't she simply loathe him and get on with her life?

Why, when she thought about him, did she remember not only the vile things he'd said just minutes ago in the luncheonette, but the way he'd looked last night in the warm glow of the fireplace? Why did she remember the way he'd smiled over their supper of sandwiches as he proudly described the dramatic cliff-hugging house his company had just finished constructing in the hills high above downtown Portland? Why did she remember the resonant power of his gaze when he'd stood beside the bed in the guest room, his eyes eloquently expressing the question he was too polite to ask out loud?

He'd wanted her to stay with him last night. He hadn't said it, hadn't given any overt indication of it—and if he had, she would have said no—but his gaze had spoken of his desire. Her heart had responded with a shameless assent. She'd escaped from the guest room before he'd had the opportunity to put their mutual attraction into words.

Thank God for that, too. What if he had asked and she hadn't said no? What if she'd decided to do something totally out of character and give in to the passion throbbing between them in the guest bedroom?

She doubted she would ever love anyone the way she'd loved Andrew, but love and physical pleasure were two different things. Gary was always nagging her to indulge in some healthy sexual activity. Last night, if Matt had dared to verbalize what they'd both been feeling, she might have been impetuous enough to say yes.

And then today... she would have hated not only him but herself. The mere thought of Matt Calloway touching her made her shudder. The mere thought that she'd found him desirable, that she'd happily welcomed him into her home...

A knock at the door jolted her. She took a moment to focus on her surroundings—the colorless walls enlivened by a few bright posters, the gray steel file cabinets, the clean blotter centered on her desk, the pens and stacking shelves to her right and the Rolodex and telephone to her left—then lifted her gaze to the door. "Yes?"

Kay pushed the door open. "Are you okay?"

"Of course I'm okay," Linda answered peevishly.

"Your lunch date—"

"It wasn't a date, Kay, all right? Is my next appointment here?"

Kay studied her for several long seconds, then shrugged and mumbled something that sounded like,

"Physician heal thyself." In a louder voice she said, "Eleanor Vespi arrived for her one o'clock appointment. I'll send her in."

"You could have buzzed me on the phone, you know," Linda reminded Kay before she could close the door.

Kay turned back, her eyes narrowed on Linda. "When I buzz you on the phone, everyone in the waiting room can hear everything I say. I thought I was doing you a favor walking down the hall."

"You were." Linda sighed and sent her colleague a sheepish smile. "Sorry."

"Did that guy give you any trouble? Do you want to talk about it?"

"No, and no," Linda said. "No trouble, nothing to talk about. He's a friend of Gary's, that's all."

Kay studied her a minute longer, her expression implying she assumed Linda's problem was that Matt was a friend of Gary's and that was all.

But he *wasn't* a friend of Gary's. He was a ruthless scoundrel who had charmed his way into Linda's house with the goal of destroying her brother. That was the real problem.

"Listen, Kay," she said, comprehending for the first time that Gary could be in danger. "Give me five minutes before you send Eleanor in."

"All right." Kay stepped back into the hall and closed the door.

Linda stared at her telephone. She had to call Gary in Somerville and warn him. She had to alert him to Matt's "surprise" and let him know his alleged friend was saying terrible things about him. Properly forewarned, Gary could defend himself against Matt's malevolence, or else he could avoid Braxton altogether.

Her hand closed around the receiver and she lifted it to her ear. Her fingers perched above the buttons, she hesitated.

What if Matt was telling the truth?

The shocking disloyalty of the thought made her stomach clench into a painful knot and her eyes fill with tears. How on earth could she even consider such a possibility?

But... What about Gary's temperamental behavior of late, his flying to Massachusetts and not even telling Debbie where he was for two days, his snapping at Linda whenever she tried to help? What if...?

No. Gary was her brother. Her only family. Her friend and confidant and the dearest man in the world. No one was going to destroy her relationship with him, not even Matt Calloway. Especially not Matt Calloway.

She punched the buttons and listened to the clicks as the call was connected. The phone rang ten times unanswered. With a doleful sigh, Linda lowered the receiver into the cradle.

"I tried, Gary," she whispered into the air. "I tried to warn you. Please, *please*, don't shut me out. Let me help you."

Not that she thought Gary needed her help. Not that she presumed for an instant that he was shutting her out. She didn't believe a word of Matt's insidious accusation, not a breath of it. It was a lie.

Gary was all she had in the world. If she let Matt steal her faith in him, she would have nothing.

CHAPTER FIVE

"So, LISTEN," Steve said as Gary slammed shut the trunk of the car he'd rented, "if you want to spend a little time here on your way back to the airport, that'd be cool."

"Yeah, thanks," Gary grunted. He was too busy thinking about the limits of courage to give Steve his full attention.

"Marlene won't mind. I think she thinks if I've got you to keep me company I won't get into trouble."

"Ha." Gary managed a feeble grin as he picked his way around the slush puddles to the driver's side door.

"Hey, look, I'm bored out of my skull. Once every other week I stand in line at the unemployment office. The rest of the time, I read the want ads and get depressed. You cheer me up, Gary. I like having you around."

"Thanks," Gary said, this time putting his heart into his words. "I like being around. You and Marlene are too good to me."

"Say, here's an idea—I could drive out to Braxton with you. What do you think? I've got nothing else going on right now, and it's been ages since I've seen Linda."

Gary lowered his eyes and dug his toe into a mushy pile of sand left by the snowplows last night. "We've got some family business to take care of," he explained vaguely. "This isn't a good time."

"Oh. Well, give her my regards. And stop by on your way back."

Gary climbed into the car, waved at Steve and pulled away from the curb. His voice echoed grimly inside his skull: *This isn't a good time.*

If he had told Steve he wasn't going straight to Linda's, he would have been barraged with questions, questions he had no answers to. Honesty required courage, and at the moment Gary's courage was in short supply.

He'd been courageous enough the first couple of times the goons had called on him, looking for their $25,000—courageous or foolhardy, depending on one's perspective. At least he hadn't offered an immediate and unconditional surrender. He'd been fearless, admitting nothing and refusing to talk to them until their third visit, when one of them jammed a gun into his ribs and explained that if he didn't come up with the money pronto, Debbie Montoya was going to be a widow before she ever got to be a bride. Maybe a widow with an ugly scar on her face.

As frightened as he'd been about his own life, he'd been even more frightened that they had known Debbie's name and her relationship to Gary. He would do anything before he'd let a couple of gangsters hurt Debbie.

There it was, then: his limit. His courage had gone so far and no farther.

He got on the interstate northbound, toward New Hampshire. He had no idea where he was heading. All he knew was that he couldn't stand to be around Steve and Marlene anymore. Their lives were no better than his—Steve out of work, Marlene desperate to start a family but putting it off until Steve was employed again. Yet they maintained their high spirits. They were cheerful and generous. If Steve found twenty-five thousand dollars lying around, he'd know better than to keep it.

Maybe not. Maybe what Gary had done was normal. Finders keepers and all that.

He tried to convince himself that he hadn't done anything all that terribly wrong. Keeping the money had been, if stupid, at least understandable. Ignoring the first few threats of the gorillas who'd come to collect the money had taken guts. Crumpling at the sight of a gun aimed at his vital organs had been smart.

Ripping off Matt Calloway...

Very wrong. Disastrously wrong. It had been the most wrong thing Gary had ever done. But he'd done it because the gorillas had threatened Debbie. Gary had needed no more motivation than that.

He had come east to see if he could work something out with Linda—and to get away from L.A. Once he'd done what was necessary to protect Debbie, he couldn't bear to be around her. Seeing her reminded him of what jeopardy he'd put her in with his one rash act. It reminded him, as well, of how much he loved her and how little he had to give her. She was safe, so he'd left.

Besides, if he'd stayed in Los Angeles, Matt would have been able to find him before he'd figured out a way to make things right.

He had to talk to Linda. She would understand what he'd done, and why. She would forgive him. No matter how stupid he was, no matter what it might cost her, she would never stop loving him. She was family.

So why was he heading north to New Hampshire instead of west to Braxton? He couldn't see her until he'd replenished his stores of courage.

More stupidity on his part, charging a car rental to his credit card, driving someplace where he knew no one—so he'd have to put a motel room on plastic, too. He was behaving irrationally, spending money he didn't have, running away from everyone who cared about him. As if in time he would ever regain enough courage to face Linda, who believed he could do no wrong, and say, "Your big brother screwed up," and ask her for help.

He had nowhere else to turn. Banks didn't grant loans to forty-one-year-old losers. Finance companies charged loan-shark rates. Debbie...he couldn't borrow it from her. He felt bad enough that they were so dependent on her income to make ends meet. He wanted to support her, to pamper her, to buy her a big diamond ring and announce to the world that she was his. How could he ask her for money when all he'd ever wanted to do was shower money on her?

Gary knew only one person with the kind of wealth that could bail him out. And he'd already bamboozled that one person. If Matt Calloway ever caught up with him... Hell, he'd rather face the gorillas with the guns. Better to get killed by someone who hadn't been his closest buddy during the most intense twelve months of his life.

Linda was the only person he could trust to help him out of this mess. He ought to drive straight out to Braxton.

If only he had the courage. But he didn't, not yet. So he continued north, where the snow hadn't yet turned into slush, where no one knew who he was or what he'd done. He kept driving north, kept running away.

AT FIVE O'CLOCK, Linda left her office feeling wretched. Bad enough that a man she'd idolized since her preadolescent days had planted seeds of distrust in her about her own brother. Worse, when she'd finally gotten through to Steve in Somerville, he'd told her Gary was on his way to Braxton, so she was going to have to deal with him before she even knew what to think.

Worst of all, she'd let her distress over Matt and Gary interfere with her work.

She had clients who depended on her, people in dreadful shape, their lives falling apart in all sorts of ways. They came to her office to sound off, to cling, to beg for guidance. Linda had a genuine talent for listening, supplying all the emotional support they needed and pointing them in the right direction. She put her heart and soul, as well as her mind, into her work.

That afternoon, however, she'd been too distracted to help her clients. As first Eleanor Vespi and then Louise Block, Sue O'Leary and Joey Catalano had unburdened themselves to her, she'd mumbled the standard reassurances and outlined the obvious courses of action, and all the while her thoughts had wandered off in their own direction, searching for something—anything—to believe. "Sometimes," she'd remarked to Sue, who'd been in one of her martyrdom moods, complaining about how rough her

life was and how badly everyone treated her, "it's hard
to say who's right and who's wrong. Sometimes it
seems like there's more than one truth."

Unfortunately, Linda knew there was only one truth
when it came to her brother and Matt. Accepting that
meant accepting that one of the men was deceitful.
She couldn't bear the possibility that Gary might be
the deceitful one.

Yet throughout her long, agonizing afternoon, the
spark of doubt that Matt had ignited inside her refused to die.

Not that it mattered anymore. She had all but told
Matt to drop dead. When she got home, Gary would
be waiting for her, prepared to explain everything. She
only hoped he wouldn't be angry with her for having
been so considerate to Matt last night, opening her
house to him, feeding him . . . wanting him.

She drove toward her house through the thawing
landscape, navigating the winding back roads, dodg-
ing deep slush puddles and scowling at the rimmed
mud patches that stretched across the rural acreage
outside town. One belated snow squall wasn't going to
destroy anyone's daffodils, but that thought brought
no solace. She recalled clearing the damp, heavy snow
from her porch that morning, not shoveling it so much
as shoving it off the sagging planks. The snow on the
driveway was almost completely melted by the time
she'd started maneuvering Matt's car and hers in and
out of the street. By now, after a day of mid-forties
temperature, her front yard was going to be a swamp.
By next week it would be grassy once more.

As if she cared. As if she could even think about
springtime when her brother and his fearless-foursome

friend were locked into some sort of sickening con game, and she was caught in the middle.

She steered deftly up the hill at the fork, her tires spraying arcs of muddy slush behind her, and then followed the road around the curve. Almost at once she spotted a car parked on the shoulder in front of her house. It had to be Matt's; Gary would have parked in the garage barn. As she drew closer she recognized the car she'd cleared of snow and backed down the driveway that morning.

To her chagrin, her heart fluttered with excitement at the thought of seeing Matt again. She quickly squelched that traitorous response. He had come to her house only to cause trouble. Maybe he'd found out somehow that Gary was on his way here, and he was lying in ambush, ready to wrestle eighteen thousand dollars from Linda's hapless brother.

A broken sigh slipped past her lips. Foolish as it seemed, she would have preferred that Matt had returned to her house not for his money but for her.

Foolish? Brainless was more like it. Brainless and dangerous. Just because he had dark, soulful eyes, just because having him in her house last night had provided too stark a reminder of how long it had been since she'd spent any time, let alone a night, with a man...

Damn him. Why couldn't he leave her alone?

At least he hadn't blocked her driveway with his car. She pulled in, bouncing over the ruts and loose pebbles, driving too quickly past the house to the barn. She glimpsed him lurking on her front porch and despised him for being there, for disobeying her when she'd ordered him to stay away from her. She loathed

him for fanning that spark of disloyalty into a flame
of pleasure at the mere sight of him.

Furious with herself as much as him, she got out of
her car, stalked to the garage barn, unlocked the door
and yanked it open. After driving in, she turned off
the engine and slumped in the driver's seat, wondering how long she could remain hiding in the barn before he came after her.

She wouldn't let him come after her at all. It would
be a sign of defeat for her to sit stewing and simmer-
ing in the gloomy barn, refusing to confront him.

Damn him to hell.

She got out of her car and slammed the door with
therapeutic force. Then she stormed out of the barn
and along the soggy driveway to the front of the
house. Matt descended from the porch, then glanced
over his shoulder at its crooked, sloping planks.

Pivoting back to the driveway, he took a step toward her, and another. She wished she were brave
enough to approach him, but she wasn't. She simply
stood where she was, raising the collar of her coat
around her neck and feeling the damp chill of the
slushy driveway seep through the soles of her shoes.

He continued across the front yard in long, confident strides, his hands in the pockets of his leather
jacket and his shoulders slightly hunched. She
shouldn't have been able to make out his features in
the gloomy dusk light, but she could. She could see the
rigid set of his jaw, the harsh slope of his nose, the
dark fire in his eyes.

He wanted his eighteen thousand dollars. She didn't
have it. Why couldn't he leave her in peace?

"Let me fix your porch," he said, his voice low and
husky in the cold air.

Of all the things he could have said, that was one possibility she wasn't prepared for. She'd been ready to tell him to get lost, to clear out and never come back. She'd been ready to have him arrested for trespassing.

But her porch...

It listed to the left, and some of the boards were loose. She suspected that one of the underpinnings was crumbling. She had figured she would get Gary's okay first—it was his house, after all—and perhaps talk him into splitting the cost of the repair with her. Then she would get a few estimates and have the job done by a professional.

No question about it, the porch required fixing. But she wasn't going to let Matt fix it. She wouldn't have him doing chores for her in some half-baked attempt to soften her up. Besides, if he did the repair he'd have to stick around for a while, and that was something she definitely didn't want.

"The thing's about to collapse," he said. "It's not bad yet, but if you don't take care of it it's going to get worse."

If she spoke her voice would crack, or else she would say things she might regret. She only nodded.

"You put me up last night," he rationalized. "I would like to pay you back, and this seems like a good way. I'm in construction—I know how to do the job right."

She had to say no. She couldn't have him working on her house, not after he'd accused her brother of being a criminal, a crook, a burglar, a mugger. What was that nasty word he'd used?

A bum.

Maybe Matt was mistaken. Maybe someone else had swindled him. Maybe Gary just happened to be in the wrong place at the wrong time, he'd visited Portland just when someone else was embezzling from Matt, and...

Oh, God, what if it were true? What if Gary *had* robbed Matt?

How could she even think—?

A quiet sob filled her throat. She tried to swallow it down, but it rose to her lips, demanding release. She stood mute, afraid of what would happen if she opened her mouth.

"It wouldn't take me more than a day to do the repair," he said. "Let me do it for you."

His offer had nothing to do with paying her back for putting him up. It had to do with compensating her for the horrible things he'd said at lunch. It had to do with helping her to accept his version of the truth, helping her to bear it.

The sob broke from her. She clapped her hands over her eyes, humiliated by the thought of falling apart in front of him. She couldn't stop, though. It was too much; she couldn't hold in her misery.

The tears began, first a trickle and then a flood, leaking through her fingers and spilling down her cheeks. She cupped her palms against her face and prayed that by some miracle Matt would disappear into the night so she wouldn't have to face him after this.

She felt his arms closing around her, at first hesitantly and then protectively, circling her back, drawing her against him. Just as her clients turned to her for support, now she turned to him and leaned on him, needing someone strong and steady to get her through the next minute, the next wrenching sob.

"It's all right," he murmured, his breath warm and soothing against her hair, her brow. "God, I'm sorry, Linda, I'm so sorry. It's all right."

She pressed her face into the hollow beneath his jaw, inhaling the aroma of his leather jacket and the lingering spicy scent of his after-shave. Her hands relaxed, fell from her cheeks and shifted to grip his shoulders. He tightened his hold on her, his arms ringed solidly around her, his fingers toying with the locks of hair that had unraveled from the twist into which she'd pinned it a lifetime ago. He felt sturdy and powerful. Ironically, she felt safe in his embrace. Matt Calloway, the man who had brought her all this pain, was making it go away, at least for this one moment.

"I'm sorry, Linda," he whispered, his lips moving against her brow with a gentle, comforting murmur of breath. "It isn't your fault. I shouldn't have dragged you into it. I never wanted to hurt you."

He wasn't hurting her, not now. The heat of his body spread to her. She felt it radiating from his mouth to her forehead, from his chest to the sensitive swells of her breasts, from his hips to hers. She wanted to curl deeper into his embrace, to feel the possessive strength of him all around her, shielding her from her grief.

His lips danced across her forehead once more. Surely he meant only to console her, but she felt her scalp tighten and her breath catch; she heard her moan of sorrow become a moan of yearning. She wanted him, wanted him to save her from all the bad things in the world, from deception and dishonesty and the awful fate of losing yet another loved one.

She couldn't endure another loss. She wanted Matt to guard her from the pain, even though she knew he'd been the one to bring it down upon her in the first place. If Gary was guilty as Matt claimed, then he was already lost. All Matt had done was open her eyes.

Unless Matt was lying. Unless *he* was the one she had lost.

But she'd never had him to lose. All she'd had was a disembodied idol, someone she'd adored from halfway around the world. All she'd had was an old photograph and a memory of her overheated eleven-year-old imagination.

His arms tightened around her for a moment, then relented. "Don't cry, Linda," he murmured. "Please. I'm sorry it had to happen like this."

"Liar," she groaned, struggling against his gentle embrace and her own unjustifiable longing. "You're not sorry." She pushed against his chest, relief and regret vying within her as he let his hands drop to his sides. "I hate you."

"I know." He sounded rueful.

"My brother is a good man."

"I have papers with me that prove he isn't."

"Shove your papers," she retorted, too stubborn to give in. She was fighting not just Matt's charges against her brother but the unwelcome warmth he'd kindled within her. She didn't want to see his proof, and she didn't want to want him.

The moon sharpened in the sky behind her, layering the planes of his face with silver. His eyes were dark, hardening with an obstinacy to match hers. "I don't care how much you hate me," he said. "Your brother ripped me off, and I'm going to see justice done."

"Fine. See justice done. Just get the hell off my property."

His eyes grew even darker. He sized her up, apparently aware that his gentle hugs and whisper-soft kisses couldn't convert her to his side. "Linda—"

"Gary's the one you're after, and he isn't here. So leave."

"He will be here, though. Sooner or later he's going to come to you."

"That doesn't give you the right—"

"Linda, please." His voice grew soft, imploring. "I have proof."

She exhaled. She could say she didn't believe him only so many times before she stopped believing herself. Another breath left her, raw and rasping along her throat, leaving in its wake a staggering weariness.

"All right," she muttered, too exhausted to argue. "Let me see your proof."

He clearly understood how difficult her capitulation had been. He took a moment to absorb it. "I'll have to get it from my car. Then can we go inside?" he asked. "It's cold out here."

She didn't want him in her house. She knew how his presence could change the atmosphere, charge it, make it hum with awareness, with a sensual undercurrent. If he came inside, she might want him to take her in his arms once more.

No, she wouldn't want him. Never. As long as he didn't touch her, as long as she focused on his proof, his incriminating evidence, whatever papers he had that damned and doomed Gary—as long as she remembered that Matt Calloway was aiming to demolish the only family she had left, she would never feel anything more than hate for him.

"All right," she said. "Come in."

HE PAUSED at his car, his suitcase lying open on the seat, and stared across the yard to her house. She was scarcely visible, a shadow moving on the porch.

It was always possible that she would slip inside and lock him out before he could reach the door. If she did, he would deal with it. In a sense, she already had locked him out.

Except . . . except for the way she'd felt in his arms, the way she'd melted against him, pressed against him, curled her fingers around his shoulders and wept into the hollow of his neck. Except for the way she'd clung to him and sighed, awakening every cell in his body, heating his blood, arousing him.

He shouldn't have touched her. If she hadn't started crying, he wouldn't have. But she had, and he did, and she'd felt so fragile in his arms. So vulnerable. So very alone in the world. She *was* alone—her lover dead, her parents gone, her brother a snake—and Matt had wanted to hold her tight and swear to her that as long as he was around she would never be alone.

God help him, he wanted her more than ever.

A glance down at his suitcase drew him back to reality. Two items tucked into an inner pocket would prove to her that her brother was everything Matt had accused him of being. She was going to despise Matt for having those papers, for showing them to her and forcing her to acknowledge the truth. She was going to hang the messenger for his message.

Maybe it was just as well. He couldn't have her, anyway. Linda Villard wasn't the sort of woman a man took to bed and then kissed goodbye. Matt ought to forget about her and stay focused on his ultimate goal: finding Gary and making him pay.

He was going to make the bastard pay twice—once for conning Matt, and once for conning Linda. Matt suspected that her brother's dishonesty was going to hurt her far worse, and far longer, than it hurt him. He would recover. He'd get his money and walk away.

Linda couldn't walk away. Money would never ease her pain. She would suffer from this forever.

He closed up the car and peered at the house again. Linda had gone inside, but she'd turned the porch light on for him.

He strode up the driveway and along the path to the porch, where he'd spent most of the afternoon, waiting for her. As one hour had dragged into the next, he'd stumbled onto the idea of repairing the dilapidated structure for her. He'd examined the supports, knelt down to inspect the underside and decided the job wouldn't take much, in materials or labor.

He wanted to give her something—a mended porch, at the very least. But he couldn't imagine her accepting anything from him.

He rapped lightly on the front door, then tested the knob. She'd left it unlocked and he let himself in. After wiping his feet on the rug in the entry, he headed toward the glow of the kitchen light.

Linda sat at the table, her head bowed, her forehead resting in her palms and her fingers threaded into the loose tendrils along her hairline. She had removed her coat, and he noted the pastel-pink sweater she had on. She'd looked so pretty and cheerful when he'd met her for lunch just hours ago, so pleased to see him. So utterly desirable.

His memory wheeled back further, to the pink stationery he'd found on the table that morning, inviting him to help himself to her food. Then even further, to last night, to her insistence that he stay at her house instead of forging out into the storm, to the crisp linens with which she'd made up his bed, to her kind smile and her radiant eyes.

If she didn't let him fix her porch he'd go crazy.

She glanced up briefly at his entrance, then rested her head in her hands once more. Not knowing what else to do, he took the chair across the table from her and pulled his evidence from a Calloway Construction Company envelope.

"Here's the IOU," he said, nudging the papers across the table to Linda. "For two thousand dollars. That's Gary's signature. And here's the check he altered."

She lifted her head slightly—enough to view the papers while avoiding Matt's gaze. She focused first on the sheet of Three-C letterhead with the terms of Matt's loan to Gary specified and the men's signatures at the bottom. The amount of the loan was printed in digits and spelled out; there was no question that it was two thousand dollars.

Matt noticed her fingers trembling as she lowered the IOU and picked up the canceled check for twenty thousand dollars, with Gary's skillful modification of the numbers and spelling. The ink matched; the letters slanted uniformly. The dates on the documents computed. Linda couldn't refute what she was seeing.

Her eyes welling over with fresh tears, she dropped the canceled check onto the table. Matt braced himself for the heartrending sound of her sobs.

Maybe he could repair her roof, too, he thought. The barn out back. He could repaint the shutters, repave the driveway. Anything. He would do anything to keep her from crying over her idiot brother.

Tears ran in rivulets over the smooth ivory of her skin, but she didn't make a sound.

"I'm sorry," he said for the umpteenth time.

She shook her head, apparently unable to speak.

It was a strange thing, this overpowering need to comfort her. Ever since he'd discovered Gary's treachery, Matt hadn't been able to think of anything else—until now. All of a sudden, consoling Linda seemed infinitely more important than wresting justice and revenge and eighteen thousand dollars from her brother. Easing her pain was the most important thing in the world.

"He wasn't having money problems," she whispered.

Maybe he wasn't. Maybe he'd ripped Matt off for some other reason. At least Linda wasn't calling Matt a liar anymore.

"He must have misunderstood..."

"He signed the IOU," Matt pointed out. "I don't think he misunderstood anything."

"He's not a criminal, Matt. He's not an imbecile. You must have misled him or something. What's the word? Entrapment. You must have entrapped him—"

"You know I didn't."

"If he needed money he would have told me," she said in a wavering voice. He admired her loyalty; no matter how upset she was, she wouldn't stop defending her brother. "He owns this house, Matt. If he needed money he could have borrowed against it. It just doesn't make sense."

"Do you know where he is?" he asked.

Her eyes flashed, hot and bright through the dampness that misted them. Then she looked away, past Matt, toward the window above the sink, down at the canceled check. "No."

He wasn't sure he believed her, but if she was lying he couldn't blame her. She'd come a long way that afternoon, from ordering Matt out of her life to seeking comfort in his arms. If concealing her brother's whereabouts for a while longer made her feel better, Matt could accept it. Right now, making Linda feel better was more crucial than locating Gary.

"Are you hungry?" he asked. "Would you like some dinner?"

"Oh—I couldn't..." She shook her head again.

"I'll take you out somewhere," he offered. "You said we could find a decent restaurant a half hour away."

She sighed. "I'm not hungry."

"You've got to eat something." When she started to shake her head yet again, he pressed on. "I could bring in a pizza or something. Is there a pizza place in town?"

"A pizza." Her eyes met his fleetingly. They looked just a touch less watery to him, although her complexion retained a frail pallor.

"How about it? I'll go pick one up and bring it back, and you can eat as much or as little as you want."

"I'm not hungry. All I want is a bath."

"Take a bath while I get the pizza. Maybe you'll feel hungry by the time you're done."

She held his gaze once more, longer this time. "Okay," she said. For all he knew, she had agreed just to get him out of her house.

He pushed away from the table and stood. "I'll be back in a while. Do you like any toppings?"

"Mushrooms?" she half asked.

If she'd wanted caviar and truffles he would have arranged it. "Mushrooms," he promised, starting toward the door.

"Matt. Take the key."

He froze in the doorway, then turned slowly, afraid to jump to the wrong conclusion. One of her arms was extended toward him; cupped in her palm was her house key.

He stared at the key for a moment, and then at her. "So you can let yourself back in if I'm still in the bath," she explained.

"All right." He managed to pluck the key from her hand without letting his fingers graze her palm.

"Go to DeVito's on Main Street. That's the best pizza in Braxton."

"DeVito's on Main," he repeated. "I'll be back in a while."

As he walked out into the chilly night and shut the door behind him, he felt better. Stepping off the decaying front porch, he felt better yet. He closed his fingers around the key and squeezed it, as if it were an amulet, an antidote, a magic talisman that could make everything good again.

Linda had given him her key. She trusted him that much.

His pleasure was short-lived. He understood that trusting him had cost Linda her trust in her brother.

He could only guess at the depth of her pain. But he would do what he could to comfort her. He would take care of her. He would feed her and fix her porch.

And maybe she would hate him just a little bit less.

SHE DIDN'T BOTHER with bubble bath. She was not in a bubbly mood. Instead, she poured a capful of baby oil into the steamy water, then climbed into the footed ceramic tub in the bathroom off the bedroom.

Originally the master bathroom had been one of two family baths on the second floor, but her parents had sealed the door to the hall and added a door opening directly into their bedroom. The modification gave the old farmhouse an almost suburban feel, but Linda liked it. At the moment, she wasn't sure she would be able to cross the threshold from her bedroom back into the hall. She wanted to languish in the tub until the water grew cold, and then languish in bed. She wanted to pretend a world of woe didn't exist beyond the boundaries of her room.

She sank slowly into the water, giving herself time to adjust to its scalding temperature. She'd made it as hot as she dared, hoping the heat would purify her somehow. She felt befouled, as if Gary's crimes had left a stain on her.

Her skin erupted in goose bumps, then smoothed as she grew acclimatized to the steamy water. She rested her head against the high lip of the tub and closed her eyes.

She couldn't fight it anymore. She couldn't think of any way to justify the papers Matt had shown her. Gary was guilty. He'd done what Matt had accused him of doing. He'd cheated a good man out of a great deal of money.

And now, according to Steve, Gary was on his way here. What would she say to him when she saw him? "Turn yourself in!" Or, "How could you?" Or, "You're the only family I've got, and I have to side with Matt. I have to turn against you."

She understood Matt's anger; she felt as betrayed by Gary as he did. She had fought his fight, defended his honor, pleaded his case, believed in him—and he was guilty.

More tears trickled down her cheeks. She let them drip off her chin into the water. Eventually, she supposed, her tear ducts would run dry. Her brother's dishonor would never stop hurting, just as Andrew's death had never stopped hurting, but eventually she would be too drained to cry anymore.

"DEBBIE? It's Gary."

Debbie twirled her diet cola and listened to the ice cubes clink against the glass. She'd had a lousy day at work and she'd come home to an empty apartment, and she was furious with Gary. When he'd called last night, he had told her he was at his friend Steve's house in Somerville. He hadn't told her why he'd left Sunday and neglected to phone her until Tuesday.

She wanted to chew him out. Before she could, he said, "I miss you."

She took a sip of cola to keep from blubbering. She missed him, too. How could she chew him out when they both missed each other so much? "Are you at your sister's?" she asked.

There was a long silence on the phone. She listened to the hiss of the air conditioner pumping cool wind through the vents in the living room. She listened to the refrigerator's motor hum in the kitchen.

She listened to the ice cubes clinking and her anger returned, full-blooded and healthy. "It's not such a difficult question, Gary," she chided, a sarcastic edge to her voice.

"I'm not at Linda's," he said.

"Where are you?"

He groaned. "I'm in Nashua."

"Where?"

"Nashua, New Hampshire. Listen, Debbie, everything's so messed up. I just—I want you to know how much I love you."

It was her turn to groan. He always did that—told her he loved her an instant before she was about to tell him to go to hell. Hearing him say he loved her was like taking a punch to the stomach; it knocked the wind out of her, kept her from being able to reply.

"I *will* be going to Linda's," he went on. "I just couldn't go yet. Everything's a mess. I need to straighten out my head first."

"You sure do," Debbie muttered.

"Listen, honey, you haven't . . . you haven't heard from any strange men, have you?"

"Heard what?" She stood taller. Something in his voice held a warning.

"I don't know, any strange phone calls or anything?"

"This is the strangest phone call I've had in months," she told him.

He laughed, but he didn't sound very happy. "I love you, Debbie. I need to know you're okay."

"Of course I'm okay," she snapped. "Why shouldn't I be okay? I'm standing in the kitchen of our apartment, and you're God knows where. Yeah, I heard from a strange man today. He came into the

store and asked if we sold designer toothpicks. He said
he heard we sold them, and he wanted to buy two
hundred dollars' worth. That sounded pretty strange
to me.''

"Great." Gary breezed right past her story. "Nobody malicious, though? Nobody giving you a hard
time?"

She recalled the hoots she'd earned from a couple of
Chicano youths after work that afternoon, when she'd
been walking out to her car in the parking lot behind
the boutique. They'd made some remarks about her
legs, the sort of remarks that could be interpreted as
sleazy or flattering or both. The boys had shouted at
her in Spanish and she'd understood most of what
they'd said. Her father had been born in the United
States, and he rarely spoke Spanish around the house,
but he had a few pet phrases for her mother, Latino
expressions of appreciation for her figure and her way
of walking and her pretty red lips.

Debbie ought to have tuned out the guys in the
parking lot. But she'd secretly enjoyed their whistles
and shouts. She knew she was about to go home to an
empty apartment, her boyfriend was thousands of
miles away, and there was no man around to call her
bonita.

"When are you coming home, Gary?" she asked,
not caring if she sounded like an impatient nag.

"As soon as I can, I promise. You haven't heard
from anyone named Matt, have you?"

"Matt?"

"Matt Calloway."

"Oh, yeah... he called, when was it? Monday, I
think."

"What did you tell him?"

"I told him you were going to visit your sister."

"Great." Gary sounded angry. "Great."

"All right, so you're not at your sister's. I didn't know. You said you were—"

"No, it's all right. Never mind. I'll work it out with Linda."

"Listen, mister," she said, tired of his cryptic questions. "You work it out however you want to work it out. You work it out with Linda, you work it out with your friends in Somerville, you work it out with Matt Whoever and the strange men. I don't want to hear from you till you've worked it out, okay?"

"Don't say that, Debbie. I love you."

"That's your problem. I guess you're going to have to work that out, too."

"I really do love you," he insisted, a pleading tone in his voice. "Maybe you'll never believe me, but whatever happens, I did it for you. For both of us."

"You did what?"

Another long silence. "I better go. Someday, baby, maybe I'll be good enough for you."

She heard the click as he hung up the phone on his end, and then she hung up, too. She belted down her soda and wished it was booze.

What was he talking about? He was more than good enough for her—if only he would be where he was supposed to be, and not go running off on a whim, and pitching riddles at her over the phone. He would be good enough if only he'd spend less time dreaming about becoming better and more time recognizing how very good things were between them. She loved him, he loved her—what more did they need?

Just weeks ago, things had been phenomenal. Gary's boss had come up with delayed bonuses for the drivers, and suddenly Gary had all this money to burn. And oh, how they'd burned it. They'd gone to the racetrack. They'd bought the new TV. Gary had gotten one of his regulars, a star on a top-twenty sitcom, to arrange entry for them into one of the hottest restaurants in town, where the bill they ran up was almost as high as the price of the new TV.

"It's a bonus," Gary had said, whenever Debbie suggested that they should put a little aside. "Let's enjoy it. We deserve it."

So they'd enjoyed it.

What had happened? Why had things changed from so good to so bad, so fast? If the bonus was gone it was gone. They'd had their fun, and they still had the television and lots of memories. Maybe next year there would be another big bonus. Was that a reason for Gary to flip out?

Or was this just some more of his moodiness?

The hell with it. She didn't care. She had a life. A couple of good-looking *hombres* in the parking lot behind the store thought she was *bonita*. She didn't need this garbage from Gary.

Then why was she crying? Why was she standing in her nice clean kitchen, with an empty glass in her hand and tears streaming down her cheeks?

CHAPTER SIX

MATT DROVE UP the serpentine back road to Linda's house, a flat white box resting on the seat next to him and a bag containing a chilled six-pack of beer on the floor. The car was redolent with the aromas of oregano, tomatoes, mushrooms, hot oil and cheese. He hoped she'd gotten her appetite back. He was starving.

He pulled into her driveway, not concerned about blocking her car. He wasn't going to spend the night at her house again. He would stay only long enough to make sure she was all right, and then he would head back to town and take a room at the Braxton Motor Inn.

He shut off the engine, gathered the pizza and beer and strode up the walk. Unlocking the door, he stepped inside. The lights in the kitchen and up the stairs in the second-floor hallway were on.

"Linda?" he called out on his way to the kitchen.

She wasn't there. He set the pizza and her key on the table, removed the beer from the paper bag and found a place for it on a shelf in her refrigerator. Then he pulled off his jacket and slung it over the back of a chair.

"Linda? I'm back."

Silence.

A frown tensed his brow. He returned to the hall, to the foot of the stairway. "Linda?" he hollered up the stairs.

Not a sound.

Fear began to gnaw at him. When he'd left her she had been distraught. Maybe she had done something drastic—run away, polished off the bottle of brandy and passed out, gone to the police . . .

Maybe Gary had shown up, and they'd fled together.

Matt climbed halfway up the stairs, halted and shouted her name. "Linda!"

Nothing.

He hurried the rest of the way upstairs, taking two steps at a time. His heart pounded. If she was in a drunken stupor or crying her heart out again, it was his fault.

"Linda!"

He sprinted down the hall to the master bedroom, grabbed the molded doorframe to brake his speed, and swung into the room just as an inner door opened and Linda stepped through it, wrapping a thick white towel around herself.

He fell back, retreated into the hallway and leaned against the wall, shutting his eyes against the fleeting vision of her slim, glistening body. In the instant before she'd closed the towel around her, he'd seen everything—her unbearably graceful shoulders, the high, taut spheres of her breasts, the vertical dent of her navel, the triangle of tawny curls tapering below her abdomen . . .

His heart was still pounding. Not from fear.

He remained where he was, his spine pressed hard against the floral wallpaper. His skin felt feverish; his muscles ached. He wanted her, wanted her more than he wanted justice, revenge—more than everything that had driven him to her home in the first place. He wanted to touch that golden, bath-softened skin, to kiss those high round breasts, to slide his fingers through the tangle of curls between her legs, to unlock her body the way the key she'd given him had unlocked her door. He wanted to plunge into her, explode inside her, bring her so much pleasure that she would never hate him for tearing her brother to shreds.

Definitely the Braxton Motor Inn tonight, he thought with a wry smile.

Through the open door he heard no sound. Maybe she was as stunned as he was. Maybe she was embarrassed, mortified, infuriated. Maybe the minute she was dressed she would slap his cheek, or kick him someplace lower.

"Matt?" Her voice was muffled, as if it came from a great distance.

"I'll...I'll be downstairs," he mumbled, shoving away from the wall and walking stiffly to the stairway. By the time he reached the bottom step his body was almost back to normal.

Almost. But then he foolishly closed his eyes and visualized her all over again, her lissome curves and sleek, dewy skin, her dusky nipples and her hips just broad enough to fit into a man's hands, to fit a man...

And his temperature soared back into the danger zone.

LINDA PADDED BAREFOOT over the braided rug to the door and closed it. Then she let out a long, tremulous breath.

He hadn't seen her. He couldn't have. She'd had the towel wrapped around her before she'd left the bathroom, hadn't she? All he'd seen was her tucking in the corner of the towel to hold it in place under her arms. She was sure of it.

Still, she felt tense, oddly expectant. The bath had helped her to relax some, but not enough. She had spent the entire time straining to hear Gary's arrival, or Matt's. The thump of Dinah leaping from the rocker onto the rug in her bedroom had made her flinch.

She'd lain in the tub, wondering what would happen if Matt and Gary ran into each other on the front porch. Would they have it out right there while she hid inside, wet and naked? Afterward, would she be expected to pick up the pieces and bandage their wounds? Would she want to have anything to do with either of them again?

How could Gary have committed such a heinous act? How could he have done it to Debbie? To himself? To Matt, his brother-in-arms, one of the fearless foursome?

There had to be a reason, something more significant than a mid-life crisis and a few mood swings. Something must have happened, something so appalling he couldn't turn to his sister or his girlfriend for help. Something so dreadful he'd felt it necessary to cheat a man whose life he had saved twenty years ago, a man to whom he owed his own life.

If only she'd known. If only she could have helped Gary before it was too late.

She pulled on a pair of worn jeans, thick socks and an old fisherman's sweater. Who cared about donning her best green pullover for Matt? Who cared

about making a good impression on him? They were
both beyond that now.

Once she had brushed the tangles from her hair, she
wandered down the stairs and into the kitchen. The
room smelled of sauce and spices. Next to the De-
Vito's box on the table lay the canceled check and the
IOU her brother had signed. Wincing, she left the
room.

She found Matt in the living room building a fire.
Dinah sat on the hearth next to him, switching her tail
back and forth and overseeing his efforts. He touched
a lit match to the crumpled sheets of newspaper
wedged under a tepee of kindling, then sat back on his
heels to gauge the result of his efforts. The flames
licked high, causing the kindling to snap and spit. He
added a split log to the pile.

Dinah seemed to approve. She groomed her paws
and then stretched, arching her spine into a question
mark. Linda realized she'd forgotten to feed her.

As she stepped back through the doorway, Matt
rose and cleared his throat. "I hope you don't mind,"
he said. "The fire, I mean."

"No, of course not." She minded too many other
things to enumerate, but the fire was fine with her.
"Any sign of Gary?"

"Is he coming here?"

She recalled her conversation with Steve earlier that
afternoon. He had said Gary was on his way to Braxton, but God only knew whether Gary was lying to
him along with everyone else. "I don't know," she
said, pleased that it was the truth. She gazed at the
embryonic fire and then glanced away. "I've got to fix
Dinah's supper, and then, if you'd like, we can eat the
pizza in here." She couldn't stand the idea of eating at

the kitchen table. The IOU and the canceled check lay there, condemning Gary, polluting the entire room.

"Eating in here would be nice," Matt said.

It didn't take her long to fill Dinah's bowls with food and water. She opened the refrigerator in search of soda and saw the beer.

She opened two bottles, collected a couple of plates and the pizza box, and returned to the living room. Matt was kneeling in front of the hearth again, adding another log to the blaze. At Linda's entrance, he stood and crossed the room to help her.

His hand brushed hers when he took the bottles from her. As their eyes met, she recalled how safe she had felt in his arms outside, and how helplessly, foolishly aroused. The stark power of his gaze reawakened those two contradictory sensations, and she turned away. She wasn't safe with him. She couldn't afford to feel aroused by him.

She wondered if he knew how uneasy he was making her. She felt his gaze lingering on her, his expression inscrutable. Then he passed her a plate with a wedge of pizza on it. Lowering himself onto the couch, he settled deep into the plump cushions.

She sat as far away from him as she could. The arm of the sofa pressed into her back. She lifted the pizza slice, then lowered it back to the plate and sighed.

"Are you all right?" he asked.

His solicitousness embarrassed her. She wasn't all right. He knew she wasn't, and he knew why.

She took a deep breath and ordered herself to remain calm. Matt wasn't the bad guy in this ghastly situation. He was the honest one. She couldn't forgive him for having shattered her beliefs about her brother, but she could trust him. Probably.

"Sure, I'm all right," she said, forcing herself to take a bite of her pizza.

He continued to watch her. She studied her pizza, the fire, the bookshelves—anything to avoid looking at him.

"I shouldn't have involved you in it," he said.

"No, you should have." Her tone was quiet, heavy with resignation. "Gary is my brother. What he does matters to me."

"You do know where he is, don't you?"

"I really don't," she insisted, then forced herself to take another bite. "Please don't ask again," she said, putting her plate on the coffee table and reaching for her beer. Assuming he didn't show up in the next hour or so, Gary might give her a call and update her on his plans. If she found out where Gary was and informed Matt, he would surely leave Braxton.

Which would be for the best, she reminded herself. Better to have Matt chasing after Gary than hanging around here, making her long for the dangerous warmth of his arms, making her remember how strong and solid he'd felt, how gently his lips had whispered against her hair.

She didn't want to fall apart again in front of Matt. She didn't want to need him to hold her. But there were things she had to know, even if learning them might demolish her.

"Tell me about Vietnam," she said.

Her request seemed to surprise him. He shot her a sidelong glance, then took a long drink of beer. "It's not my favorite subject."

"Tell me anyway. Tell me what it was like between you and Gary back then."

He took another swig of beer, then planted the bottle on the table and leaned forward, resting his forearms across his knees and staring at the bright yellow blaze dancing in the fireplace.

"We were friends," he finally said.

She waited patiently, knowing there was much, much more to it than that. Now that he was no longer focused on her she felt safe looking at him, absorbing the manly arch of his back, the sinewy strength of his wrists and forearms below the pushed-up sleeves of his sweater. She took note of the rigid angle of his jaw, the grim set of his lips, the fire's flames reflected in his eyes, imbuing them with an animated brilliance.

"I don't think I've ever had any friends as close as the four of us were then," he went on, a trace of Missouri drawl filtering into his voice. "We were thrown together. It wasn't a normal environment, but... What we had was special."

"Gary thought the world of you."

Rather than snort in disbelief, Matt only nodded. "We all thought the world of each other. We *were* the world to each other."

"Did you really save his life? Literally?"

Matt turned back to her. His mouth had softened with the hint of a smile and the glow remained in his eyes. Perhaps he detected a touch of adolescent hero-worship in her tone, or perhaps he was just happy to be talking about something other than his current clash with Gary. "I really did," he said.

"How? What happened?"

He sighed, then turned back to gaze at the fire. "We were on patrol, and he was about to step into a clearing. It was an abandoned farm, maybe thirty, forty acres that hadn't been planted. I got this weird flash that the field was mined, and I stopped him from marching through it."

"And it was mined?"

"Yeah. I threw some stones out into the clearing, and sure enough one of them triggered a mine."

"Gary must have been overwhelmed with gratitude."

Matt chuckled and shook his head. "You couldn't let yourself get overwhelmed over there. 'Overwhelmed' wasn't the right state of mind to be in. As I recall, Gary made a joke about it, something about how now we were even."

"Because he'd saved your life?"

"Yeah." Matt's smile grew wistful.

"Tell me." She was desperate to hear good things about her brother, desperate for proof that, despite what he'd done to Matt a few weeks ago, he wasn't completely evil.

Matt polished off the remainder of his pizza slice, picked up his bottle of beer, then settled back into the sofa, kicking his feet up onto the coffee table. "Your brother was a wheeler-dealer," he said. "We all had our strengths, and Gary's strength was getting things done. He always knew someone who could fix something so things would go our way, or he'd get us some special privilege or rustle up some goodies when we needed them most. I don't know, maybe he was a con man even then."

Linda ought to have bristled, but she didn't. The beer, the fire, this glimpse of Matt's past, all worked together to soothe her nerves more effectively than the bath had.

"One time—I don't know how he did it—he found out my name was on the wrong list. I was assigned to what wound up being a suicide mission. It was billed as a simple maneuver—flushing out snipers near a village where there'd been a lot of activity. The CO was assigning grunts at random, and my name wound up on the list. Gary wheeled and dealed and switched some files around, and the next thing I knew, my name was off the list.''

"So he saved you from a dangerous mission?"

"Dangerous?" Matt's smile evolved again, becoming bittersweet. "Every damned soldier on that list went home a statistic. There's a date on the Wall down in Washington—I could show you the names. If it weren't for Gary, 'Matthew Calloway' would have been carved right alongside the others." He lapsed into silence for a minute, deep in thought, and when he resumed talking, his voice had a pensive edge to it. "It was a strange business, Linda. It's hard to explain to someone who wasn't there, but... When you were over there, you'd spend all your energy placing wagers with Lady Luck. It had nothing to do with skill or smarts or anything else. Survival was simply a matter of chance. You'd measure the odds and take a chance and hope luck was with you. And if it wasn't, you'd fight chance. You'd try to make it go the other way." He took another drink of beer, then set down the bottle and shook his head once more. "We went over there wanting to do our duty to our country, wanting to fight for freedom and the American Way and all that. But after a few weeks in-country everything changed. All that mattered was getting through it and going home. It had nothing to do with patriotism. It was all about chance. And Gary..." Again Matt fell silent, reminiscing. "There was something about him.

He had a way of stacking the deck so you'd win more than you lost."

Linda digested Matt's words. It was true; Gary had always had a talent for getting things to work out. After he'd returned home from the war, he had been Linda's ally in her constant battles with their conservative parents. They'd been in their late fifties by then, set in their ways, perpetually carping about curfews and loud music and, later, adamantly refusing to let Linda go away to college. But Gary had fixed things, pulled a few tricks out of his bag, persuaded her parents to let her attend school in Boston. "It's not so far away," he'd reminded them. "And you know, I've been thinking about crashing with some buddies in Somerville for a while, looking for work in the city. I'll be right across the river from Linda. I'll keep an eye on her."

When her father died, Gary had returned to Braxton and somehow managed to get the local bank to release the funds in his parents' joint savings account before they became subject to probate. When his mother had decided to move to Florida, he'd negotiated the price down twenty thousand dollars for the condominium she liked. Gary had never been a whiz at school, but he had his own distinct brand of intelligence, a way of getting things done and making things work out in his favor.

"What else?" Linda asked, nestling into the corner of the sofa, tucking her legs under her and propping a throw pillow behind her back. "Tell me more."

Matt seemed to recognize that she needed something positive about her brother to cling to. "Well," he said, "there's more than one way to save a life. Half the time we were over there we thought we'd die from boredom, or just from the irrationality of what we were doing. But the four of us, Jimmy and Darryl and Gary and me... We'd cut up or get wild. We'd keep each other sane, and that was an important part of staying alive.''

She felt eleven years old again, dying to learn about the world, dying to share in Gary's dramatic adventures. "His letters were always so upbeat, full of news about trips to Saigon or descriptions of the native food—and descriptions of you and the others. Things had to be hard for him, but he never complained or said he was scared. The only way I knew the truth was from what he wrote about you.''

"What do you mean?''

She closed her eyes and pictured the crinkly pages crammed with Gary's scrawly writing. Where were his letters? Where had she stored them?

It didn't matter. She remembered enough. "He wrote that if anyone got spooked, you were the man who brought them down. He wrote that if anyone had nightmares, you'd shake them awake and talk it through with them. He never came right out and said *he* was the one getting spooked and having nightmares, but I assumed he was.''

"Everyone was spooked.''

"Not you,'' Linda insisted. "You were the rock.''

Matt opened his mouth and then closed it. "Maybe I kept my demons to myself better than the others.''

"He said you could always read the locals better than anyone else,'' she recalled. "If some peddler came around trying to sell junk, you always knew whether the peddler was legitimate. Gary wrote that you once figured out a peddler was really an enemy trying to smuggle explosives into the camp. He got taken prisoner before he could do any damage, thanks to you."

Matt shrugged. Apparently he didn't remember his life as well as Linda remembered the letters she'd received. His smile gone, he emptied his bottle and placed it on the table with a hollow thud. "Maybe I used to be able to read people," he drawled, his eyes turbulent as they mirrored the fire. "Obviously I'm not too good at it anymore."

Gary, she thought. They were back to the present, back to the bitterness. She ached to return to the past, to hear Matt tell her more about how good things used to be between him and her brother. But the past was no longer relevant. Matt had misread Gary, and all those good memories were gone.

"Would you like another beer?" she asked, knowing the offer was futile. The nostalgic mood had dissipated, leaving only anger and hurt.

He shook his head. "I ought to go."

She wanted to beg him to stay, to help her ward off the present, the truth. "Where will you go?"

"The motel in town."

"All right." She reminded herself that it would be better if he left. If he stayed, she would want to cuddle in his arms and listen to him tell her every happy story he could remember. She would want him to brush his lips over her forehead again, and tell her everything was all right.

He couldn't do that. She couldn't let herself want him to.

"Do you know how to get there?" she asked.

"I passed the place on the way to DeVito's." He stood, looming above her. She sprang to her feet, but she still felt small beside him, fragile, already lonesome even though he hadn't left yet. "Do you want me to help you clean up first?" he asked, gesturing toward the leftover pizza and the dirty dishes.

"No." *Just go,* she thought. *Get it over with.*

As if he could read her mind, he strode briskly out of the living room and down the hall to the kitchen. When he returned, he had on his jacket. "Will you let me know if Gary shows up?" he asked.

She gazed up at him. Without the fire to illuminate them, his eyes looked infinitely dark. She saw no hope in them, no warmth. He had shut down his memory; all that mattered was now, his money, his betrayal. All that mattered was Gary.

"I don't know," she replied.

A sad smile flickered across his lips and then vanished. He seemed to appreciate her honesty, even if he didn't like her answer. He reached for her shoulder, curved his fingers around it, started to pull her toward him and then abruptly let his hand fall. "Take care of yourself, Linda," he murmured, turning away and stalking out the door.

Take care of yourself, she echoed silently. She had to take care of herself, because no one else was going to take care of her. She was on her own. No one was going to help her to endure her oppressive sadness. No one was going to shelter her in his arms and swear that everything was all right.

Nothing was all right. And she was going to have to deal with that reality by herself.

WHEN SHE'D SAID the Braxton Motor Inn wasn't the Ritz, she hadn't been kidding. The room was drab and dreary, furnished with laminated furniture and floored in a mustard-colored shag carpet with cigarette burns in it. The radiator clanked and the mirror above the dresser was flawed, warping everything it reflected. Matt congratulated himself on having had the foresight to detour to the liquor store before he checked into the room. The bottle of bourbon he'd purchased was going to come in handy.

He had already called Jean in Portland, catching her just before she'd left the office for the day. Three-C was running smoothly, she'd assured him. The contracts on the health club renovation were being vetted by the lawyer, and the final payments on the medical building in Troutdale had come in. And she still felt guilty for having accidentally approved the transfer of funds to cover the check Gary Villard had doctored.

Matt had told her to stop being so hard on herself, then hung up and poured two inches of bourbon into one of the sanitary-wrapped plastic cups that stood in a stack on the bureau. He took a stiff belt, felt the liquor sear and then numb his throat, and stared out the window at the parking lot. Mercury streetlights cast an eerie orange glow across the asphalt and the cinder block side wall of the car wash next door. He craned his neck to see if the splashing sound he heard was caused by snow melting from the roof of the motel, then realized it was coming from his bathroom. He entered the tiny room, which smelled faintly of disinfectant, and discovered that the shower faucet leaked. He twisted it as tight as he could, but it continued to drip.

He left the bathroom and stretched out on the bed. Another slug of bourbon, and he put the plastic cup on the night table, gazed up at the water-stained ceiling and thought about Linda's house, the cozy guest room under the eaves, the bucolic vista outside the window. He thought about the homey wallpaper, the comfortably worn rugs, the old-fashioned molding that framed every doorway.

He thought about curling his hand around the molding of her bedroom door and seeing her.

It was torture, but he couldn't seem to stop picturing her smooth, creamy skin, her feminine curves, the rosy crests of her nipples just before she closed the towel around herself. He couldn't blank out the delectable shadows underlining her collarbone and tracing the edges of her hipbones. He couldn't erase the sleek, inviting contours of her thighs.

He cursed and reached for the bourbon.

Think about Gary, he ordered himself. The only way to counteract his erotic visions of Linda was to revive his outrage over her brother.

Yet when he tried to think about Gary, his fury was nudged aside by other emotions. He shouldn't have told Linda about all the good times he'd shared with Gary. He shouldn't have given in to recollections of the past. Those memories had been nullified by Gary's treachery. They no longer counted.

Unfortunately, now that they'd been awakened he couldn't put them back to sleep. They haunted him.

"You've got to get off that list, Calloway," Gary had said. "You can't do that run."

Matt had chuckled. Gary's accent always made him think of the Kennedys. It had such a rich, proper, well-educated quality.

"Don't laugh," Gary had scolded, only it sounded like "Don't *loff*." "People are going to die on that trip. You want me to get your name off the list?"

"Just supposing you're right that it's a dead-end gig," Matt had drawled, "how do you reckon to get my name off?"

"Magic, Calloway. Remember those stitches on the bottom of your foot?"

"What stitches?" Matt had suffered a twinge of apprehension. He'd heard about guys inflicting injury on themselves to avoid combat, but he wasn't going to sacrifice his foot because of some half-baked premonition of Gary's. "Don't you dare cut my foot, Villard. If you do, I swear I'll cut parts of you that you don't want to live without."

"Mellow out, Matt. Your stitches are on Rusty Becker's foot."

"What?"

"I've just got to rearrange a couple of medical records, and presto! Your file will have Rusty's injury erroneously entered onto it, and you'll be scheduled for the medics when that mission takes off."

"Gary. You're gonna get yourself strung up, fooling with the medical records."

"Nah. O'Reilly owes me a favor. I got him a case of tequila through back channels. He owes me."

"You shouldn't be wasting your favors on me."

"The hell I shouldn't. We're brothers. All for one and one for all. I'll get you off that list, Matt."

We're brothers, Matt thought, staring at the ceiling and listening to the continuous dripping of the bathroom faucet. They'd been brothers, and Gary had gotten Matt off the list.

Wasn't his life worth eighteen thousand dollars? Couldn't he bring himself to forgive Gary?

It wasn't the money. He'd known that almost from the start. Losing ten bucks to a mugger on the street would bother him more than handing eighteen thousand dollars over to Gary. The money had never mattered as much as the trust. The broken trust.

After he'd come home from Vietnam, it had been so hard to trust anyone. Ellie had thrown herself at him, jabbering about their wedding, the house they would buy in town, the way Matt would fit himself back into the community. When he'd tried to describe to her what he'd seen, what he'd lived through, she hadn't wanted to listen. He couldn't trust her to share his pain, to help him readjust to the real world.

No one else had wanted to listen, either. Not his family. Not his neighbors. Not his classmates when he'd started college, those privileged suburban kids who gawked at him as if he'd spent his entire tour of duty slaughtering babies and burning down villages. Not his professors, who wallowed in their theories and didn't want to hear anything contradictory. And still not Ellie, who was too involved with her own grievances to care one way or the other about his.

He hadn't started trusting again until he'd founded Three-C. At long last he could trust his boss because *he* was the boss. No one else spoke for him, no one else made decisions for him. He would never wind up on the wrong list due to an accident of fate. He was his own person at last.

God, it had taken so long. So long to rejoin the human race, to regain his faith. And now it was gone again.

He refilled his glass of bourbon, turned off the bedside lamp and let the salmon-hued light from the parking lot seep into the room. For all he knew, Gary could be with Linda right now. She had been honest enough to admit that she wasn't sure she would tell

Matt if Gary showed up in Braxton. He could trust her only enough to know that he couldn't trust her.

She didn't trust him, either, at least not when it came to her precious brother. She trusted Matt enough to weep in his arms, and to lend him her key, and to let him traipse around her house while she took a bath. She trusted him enough to permit him to bring her a pizza and build a fire in her fireplace. She trusted him enough to remain alone in her house with him, even though that was one area where she probably shouldn't have trusted him.

Just before he'd left her, he had come close to pulling her close and letting her discover in the most graphic way the effect she had on him. He had touched her shoulder and gazed down at her, and it was only the astonishing trust he'd seen shimmering in her lovely hazel-green eyes that had kept him from crushing his mouth to hers.

The trouble he could cause her was far worse than anything he could do to her brother. Why was she more anxious to protect Gary than herself? Why wasn't she smart enough to deliver Gary into Matt's custody and then run for her life?

Why couldn't she trust him a little bit more—or not at all?

CHAPTER SEVEN

LINDA ARRIVED at the Braxton Health Center at eleven-thirty, feeling out of sorts. The day was overcast but warm enough to keep the lingering slush from freezing up. Despite the milder temperature, she had forgone pastel-colored spring apparel and dressed in a pair of corduroy slacks, sturdy walking shoes and a Fair Isle sweater under her down vest.

Her Thursdays were spent visiting clients in their homes. In the mornings she paid calls to several unwed mothers on public assistance; the county required on-site inspections to make sure their apartments were clean and safe for their babies. She devoted the afternoons to shut-ins: two elderly women who relied on canes and walkers to get around, a wheelchair-bound man, and a divorced woman with four children whose car had been repossessed.

Ordinarily, Linda enjoyed her Thursdays out in the field. She liked seeing her clients on their own turf. They usually felt more relaxed away from the bureaucratic setting of the center, and she was able to pick up clues about their lives, things they might not readily admit to in their conversations with her—that a stove didn't work properly, for instance, or that a boyfriend liked to leave his hunting rifle in a place where a child could reach it.

She hadn't enjoyed herself today on her morning rounds. She was running on too little sleep and too much tension, and she had to labor hard to push her own concerns out of the way and give her full attention to the clients.

Gary still hadn't shown up. She had waited half the night for him to arrive, and by the time she'd conceded that he wasn't coming, it was too late to call Steve in Somerville.

Before she had learned that her brother was a fraud, she wouldn't have minded his unexplained absence. But now, everything he did—like not coming to Braxton after he'd told Steve he *was* coming to Braxton— struck her with a staggering impact. Suddenly his being unaccounted for on Wednesday night reared up like some sort of monstrous evidence, condemning him.

She was annoyed at Gary, and at Matt for bringing this misery down upon her. All his apologies didn't alter the fact that he had rammed into her world and battered its foundation. She felt precarious, as if one light breeze, one tiny mishap, would topple her.

Mostly, she was annoyed at herself for not hating Matt. For not being able to dismiss him and his incriminating documents. For allowing him to undermine her love for her brother. She was annoyed at herself for lying awake long after she'd concluded that Gary wasn't going to show up, and reliving the way Matt had held her, the way his arms had enveloped her. The way his lips had browsed through her hair and his voice had lulled her. The way every time he'd gazed at her she'd felt as if he could see through her clothing, through her defenses.

As if he knew how powerfully attracted she was to him.

Maybe her having been single for so many years magnified Matt's appeal in her eyes. Maybe she had gone for such a long time without a man's touch that even the most innocent embrace aroused all sorts of latent passions inside her. Gary kept telling her she needed to socialize more, to put her memories of Andrew away and have herself some lighthearted fun.

She couldn't have lighthearted fun with Matt, though. Not when he was gunning for her brother. Not when he was the embodiment of all her fantasies from way back when her fantasies were safe and simple and utterly divorced from reality.

She parked her car in the lot adjacent to the clinic and headed toward the sidewalk, trying to bolster her spirits. She needed to put up a cheerful front in Kay's presence, or Kay would ask questions Linda didn't want to answer. Linda wouldn't be in the office long, anyway. She would just check her mail, her messages and her appointment calendar, and then—

Damn.

Matt was standing on the top step in front of the glass door. The collar of his leather jacket was turned up against the cold, and his hands were in his pockets. The wind tugged at his thick, dark hair, mussing it. His eyes met hers and he started down the steps.

She didn't want to see him. She had no idea what to say to him. No doubt he was interested only in finding out whether her brother had arrived in town overnight.

Matt was using her. She knew it, and she resented it.

He reached the bottom step at the same time she did, and they stared at each other beneath the gray light of the overcast sky.

"Hi," he said.

Go ahead, she thought churlishly, *ask me about my brother.*

"The receptionist said you might stop by around lunchtime," he went on when she didn't speak.

"Well, here I am," she said none too politely.

"Have you got enough time to eat somewhere nicer than that dive across the street?"

She hadn't expected an invitation to lunch, and she wasn't sure how to react. She wished he would simply stick to business, ask about Gary and go away, before she fell under the spell of his beautiful eyes and started thinking of him as a man, someone whose touch could bring her to life, whose smile could ignite her soul.

"I have a bag lunch in my car," she told him.

"Then we'll take my car," he said, pulling his hand from his pocket and slipping it around her elbow. Her body responded to the casual gesture much too strongly, yet to yank her arm away would reveal how vulnerable she was to him. She bit her lip and kept her gaze focused on the sidewalk.

"You'll have to give me directions," he said once they were both seated inside his rental car.

She didn't want to give him directions. She didn't want to be seated so close to him, inhaling his clean scent and fighting her awareness of his hands, his lean thighs, his athletic physique, his sensuous lips. "Go down to the light and make a left," she mumbled.

He shot her a quick glance, then started the engine. Linda tried not to brood, but if she could scarcely manage to fake a cheerful disposition for her morning clients, she certainly couldn't fake one for Matt.

She waited for him to ask about her grouchiness, about the shadows under her eyes, her uninspired outfit, the haphazard braid into which she'd woven her hair that morning—and about her truant brother. All he said was, "Should I stay on this road at the intersection?"

"Follow the signs to Route 63," she answered. And that was it, for the next thirty minutes. They sat side by side in silence, Matt concentrating on the winding road and Linda shoring herself up, waiting for the subject of Gary to cast its long, cold shadow over them.

OWING TO THE PRESENCE of the University of Massachusetts and two private colleges within its borders, the town of Amherst had a variety of charming restaurants to choose from. Matt drove slowly along the main street, passing chic boutiques and bustling book shops, convenience stores and sporting goods emporiums. The prosperous town offered a sharp contrast to Braxton's bleak business district, where the economy was hurting and Braxton Gravel and Asphalt was repeatedly laying people off.

"Where should we go?" Matt asked.

Linda gestured toward a glass-walled eatery. She'd had dinner there a year ago, when she and Phil Richards had driven down to see the university's production of *Romeo and Juliet*. The play and the food had been excellent, but Phil's attempt to transform an old friendship into something romantic had been a dismal failure. He had driven her home and they'd kissed . . . and she'd felt nothing even remotely as exciting as what she felt merely glimpsing at Matt's work-hardened fingers, his rugged jaw and his coal-dark eyes.

He parked the car and they entered the restaurant. Linda wondered when he was going to broach the subject of her brother. She knew it was coming; she just wished he'd get it over with. The anticipation was building inside her like steam in a pressure cooker. She felt ready to explode.

A hostess led them to a table nestled into a grove of potted plants. Having been too sleepy to bother with breakfast that morning, Linda ordered an omelet. Matt requested a roast beef sandwich, and coffee for them both. "You look tired," he explained when Linda frowned at his presumptuousness.

"I am," she admitted. Now it was coming. He'd made a personal observation. Soon he would turn the discussion to the even more personal subject of whether she was harboring her fugitive brother.

He leaned back in his chair and sent her a lopsided smile. "I'm tired, too. I had a hard time falling asleep last night. The Braxton Motor Inn is the pits."

She didn't want to share his opinion; it drew them together, somehow. But she couldn't help returning his smile. "I warned you not to stay there."

"I haven't got too many alternatives."

You could go back to Oregon, she thought, knowing full well that he wouldn't. Not until he'd confronted Gary.

"I shouldn't stay at your house, Linda, but if you offered, I wouldn't be able to say no. So please don't offer."

She gaped at him in surprise. The waitress came with their coffee, and Linda took advantage of the interruption to sort her thoughts. She wanted to maintain her distance from him, yet as soon as he'd spoken she realized she had been very close to telling him he was welcome to make use of the guest room in her house.

She felt his eyes upon her, measuring, trying to decipher her mood. "The motel is okay," he finally said. "I'll survive."

"You're staying in Braxton, then," she half asked.

"You want me to leave?"

"I don't know what I want," she replied, not bothering to hide her exasperation.

"Yes, you do," he argued quietly. "You want to wake up and discover this whole thing has been a bad dream."

But it hadn't been all bad, she almost protested. She'd gotten to know one of the fearless foursome. She'd gotten to feel something for a man again. "Wishing that things were different is a waste of time," she said. "All I wish is that..." She sighed. "That there could be some peaceful way to work everything out."

"Peaceful, huh."

"Why don't you think you should stay at my house?" The question slipped out before she could stop it.

He didn't answer immediately. The waitress arrived to deliver their meals, but Matt only gazed across the table at Linda. For a moment she felt inhibited by his stare—maybe a film of coffee clung to her upper lip, maybe her braid was unraveling, maybe the sleeves of her sweater were sagging at the elbows. Surely something must be terribly wrong with her appearance, given the hard, relentless way he was staring at her.

"I want you," he said. His implacable eyes echoed the sentiment, allowing her no chance to misinterpret his words.

She swallowed and examined the cheese oozing from the center of her omelet. Had she dreaded talking to Matt about her brother? That seemed like a delightful subject compared to this.

"There's no peaceful way to work it out," he added, sounding pensive. "I want you, and I can't have you."

"Then why are you taking me out for lunch?"

He laughed grimly. "To torment myself."

"I don't believe that." She poked her omelet with the tines of her fork, then tasted it. "I believe you've taken me to lunch so you can find out if Gary is in town." If he wasn't going to say it, she would.

Matt took a bite of his sandwich and shook his head. "I don't want to talk about him."

Neither did she. But if they didn't talk about Gary they might revert to talking about Matt wanting her. "I honestly don't know where he is," she said. "His friend Steve said he was coming here, but Gary himself told me he might not show up until the weekend, so I really don't—"

Matt reached across the table and covered her hand with his. Until that moment, she hadn't realized that her hand was trembling.

"I don't want to talk about him," he repeated.

"Why not?" It was half a challenge, half a plea.

"It'll only make me angry. I'm tired of being angry, Linda. I'm tired of hurting. I just..." He considered his words. "I just want to have lunch with someone I like."

"I don't know why you like me," she muttered, easing her hand from his the instant she felt his clasp relax.

He smiled. "You're smart, you're beautiful, you're sympathetic, you're generous... Should I keep going?"

She felt her cheeks flush. "Oh, my. Maybe I should get fitted for a halo and wings."

"Maybe you should," he agreed, lifting his sandwich to his lips. "If you were an angel I wouldn't want you the way I do."

"Don't say that."

"Forget it," he assured her, his smile gone. "I'm not real big on wishing for things that can't be, either. So let's just enjoy our lunch. Have you given any thought to my doing the repair on your porch?"

She busied herself with her omelet for a minute, struggling to shift gears. How could Matt expect her to make idle conversation with him after he'd expressed his desire for her so bluntly? Had he any idea that she wanted him, too? Or had he dropped his bombshell simply as a way of shaking her up, hoping to weaken her so he could get to her brother more easily?

No. Matt wasn't the sneaky one in this scenario. "You can't repair the porch until I've checked with Gary first," she told him. "It's his house."

"Then he should fix the porch. What's he waiting for?"

"I haven't bothered to tell him how bad it is. I was figuring that when the weather improved I'd get some estimates and discuss it with him."

"I'd do the job for free."

"Why?" she asked. "You're a professional. You ought to be paid for your labor."

"What's wrong with doing a favor for someone?"

"You might expect something in return," she said.

He regarded her thoughtfully, then took a long sip of coffee. "I expect nothing from you," he assured her, his voice low and intense. "What I want and what I hope to get are two different things."

"What do you hope to get?"

His gaze tightened on her, the fiery darkness of his eyes burning through her. "Your forgiveness."

"You've done nothing I have to forgive," she said, knowing as soon as she spoke that it wasn't true. He had torn her apart. He'd destroyed her illusions. He'd come very close to wrecking her relationship with her brother.

He didn't challenge her assertion, though. Her words hung between them, making her omelet taste gummy, making her coffee taste bitter, making her unable to look at him.

He wanted her forgiveness. He wanted her.

His life was out west, and his goal was to ruin her brother. There was no place for her in any of it, no room for love to blossom, no chance for her and Matt to discover what could exist between them. No peaceful solution.

So he would spend tonight in the Braxton Motor Inn, and tomorrow night, and however many nights it would take until he either found Gary or gave up. And she would spend her nights alone.

IT WAS TORMENT, he thought, gazing across the table at her, knowing she saw him only as a troublemaker, an instigator, the embodiment of a dilemma. It was torment to have caused her such problems, and yet yearn for the feel of her graceful body against his. Torment to know that if he ever got what he truly wanted from her, it would only cause her more problems.

But he couldn't stay away.

While he ate his sandwich, she told him about one of the clients she'd visited that morning, a nineteen-year-old girl with a two-year-old son, another baby on the way and a boyfriend in prison. It sounded depressing to Matt, but Linda was optimistic. The client was working hard to earn her General Equivalency Diploma, and Linda had enrolled her in a health program for pregnant women. "This pregnancy has gone so much better for her than the last one," Linda related. "Her best friend is going to go to the prepared childbirth classes with her. She's really turning her life around."

Matt liked to hear success stories as much as anyone. But in this story success was only a possibility. What enthralled him was Linda's confidence. She was making a difference in the girl's life, not just by steering her into the proper health and education programs, but by being so hopeful. Merely talking about the girl's prospects filled Linda's eyes with lustrous pleasure. Her voice grew melodic, her kittenish mouth curved in a delectable smile, and...

And he found himself thinking about her big brass bed.

That was the real trouble, of course: not that her brother stood between them, but that Linda still knew how to hope and care and believe in the goodness of people. Matt didn't. Not anymore.

The drive back to Braxton was as quiet as the drive to Amherst had been. As they approached the town from the south, he asked her for directions, and she told him where to turn, which road to take. It wasn't the same route they'd taken when they'd left Braxton. "Is this a short cut?" he asked.

"About the same distance," she said. "Right after this turn, take a left."

He recognized where he was then: the fork in the road, the incline, the twisting lane to her house. She couldn't possibly be navigating him there to invite him to act on the passion he'd admitted to at the restaurant. "You need something at your house?" he asked, slowing at a bend in the road.

She said nothing, only leaned forward as the property loomed into view. The driveway was empty, the interior lights off. "No," she finally answered. "We may as well head back to town."

"Looking for Gary?" he guessed.

She sent him a quick, oddly guilty look. "I honestly don't know where he is."

"I believe you," Matt said, meaning it. At another time, in another context, he might not have. But how could he not believe her when her house was obviously unoccupied?

"It isn't like I want to protect him, Matt, but . . . I don't know, I feel like one of those Nazi youths, turning in their parents."

"You don't have to turn Gary in," Matt said cautiously. He didn't want to discourage her from turning her brother in, either.

"I mean, he *is* my brother."

"I know."

The tension he'd sensed in her when he'd first spotted her approaching the health center was returning. Her eyes lost their sparkle, her lips their gentle curve. Her posture grew slack. She seemed on the verge of saying something, but he was afraid of what it might be.

Before she could speak, he reached across the seat and patted her shoulder. Touching her reminded him of how tempted he was to touch more of her, all of her. "It's all right, Linda," he said. "I'll deal with him. You can stay out of it."

"I can't. I'm already in the middle of it." It wasn't an accusation or a plea, it was simply a statement of fact. A grievously sad fact.

Fixing her porch wouldn't begin to compensate for what he'd done to her. Apologizing wouldn't make things right. Letting his hand linger for another instant on her shoulder would make things worse than they already were. It would compel him to pull off the road and gather her into his arms, and kiss her, and make promises he couldn't keep.

He returned his hand to the steering wheel and kept his gaze riveted to the road ahead.

"I'm late for my afternoon appointments," she said as they reached Second Street. "You'd better just drop me off by my car."

He steered into the parking lot adjacent to the health center. She pointed out her Subaru and he braked to a halt beside it.

"Thank you for lunch," she murmured, opening her door.

Once again he wrestled with the urge to touch her. "Are you free for dinner tonight?" he asked, knowing he shouldn't. It wasn't fair to keep insinuating himself into her life; the less time he spent with her the happier they'd both be.

Her eyes brightened once more, glimmering with sparks of green as they searched his face. She looked hopeful again, as hopeful as she'd looked when she'd described her troubled client.

Maybe that was how she saw this mess: troublesome, but not impossible. Impossible, but not hopeless. Hopeless, except that Linda was too idealistic to give up hope.

Then common sense got the better of her. "No," she said, abruptly averting her gaze and climbing out of the car. "I'm not free."

There was a sharp metallic clap as she closed the door behind her. Matt then U-turned and cruised to the lot's entrance. When he glanced into his rearview mirror, he saw her standing beside her car, gazing after him, looking as tormented as he felt.

GARY HEARD the muffled sounds of traffic through the window of his motel room: an occasional car, the drone of a motorcycle, an eighteen-wheeler's brakes wheezing and coughing. The room smelled of mildew.

He was lonely. It was dark, late. He lay on the squeaking, sagging mattress, naked except for his earring, wrapped in the sheets and his memories.

The money. Twenty-five thousand dollars in cash. Like a message from God, sent directly to him, for his eyes only: *Here, Gary. You've worked hard, you've had it rough. You deserve this.*

He hadn't meant to spend it all. If only someone had claimed it right away, he would have spent none of it. But no one had claimed it; no one could. That much cash implied that the money was dirty. What criminal was going to sidle up to Gary's boss and say, "By the way, has one of your drivers turned in a fat wad of illegal tender?"

He'd waited, sat on the money, exercised patience. And then, after a few weeks, he'd decided it was his to keep.

It had gone so fast, all of it for fun, food, laughs and thrills. Except for the TV, and the ring he'd bought Debbie, intending to give it to her on Valentine's Day. Cripes, all of it—the dinners out, the days at the track, the shows, the dancing, the TV, and most especially the ring—had been because of Debbie, because he loved her. He had chosen a great, dazzling hunk of diamond, emerald cut because the guy at the jewelry store said she would like that best. Two-and-a-half carats, set in genuine eighteen-karat gold. He'd bought it because he loved her.

He'd robbed Matt Calloway because he loved her. Because one evening, after he'd finished cleaning his limousine and left the garage for the day, he'd gotten waylaid out back by two men. One of them had been his passenger the day he'd found the cash on the floor of the back seat. The other resembled King Kong after a skillful barbering.

"Where is it?" his passenger had asked.

Gary had tried polite innocence. "Excuse me, sir, are you talking to me?"

"My money," the passenger had said. "I want it. Explain to him how much I want it," he'd ordered King Kong.

"He wants his money," King Kong had explained.

"I don't know what you're talking about," Gary had lied.

"Think about it overnight," the passenger had said. "Maybe you'll remember. We'll be back tomorrow."

As promised, they'd been back. Gary had held them off again, playing dumb, which had been so dumb, maybe he hadn't been playing. Then they'd been back again. This time with a gun. And a threat.

"You haven't even married her yet," the passenger had said as King Kong ran the gun's barrel from Gary's sternum up to the underside of his chin and then back to his belly. "Debbie Montoya could be your widow before she's your bride. We could arrange that."

"Maybe," King Kong had added enthusiastically, "we could, like, cut her face or something, so no one would ever want to marry her. Would you like that? We could make it so no one else will want her after you die."

"I'll get your money," Gary had said. "I'll get it. Just stay away from her."

"Okay," the passenger said, signaling King Kong to lower the gun. "We'll be back tomorrow for it."

"Tomorrow! Hey, man—I need a little time to get it together. Please—it'll take me a week, at least...."

"One week," the passenger had said. "One week. We'll be back, ready to do business." He gestured toward King Kong's gun so Gary would understand exactly what sort of business they would be ready to do. "You don't discuss this with anyone, right?" the passenger had added. "Because we know where Debbie Montoya lives, where she works. You get the money, you stay quiet, and Debbie lives a long life with a pretty face. Are we clear?"

"Yes. We're clear."

He'd had to get the money. If he hadn't, they would have killed him. If he'd disappeared, they would have gone after Debbie. If he'd talked to the police, they would have hurt her. Or worse.

He would have done anything—even cheat the man who had saved his life in Vietnam—for Debbie.

The electric clock bolted to the night table beside his bed read one o'clock. The last time he'd spoken to her she'd sounded royally ticked off at him.

He didn't blame her; taking a powder after he'd paid off the thugs hadn't been the noblest thing he'd ever done in his life. But he couldn't bring himself to tell her the truth. After risking so much to protect her, he couldn't just come right out and say, "I'm an ass," and expect her to love him. And he couldn't bear the thought of losing her love.

One a.m. in Nashua, New Hampshire, was 10:00 p.m. Pacific time. Right now, she was probably drinking a diet soda and flipping through a magazine, with the TV on in the background. Maybe she would be a little sleepy, a little romantic, a little receptive to him. He'd call her up, whisper that he loved her, and promise that he'd come home soon. As soon as he could see Linda and talk to her about how he was going to raise the money to pay Matt back.

He wouldn't go into all that with Debbie, of course. He'd simply tell her he loved her.

Without bothering to switch on the lamp, he pressed the number for an outside line and then punched in the phone number at his apartment. He listened to the rhythmic purr as it rang once, twice... Three times. Four.

Twelve times.

Debbie could be anywhere, he told himself as he hung up. Maybe she'd taken a bag of garbage out to the dumpster. Maybe she'd dropped by a neighbor's apartment for a minute. Maybe she'd gone to her friend Rosie's place and they were watching a video, one of those sappy flicks Debbie was always selecting and he was always vetoing at the video rental place.

That was it. She was watching some tearjerker with Rosie. Tomorrow was a working day, so she would have to get home soon.

He tried the number again, just in case. It rang ten times and he hung up.

A half hour later, he tried again. He listened to it ring fifteen times before dropping the receiver into its cradle. Unable to sleep, he got out of bed, put on his jeans, paced the room in a circle, and stared through the window at the sporadic wee-hours traffic trickling past the motel. He walked down the hall to the soda machine, bought a cola, returned to his room and sipped it as slowly as he could. The caffeine couldn't make him any more jittery than he already was.

Once the can was empty, he sprawled out on the bed and dialed the number once more. After twenty rings, he slammed down the receiver and cut loose with a profanity. Then he fell back against the pillow, fingered the smooth gold letter dangling from his ear-lobe, and tried to smother the panic that threatened to swamp him.

Why wasn't she answering the phone? Why wasn't she home?

Where was she? What if she was gone for good?

"Damn it to hell," he muttered into the stale darkness of the room. "Everything I touch turns to mud.

Try to do things right, man, and it all comes out wrong.''

He was alone in a godforsaken motel in the middle of New Hampshire. The woman he loved was gone, away from home, out of reach. His sister was living her calm, peaceful life in Braxton, little knowing that Gary was about to throw himself at her and beg her to straighten everything out, to save him, to empty her bank accounts for him and, if that wasn't enough, to move out of the house so he could sell it to get the money he needed to make things right.

If it was even possible at this point to make things right. He didn't know if he could do it. But he knew that if he couldn't, he would spend the rest of his life running away from Matt Calloway—and from himself.

CHAPTER EIGHT

IN THE LULL between the breakfast rush and noon, the coffee shop across the street from the Braxton Health Center was nearly empty. The chatty waitress who had served him when he'd come here for lunch with Linda spotted him the moment he stepped inside. As soon as she registered the fact that he was alone this time, she shaped a coquettish smile and ushered him to a secluded booth near the back of the dining room. "Hi, there," she said, preening, brushing her blond curls back from her face. "Guess you haven't left town yet."

Matt wasn't in the mood to be pleasant, but he exerted himself. "I guess I haven't."

"What can I get you?"

"Just coffee."

She seemed mildly disappointed that he wasn't ordering more, but her smile remained in place as she sashayed over to the counter to drop off his unused menu.

Matt's eyes followed her movements, but his mind remained on the boxy public building across the street. On the tawny-haired woman inside, the one with the hazel-green eyes and the too-small nose and the body even an ensemble of bulky winter clothes couldn't disguise.

After dropping her off at her car the previous afternoon, he'd spent some time driving around town, cruising past the high school, the cemetery, the Braxton Gravel and Asphalt quarry on the western end of town. He'd driven by the library, the town hall, the police station, not sure of what he was looking for—a sense of who the Villards were, he guessed, how they'd grown up, how they'd wound up with such completely different natures. Eventually he'd returned to the motel, where he'd spent an hour on the phone with Jean in Portland, reviewing all the major and minor goings-on at Three-C.

At six o'clock, he'd left the motel for DeVito's to pick up something to eat. His car had had ideas of its own, however, and before he could stop himself he'd driven up the hill past the fork, along the sinuous country lane, beyond the bend to her house.

The front windows had been filled with light, and what appeared to be fresh tire tracks had been etched into the muddy driveway. The garage barn had been closed. If Gary had arrived, he hadn't parked in the driveway.

Matt hadn't come looking for Gary.

He'd sat in his car on the side of the road, staring at the windows, praying for a glimpse of Linda's silhouette against the drapes. He'd sat there for longer than he wanted to admit, watching for her, wishing he'd had fewer scruples. If he hadn't cared about hurting her, he would have marched to the front door and rung her bell, and when she'd answered he would have pulled her to himself and done whatever was necessary to put out the fires raging inside him. He would have taken her mouth with his, and her body, and even her love if she wanted to give it.

But he did have scruples. So he'd turned his car around and driven back to town.

The waitress returned with a pitcher of cream and a glass pot of steaming coffee. "Here you go," she said gaily as she filled his cup.

He peered up at her, assessing her elastic smile, the tiny lines framing her eyes, the softness of the skin beneath her jaw. She was probably close to his age—and Gary's.

"How are your daffodils?" he asked before she could turn away.

She appeared momentarily bewildered. Then she recalled their earlier conversation and grinned. "Hard to say. It'll take a couple of weeks to know for sure."

Hahd to say, he repeated mentally, capturing her accent. *A couple of weeks to know fuh shaw.* Her pronunciation was identical to Gary's. "Have you got a minute?" he asked, gesturing toward the banquette across from him.

Her expression brightened. "Let me go put this down," she said, indicating the coffeepot. She hurried to the counter, the soles of her sneakers squeaking on the linoleum tiles, and then jogged back to his table, once again fussing with her yellow hair.

"It's quiet right now," she said as she slid into the booth across the table from him. "If the traffic picks up, I'll have to go. But it *shaw* feels good to take a load off my feet for a minute. We were really hopping at breakfast this morning. And I'll tell you, breakfast is the worst for tips. Most folks are too tired to think about it."

She certainly was garrulous. "Are you from around here?" he asked.

"Born and bred."

"I'm here to see an old friend," he ventured, gauging her reaction. "His name is Gary Villard. Do you know him?"

"Gah-ry Vill-ahd," she repeated. She frowned for a minute, then nodded. "We were in high school together. He was a year behind me. No—a year ahead of me," she amended, as if afraid that Matt would deem her too old.

"So you know him, then?"

"I know him," she said. "He used to be a driver for Killbrun's Delivery Service. He came in here for coffee all the time."

"Has he been in lately?"

"Oh, heck, no. He doesn't live around here anymore. Not since Killbrun filed for bankruptcy. All the drivers got laid off. It was so sad. Things are tough all over, right? Where are you from?"

"Oregon," Matt said laconically, not eager to discuss himself.

"Wow. You're a long way from home, aren't you. What brings you to Braxton?"

"Just visiting. So, Gary isn't in town, then?"

"Haven't seen him since Killbrun's went under. I suppose he had to go make his fortune elsewhere. Money," she said with a sigh. "Isn't that what it's all about?"

Yes, Matt thought wryly, money was what it was all about. He would have preferred if Gary had actually *made* his fortune, instead of stealing it, but the bottom line was still the same: Money.

"So, what's on tap for you? How long are you going to be in town?"

"Not long," he said, acutely aware of how true that was. If he couldn't catch up with Gary by the weekend, he was going to have to head for home. He'd been gone from Portland almost a week. He couldn't stay in Braxton forever.

"You still going to be around tonight? Because I could make it my business to be free."

Matt remembered his first impression of the waitress had been that she was rather forward. Forward, he decided, was an understatement. They hadn't even exchanged names, and she was already trying to line him up for the evening.

Not that he minded. He didn't think there was anything wrong with friendly aggression in a female. But...damn, if he was going to spend the evening with a woman, it was going to be with Linda.

Which meant he would be spending the evening alone.

"Sorry," he said with a gentle smile.

The waitress smiled back. "Well, it was worth a try."

"Some other time, maybe," he said.

She shrugged and pushed herself to her feet. "I got customers." She waved vaguely toward a pair of burly men in work clothes who had ambled into the coffee shop. "Don't forget my tip." She winked, then sauntered to the door to seat the new arrivals.

It all comes down to money, Matt thought cynically. He realized he had just sacrificed the empty pleasure of a night with an uncomplicated woman who had enough common sense to know what life was all about. And he had nothing to put in its place. Not pleasure, not a woman, not even anger.

Gary's duplicity was worthy of anger. His subversion of Matt's trust was. His hypocrisy was. But if, in the end, it all came down to money, Matt couldn't even give in to that corrosive, cathartic emotion.

Great principles and self-righteousness were irrelevant. It all came down to money. And all Matt felt was numb.

"WHERE WERE YOU last night?" Gary was practically screaming.

Debbie stood at the pay phone in the upstairs stockroom and groaned. Behind her was a rack of Norma Kamali jumpsuits, still in plastic; in front of her was the employee washroom.

"I tried you half the night. It was eleven-thirty your time. Where were you?"

She twirled her finger through the coiled wire and took a deep breath. She didn't love him. She wouldn't. Loving him meant she had to answer him, and she didn't want to.

"Come on, honey," he pleaded. "I'm going crazy here."

"You sure are. You expect me to tell you where I was, when I don't know where *you* are."

"I'm in Nashua. I told you."

"I don't know where Nashua is—and it's no place you ought to be. Why aren't you with Linda?"

"Debbie—"

"You know what I decided? I decided I like your sister better than you. I can trust her."

"You can trust me, too," he said.

He sounded so desperate. If she let her armor crack the slightest bit, he would sneak inside and reclaim her heart. She would feel sorry for him, and worry about him, and swear with all her soul that of course she

loved him and couldn't wait for him to come home.
She wasn't going to let that happen.

"Where were you last night?" he asked. "With
Rosie?"

If she told him the truth he might never come back.
If she didn't tell him the truth, she was no better than
he was, with his game-playing and his deceit. "I went
out," she said.

"With who? With a man?"

"Yeah, with a man. What's it to you?"

She heard a sound through the long-distance cable,
a cross between a curse and a sob. It worked on her
like a chisel, chipping at her fortifications, making her
ache for him. "Who?" he asked. There was no threat
in his voice, only defeat. "Someone rich? Someone
better for you than I am, right?"

"Oh, Gary, I don't know—"

"Who? Was it Matt Calloway? Has he come down
to Los Angeles?"

Matt Calloway. Why did Gary keep mentioning that
name? "Which one is he? The guy from Portland?"

"Yeah. He was looking for me, you said. Did he
come down to see you?"

"Gary, let's not talk about this now, okay? I'm at
work."

"It was him, wasn't it." Gary sighed. "I know, he's
a good man, Debbie. A better man than me. He's rich,
he's got his own company, he builds houses. He has it
all, Debbie. I've got nothing."

"He hasn't got me."

A pause, and then Gary asked in a small, tentative
voice, "Have I got you?"

"I don't know, Gary. I don't know anything anymore. I'm going back to work."

"I love you, Debbie—"

"Goodbye." She hung up, then sank back against the clothing rack. The plastic sheeting draped over the jumpsuits made a crinkly noise as she leaned into it.

Matt Calloway, whoever he was and however good a man he was, did not have her. Neither did Gary. Neither did the man she'd met at a bar after work with Rosie. He'd been good-looking, he'd gone out dancing with her, he'd bought her a chili dog up by Hermosa Beach, and then when he'd driven her back to her car he'd turned into an octopus, all over her, and she'd had to wrestle herself free.

Wasn't there a single decent man left in the world? Someone who courted a lady, treated her with respect, told her he loved her and meant it?

Who was Matt Calloway, anyway? If he was as hot as Gary implied, she wished she could meet him.

And then what? she thought disconsolately, pushing away from the jumpsuits and heading back out onto the floor. So what if this Matt guy was Mister Perfect? So what if he was rich and had it all? She'd bet anything in the world he wouldn't pierce his ear and wear a gold *D* earring. In all her life, she had known only one man who would do something like that for her.

But he was in some town called Nashua, and she didn't trust him.

Life stank sometimes. It truly did.

THAT EVENING, once again, he drove to her house and tried to convince himself he was only looking for Gary. It would be good if he found his quarry tonight. He wanted his anger back. He wanted to feel something real and strong, something as invigorating as the emotion that had sent him on his cross-country quest in the first place.

The moment Linda's house loomed into view, he felt real, strong emotions, all right. Loneliness. Desire. A hunger for something that bore no resemblance to revenge.

The lights inside her house were on, as they'd been last night. The porch light was on, too. When he drove closer he saw her outside, hunkering down beside the edge of the porch with her face angled toward the floorboards.

The sight of her shadowed figure, with the porch light spilling down onto her lush red-blond hair, her head cocked to one side, roused not only the expected stirrings of lust but also curiosity. What was she doing?

He slowed the car and she glanced his way. He braked, and she straightened up, planting her hands on her hips. Evidently she wasn't happy to see him.

Then her arms dropped to her sides and she squatted down beside the porch again. All his doubts, all his self-protective instincts vanished. Linda was a friend, and he'd promised to fix her porch. Perhaps it was on the verge of collapse, and she was right this very minute rethinking her rejection of his offer.

He rolled down the window and shouted, "What's up?"

She glanced his way once more. The porch light threw her features into stark relief. After a moment, she shouted back, "It's Dinah."

Her cat. "Can I help?"

Another hesitation, and she called out, "Maybe."

Refusing to consider the wisdom of it, he steered onto the driveway and got out of the car. By the time he'd reached the edge of the porch, Linda was on her knees, cooing sweetly to a crack between two boards: "It's okay, sweetie. It's okay. I'm going to get you out of there."

He stooped down beside her. "What happened?"

"Dinah somehow wriggled under the porch, and now she can't get back out. I got home from work a half hour ago and couldn't find her. She wasn't in the house. I was tramping all over the yard, and then I heard her. I can't figure out how she got down there in the first place."

Matt stepped back and studied the side boards of the porch. If the ground was spongy enough, the cat could have burrowed under the bottom boards. He saw no obvious holes or indentations, however.

He climbed onto the porch and stamped his feet, searching for loose boards. The cat howled in panic.

"It's okay," Linda murmured through the cracks. "I know it sounds loud, Dinah, but it's okay. We're going to get you out."

"This one," Matt declared, finding a suspiciously shaky plank. He knelt down and gave it a sharp tug. The rotten wood around the nails gave way and the board jerked free.

"She could have gotten down that way," Linda said, studying the space. "But how is she going to get back up? There's nothing for her to jump onto."

"Here, kitty, kitty," Matt chanted, feeling silly. "Come on, kitty, come on here." The cat glided toward the narrow opening; her eyes caught the porch light and turned an iridescent gold as she stared up at him. "Here, kitty, kitty," he murmured.

Dinah strained toward the opening, but there was no place for her to gain a purchase with her paws. She meowed plaintively.

Matt shoved the board as hard as he could, buying himself a little extra room. Then he squeezed his hand down through the space and groped for the cat. At first she shied from him, but after gingerly tasting his fingertips, she nosed her head against his palm. Even with minimal maneuvering room, he managed to pinch a bit of her scruff between his thumb and his fingers.

She let out a yowl of displeasure and tried to slither out of his grasp. "Grab her," he snapped at Linda as he contorted his wrist, raising the cat up toward the narrow opening.

Linda slid her hands into place as Matt wriggled the cat's shoulders between the boards. She gripped Dinah's ribs and pulled her out. Dinah's thank you was a furious hiss.

Matt slid his hand out of the crack and shoved the board back into place. Rubbing his wrist, he muttered, "You've got to get this porch fixed."

"I know." Linda was anxiously stroking her frazzled, chilled cat, but her eyes were on Matt's hand. "Are you okay?"

He examined the red marks on his wrist and found no serious damage. On the outer edge of his hand he discovered a sliver of wood imbedded in his skin. "Just a splinter," he reported, trying unsuccessfully to pry it loose with his fingers.

"I'll get it out for you," she said, rising and opening the front door. She lowered Dinah to the rug in the entry and then turned and waited for Matt to join her.

For the first time since he'd arrived at her house, he and Linda actually looked at each other. Her beauty staggered him—her beauty and her trust. In spite of what he'd told her yesterday, she was letting him into her home.

To remove a splinter, he reminded himself. Only because he'd gotten it in the course of rescuing her stupid cat.

Still, it was an act of faith on Linda's part to allow him inside. He vowed not to let her regret it.

Entering her house reminded him of the first time he'd been there, the first night he'd seen her. Even though he wasn't escaping from a blizzard this time, her home felt like a haven to him. He saw the cozy furnishings in the living room, the fireplace, the unpretentious wallpaper and the soft, soothing lights. He felt Linda's presence in every nook, every corner, every cubic inch of air, and he wondered how in hell he was going to find the strength to return to the Braxton Motor Inn after this.

Linda signaled for him to follow her down the hall to the kitchen. Dinah was guzzling water from her bowl, but she glanced up at their entrance, shooting Matt a leery look. "Give me a break," Matt retorted. "I saved your life."

"She's frightened," Linda explained, bending down to pet Dinah's back. Matt envied the cat. He would have liked to have Linda petting his back, fussing over him.

Instead he headed for the sink and scrubbed his hands with soap. Linda removed her down vest, then handed him a paper towel. "I'll be right back," she said. "Take off your jacket."

Not exactly the gracious hospitality he'd gotten the first time he'd been in her house. But then all he'd represented to her was one of the fearless foursome. She hadn't known what he was after. And she hadn't known how he felt about her.

When she came back to the kitchen she was carrying a bottle of antiseptic, a bottle of rubbing alcohol, a box of bandage strips, a needle and tweezers. "Are you planning on major surgery?" he joked.

She barely smiled. "Sit at the table," she said, dropping her paraphernalia and carrying his jacket and her down vest to the mudroom. She returned, pulled a box of matches from a drawer, and then took a seat facing him. He tried to focus on her hands as she swabbed the area around the splinter with alcohol, then struck a match and held the tip of the needle to the flame. He tried not to respond to the satin smoothness of her palms, the graceful tapering of her fingers and the clean pink ovals of her nails. He tried to pretend her gentle competence didn't stoke his imagination with ideas of how her hands would feel on his chest, on his back, on his thighs, on his—

"Ow!" The bite of the needle shocked him back to reality.

"Sorry. It's deep."

He gritted his teeth to keep from yelping as she jabbed him again with the needle. She moved the point fastidiously, tearing gently at his skin and dabbing a tissue against the bead of blood that formed.

Much as he admired the appearance of her hands, watching her lacerate him with a sharp object wasn't pleasant. He lifted his gaze to her face, downturned and solemn, her full attention directed to the task of removing the splinter. Her eyes glowed with purpose, and she pursed her lips in an unintentionally alluring way.

"I'm sorry, Matt," she said, digging deeper.

He choked back a curse as the needle speared through his tough flesh. "You're a sadist," he muttered.

She didn't stop poking at him. "If I were a sadist, I would have left the splinter in there to get infected."

"An infection doesn't seem so bad compared to this."

"Don't be a baby. I've almost got it." She reached for the tweezers.

"Oh, my God. Now you've got two weapons."

She probed, pricked, pried and plucked. "Just be still."

He stared at her hair. She had pulled it back into a ponytail, but it was falling loose, long, silky tendrils framing her face. In the overhead light he saw the gossamer curls of her lashes. Her nostrils narrowed in concentration as she made yet another foray into his flesh.

"Ow! Next time the cat stays under the porch."

"Your skin is so callused, Matt, it's really difficult to— Aha! I got it!" She held up the tweezers, displaying the sliver of wood like a bloody trophy.

He flexed his hand. She seemed to have caused no permanent damage. "Should I file a claim with my medical insurance?" he asked. "Or can I pay you directly?"

"You can hold still. I'm not done with you." She swabbed the spot with alcohol again, then painted it pink with antiseptic and covered it with a small bandage. "There," she said, beaming with pride. "No bill. It's on the house."

"You've really got to do something about that porch, Linda."

"Even brand-new porches can give you splinters," she said, wiping off the needle and tweezers, and capping the bottles.

"New porches don't have loose boards that cats can squeeze under."

"I'll discuss it with Gary."

Gary. Matt's alleged reason for being here.

There was no sign that Gary was in the house. No sound, other than the quiet munching of Dinah devouring her dinner. No evidence that Gary had come and gone. The kitchen looked exactly as Matt remembered it. The counters were clean, the floor swept, the drawers—which Matt himself had rummaged through in a totally unethical search of her house—all shut.

"He's not here," Linda said.

"I didn't ask."

"You were thinking it, though."

He sighed and scrutinized his bandaged hand. "I'd better go."

"I still have leftover pizza."

She said it so quietly he wasn't sure he'd heard her correctly. Glancing at her, he sensed from her enigmatic expression that she wasn't sure she'd meant for him to hear it. "Is that an invitation?" he asked carefully.

She averted her gaze. "I don't want you to read anything into it, Matt. But you saved my cat's life, and it's your pizza, anyway. You bought it."

He'd bought it the last time he was here. The night she'd taken a bath, and he'd seen her body, and he'd gained her trust—at least for a few precious hours.

If he had any intelligence, any sense of honor, he would leave. Right now. Before he gave himself a chance to think about how much he wanted to stay.

"I'd love pizza," he said.

CHAPTER NINE

SHE SHOULD HAVE KNOWN that they would wind up drinking brandy in the living room after dinner. She probably did know. Maybe that was why she had asked him to stay.

He had built a fire while she'd cleaned up the dinner dishes, and now they sat on the sofa, separated by the width of the center cushion. Dinah, having recovered from the trauma of being trapped under the porch, lay in front of the fireplace, purring and licking her paws with indulgent thoroughness.

Over dinner, Matt and Linda had diligently avoided discussing anything personal. Linda had told him about a discouraging meeting she'd attended that morning, during which the health-center staff had been updated on budget cuts. "My job is more or less safe for the time being," she'd said. "We can forget about any cost-of-living raises, though. With the cost of everything from food to property taxes going up, it's like getting a pay cut."

"Why do you pay the property taxes?" Matt had asked, skirting close to a mention of Gary.

"I live here rent-free," she'd explained. "It's only fair that I pay for the taxes and utilities, since I'm the one using the house."

She'd wondered whether Matt would pursue the subject, thus inching closer and closer to the topic of her missing brother. To her relief, he had backed off. "The economy's still strong in the Northwest," he'd remarked. "Some folks think it's too strong—it's attracting too many migrants from other parts of the country."

So they'd talked about Portland, about the city's efficient light-rail transit system, the fountains in the downtown plaza, the towering skyline of mountains east of the city, and the mild, damp climate, so different from New England's extremes of sticky summer heat and dry winter iciness.

They'd avoided talking about Gary—and they'd avoided the far more hazardous subject of what was or wasn't going on between them. Over lunch a day ago, Matt had declared that he wanted her. He'd said it as if it were a dire warning, or maybe a dare. Yet the only physical contact between them all evening had been when she'd removed his splinter.

Linda didn't need to touch him to feel the pull of his charisma, the sensual undertow. Gary might have brought them together, but he wasn't what kept them together. As long as they were in the same room, under the same roof, something far more complicated than Matt's bitterness and her own anguish connected them. Feelings she was afraid to name surged and eddied between them, drawing her toward him and then dragging her back to the safety of the shore.

She shouldn't have asked him to join her for supper. Having done that, she shouldn't have asked him to stay on and have a brandy with her. But she'd been lonesome and restless ever since the night he'd held her and hugged her and then left her. Something was missing in her life, and Matt was a much too potent reminder of what that was.

She really needed to have a fling. As soon as Matt and Gary straightened out their problems, as soon as they both departed for their respective homes out west, she promised herself she would try harder to meet men and have some fun.

The fire flickered in a hypnotic pattern. Linda watched it attentively, as if it were a movie. She would rather have been looking at Matt, but she was afraid that she might see her confusion mirrored in his eyes. Or worse, she might not see any confusion at all. He might not want her as much as she wanted him—or he might want her even more. Either possibility unnerved her.

It seemed less dangerous to focus on the fire.

"This stuff is good," Matt said.

She glanced at him only long enough to understand that he was referring to the brandy. Nodding in agreement, she turned back to the fire. "Maybe it will help me fall asleep," she murmured. "I've been plagued by insomnia lately."

"Me, too."

A tiny shiver raced along her spine. Was he sleepless for the same reason she was?

Without thinking she leaned into the arm of the sofa, away from him. "I wouldn't know good brandy from bad," she admitted. "I hardly ever drink it. This bottle has been lying around for years."

"That's why it's good," he pointed out. "The more years it's been lying around, the better."

Without looking at him, she could picture his smile. She could hear it in his voice. "It seems odd to be instructed on aged brandy by a small-town farm boy from Missouri," she teased.

He gave her a sardonic look. "You're as bad as your brother," he drawled.

She decided not to let his mention of Gary rattle her. "In what way am I as bad as he is?"

"Your Boston snobbery."

Her attempt to act affronted failed as she succumbed to a laugh. "Now, wait a minute! I lived in Boston for a few years, but that doesn't mean—"

"Gary always joshed me about being a hick. I reckon he was right, too. I'm not just from Missouri, mind you . . . I'm from the Bootheel."

"The Bootheel?"

"The southernmost part of the state. There's a little wedge of Missouri there, kind of crushed between Arkansas and Tennessee."

"Of course. The brandy capital of the state, right?" She liked joking with him. And she liked the way his drawl grew heavier when he talked about his native region.

"It's the hick capital of the state," he admitted. "Your brother used to accuse me of being a hillbilly from the 'O-zahks'—I guess that's Bostonese for Ozarks. The Ozarks are way to the west, nowhere near the Bootheel. But anyone who pronounces it 'O-zahks' can't be expected to know anything about geography west of the Hudson River."

Linda chuckled. "We don't talk Bostonese here. It's a completely different accent."

"Right," he scoffed.

"I don't expect you to understand. It's so typical of hillbillies to think that if you're from Massachusetts, you must be from Boston."

He grinned. "The foursome always rode me about where I was from. Especially Gary. He used to kid me about the hay between my toes. He called me 'po' white trash.' He said I'd grown up shoveling manure."

Linda clicked her tongue. "I hope you gave as good as you got."

"Actually, shoveling manure came pretty close to reality. One of my chores as a kid was mucking the barn."

"Mucking the barn," Linda repeated, with as much Bostonian disdain as she could muster.

"That's right, Miss Hah-vahd Yahd. I mucked the barn, fed the hogs and chewed tobacco till I was sixteen and read that it caused cancer. I could take apart a tractor and put it back together again with one eye closed and one hand tied behind my back. My dad's tractor was so old, seemed like we spent more time taking it apart and putting it together than we did driving it."

Fascinated, Linda twisted to face him fully. "It sounds like a foreign culture."

His eyes vanishing into slits, he tossed back his head and laughed. "*You* sound like a provincial."

"Seriously, Matt—hogs and chewing tobacco?"

"Go ahead, hit me with quotes from the 'Beverly Hillbillies.' That's what the foursome used to do. They even nicknamed my sweetheart Ellie-Mae, like the character from the show."

"You had a sweetheart?" Linda asked. She wanted to learn everything about Matt, not just about his chores and bad habits of childhood, but about his early experiences in romance.

He grinned at her blatant curiosity, but his eyes took on a dark pensiveness as he wandered deep into his memory. He took a quaff of brandy, then balanced his glass on his knee. "I had a sweetheart," he said. "Her name was Ellie, not Ellie-Mae."

Linda felt like a moony teenager once more, aching over the loneliness of a young soldier torn from the woman he loved and shipped so far away. "What happened to her?"

Matt took another drink of brandy. Then he turned to the fire, evading her probing gaze.

Suddenly she regretted having asked. "You don't have to answer," she said. "It's none of my business."

"No, that's all right." He cast her a fleeting smile. "What happened to Ellie was, I married her."

Linda frowned. The first night he'd spent in Braxton, when he'd stayed at the house, he had told her he wasn't married. And since then, he'd told her things a married man shouldn't tell a single woman.

"We're divorced now," he clarified. "Going on ten years."

"Oh." Her hands relaxed around the bowl of her snifter. "I'm sorry."

He shrugged off her sympathy and sighed. "Ellie was a good woman. In her own way, she saved my life in Vietnam as much as the fearless foursome did."

"How?"

"Letters from home were essential to staying alive. Particularly letters from a girl. Ellie wrote me every week, just like you wrote your brother. Those letters from home were something a soldier lived for."

"I'm sure my silly letters weren't anything to live for," Linda argued.

Matt shook his head. "We all lived for letters from home. Letters from women. Even our mothers and sisters. There was something about all the dirt and slaughter and horror we were surrounded with over there.... You'd get a letter from a woman, and it would cleanse you. It would make you think of people with soft voices and soft hands and soft hearts. It would remind you of all the good, wholesome things you'd be going back to once you'd done your time."

His words moved her. So did the dark emotion in his eyes, and the gravelly roughness in his voice. Without thinking, she shifted onto the center cushion and reached for his hand. He gave her a cautious look, then rotated his wrist and wove his fingers through hers. The leathery surface of his palm felt strong and hard against hers, his fingers thick in contrast to hers. She had never thought of her hands—or herself—as soft. But compared to Matt, to the nightmare he'd lived through in Vietnam ...

"You know how it is," he went on. "War is all about being macho. Testosterone runs the show. You take a bunch of guys out into the field, not a lady in sight, and they get so wired, so overloaded with hormones, they want to go and kill somebody. It's the oldest military tactic in the world."

Linda laughed. "And your Ellie kept you wired?"

"Just the opposite. She defused me," he explained. "I'd get her letters and read all about the mundane goings-on at home, who'd gotten hitched to who, who'd gotten knocked up, whose livestock won a ribbon at the county fair, whose pie won a prize. It didn't matter what she wrote. What mattered was that I was holding this sheet of paper that she'd once held, and reading the writing she'd written. She was so far away from the hell of it, so untouched by it. Hearing from her helped me keep track of my soul."

"So ... you came home and married her?"

"Yes." He sighed again, his fingers flexing gently between hers, his thumb stroking along hers. "I was grateful to her for helping me get through it. So I married her. Don't ever marry anyone out of gratitude, Linda. It's the worst reason in the world."

Linda studied his profile in the golden light of the fire. His nose was straight, prominent, as strong as his chin. His brow was high. He glanced away from the fireplace in time to catch her staring at him. His eyes appeared depthless, dark and turbulent with memories.

With a self-effacing smile, he said, "Cripes, who am I to give anyone advice about marriage? Mine was an abysmal failure."

"You must have tried hard to make it work," she observed. "If you got married right out of the army and didn't get a divorce until ten years ago—"

"I stuck it out a long time. I wanted it to work. But...I came back to America a different person. I'd seen too much and done too much. I had changed." He exhaled and turned his gaze back to the fire, studying it absently as he organized his thoughts.

Gary had changed, too. Linda remembered it well. Before he'd left for basic training, he'd considered her just a pip-squeak pest, but when he'd returned he'd seen her as his ally, his friend. His high school girlfriend had gone off to the University of Massachusetts and was involved with another guy, and his parents had aged so much during his time away, that he'd come to rely on Linda for love and support.

"It's a tough adjustment, coming back," she observed.

Matt nodded, his gaze growing even more distant. He leaned forward and rested his arms on his knees

again, and she slid closer to him on the couch so she
wouldn't have to let go of his hand. He let go of hers,
instead, and arched his arm around her shoulders.

There was nothing seductive in the gesture. It was
simply a physical reflection of the intimacy in his
words, his confessions. He was sharing something
astonishingly personal about himself, revealing that
the man she'd always thought of as a rock was in fact
a human being, someone who had survived first a war
and then a failed marriage. She felt honored that he
trusted her enough to tell her these things.

She let her head rest against his shoulder. "It must
have been hard on Ellie, too," she remarked. "She
probably expected you to come home and be the same
man she'd sent off."

"It was very hard on her," he confirmed, toying
with the ends of her hair. "Right from the start, we
were flying in different orbits. I wanted to get out of
Missouri and use my GI benefits for college. Ellie
wanted to be a farmer's wife and have lots of babies,
just like her mother and my mother and every other
woman in town. We went back and forth, her way and
mine. We moved to Michigan because I got into the
university there, and then she became homesick, so we
moved back to Missouri for a while, and then back up
to Michigan because I got a job in construction up
there and I couldn't find work at home. And I continued going to school, night classes, and Ellie continued shuttling back and forth to Missouri on her
own. We were drifting apart in so many ways.

"She kept coming back, though, and saying she
knew I'd get better, like I had some sort of disease. My
idea of getting better was to dream big and work hard
and move up in the world. Her idea was to go back to

what we'd been before the war. That was all she ever
wanted."

"Did you have any children?" Linda asked.

"No. I couldn't bring children into something that
was falling apart." He meditated for a minute. "I
wanted her to be happy. I wanted to give her what she
wanted. But I couldn't do it."

Linda nestled closer to Matt. For some reason, he
seemed to accept the full blame for his marriage's
collapse. It sounded to Linda as if no one deserved any
blame at all.

"Fate plays tricks on everyone," she noted gently.
"Your divorce is no more your fault than Andrew's
illness was his. People love each other and they hope
for things to work out. But sometimes luck isn't with
them. It's nobody's fault, Matt."

He craned his neck to peer down at her. A faint
smile teased his mouth. "Is that what social workers
tell their clients?"

"No," she said. "That's what I'm telling you."

His smile grew wistful. Settling back into the cushions, he drew her closer and observed the flames in the
fireplace. "I hardly ever talk about the divorce," he
confessed. "It's just not something I like to discuss. I
don't know why I'm talking about it now."

Because you trust me, she wanted to say. *Because
we're friends. Because luck handed us both a rotten
deal, and we fought back. Because there's a whole lot
more going on between us than Gary and some stolen
money.*

Because you're going to kiss me, she thought with
amazing clarity as he twisted to view her face. As well
as she knew anything, she knew that Matt was going
to kiss her.

And she knew she wanted him to.

HE ABSORBED EVERYTHING about her. The natural fit
of her body within the curve of his arm. Her fingers
alternating with his, slender and pale compared to his
blunt, callused ones, his short, square nails and thick
knuckles. Her smooth, creamy skin, sprinkled with
just enough freckles across the bridge of her nose to
remind him that she was imperfect—human and real.
Her bright eyes, flawless emeralds ringed in silver and
gold.

He thought of all the differences between them. She
had lost most of her family yet clung fiercely to what
little was left. All of Matt's family were alive but totally alien to him, strangers who understood him as
little as he understood them. She had given and given
and given of herself in a doomed love affair, while he
had walked away from his own disastrous marriage,
first spiritually, then emotionally and finally physically.

So many differences between them, yet she clasped
his hand as tightly as he clasped hers. Matt might be
large and ruggedly built while she was slim and delicate, but he couldn't overpower her. Her fingers might
be as dainty in appearance as fine china, but they were
strong. They held fast.

For a brief moment, he saw her not as she looked
now, in pale blue denim jeans and a loose-fitting
sweater, but rather as she'd looked one night after her
bath, an instant before she'd closed the thick white
towel around herself, a halo-less, wingless angel dis-
appearing inside a puffy cloud.

She looked more irresistible now than she had then. She might be fully clothed, but the longing in her eyes was naked. She wanted him the way he wanted her.

If he had any shred of decency in him, he would behave as he had that night when he'd accidentally glimpsed her beautiful body through the open bedroom door. He would back off, retreat, and pretend he'd seen nothing.

Instead, he lowered his mouth to hers.

He tried to hold back, but it was difficult. She was so soft, so pliant, moving with him, whispering against him, turning his blood thick and hot. He closed his eyes to savor the sensation. As kisses went, this was actually pretty chaste. But the promise he tasted on her lips was carnal, wanton, intoxicatingly erotic.

He dared to trace her lower lip with his tongue. She sighed and opened her mouth to him. Like a fool—like a man—he took what she offered, pressing, sliding deep. He pulled her onto his lap and cupped her chin in his hand, angling her head back as he swirled his tongue in her sweet, brandied mouth. He was going too fast, pushing too hard, wanting too much. But he couldn't stop.

She lifted her hands to the sides of his head, threading her fingers through the hair at his temples. His thigh muscles tensed underneath her; his arms cramped with the restraint he was exercising when all he wanted was to tear off her clothing and bury himself inside her.

And then abandon her. Then march out of her house, resume his hunt for her good-for-nothing brother, collect his money and go home to Oregon.

He couldn't do this to Linda. He had already hurt her too much by involving her in his battle with Gary.

To take what he wanted and then walk away without a backward glance would be a betrayal even worse than what Gary had done to him.

Reluctantly he withdrew from her and leaned back. "I'd better go," he mumbled.

"Go where?"

"The motel."

"I trust you, Matt."

Don't, he almost protested. *Don't trust me.* "I can't stay here."

She gazed at him, her eyes brighter than before, shimmering, beckoning. Her lips were moist, rosy from his kiss. She slid her hands from his hair to his shoulders and traced tiny circles against his shirt with her fingertips. She said nothing.

"I can't stay," he repeated, sounding desperate to himself. "You know what will happen if I do."

"Yes."

Her eyes were too beautiful. Too ingenuous. Too goddamn trusting. "It's all wrong, Linda. You know the reality here."

"Yes," she said. "I know the reality."

He felt the womanly roundness of her bottom against his legs. He saw the rise and fall of her breasts beneath her loose-fitting sweater. "If I stay tonight, I'll be gone tomorrow. Or the next day."

"I know." She glanced away at last, releasing him from the spell of her gaze. "I haven't asked you to stay," she reminded him, her voice low but even.

Not in words, she hadn't. But her hands had asked. Her lips. Her tongue, responding with shy honesty to his aggression.

She let her eyes meet his once more, an instant of tacit communication, of desire and remorse. Then she

turned and slid off his lap. Her departure left him cold
all over. Not as cold as he would feel when he walked
out of her house, though. This was just a preview.

She stood and studied the dying fire. Dinah lay
slumbering on the hearth, snoring. Linda stepped over
her to shut the fireplace doors, cutting off the air supply.

Matt watched her, praying that she would throw
common sense to the wind, that she would tumble
back into his arms and open herself to him. She simply directed her stare from the hearth to the crystal
brandy glasses, her lips pressed together and her eyes
avoiding his.

With a sigh, he pushed himself to his feet. He
started toward the entry and she fell into step beside
him. They didn't speak, didn't touch. At the front
door he paused. "I need my jacket."

She lifted her gaze to him. Her eyes glistened with
hope—or maybe it was tears. "I'm asking you now,"
she whispered. "If you say no, I won't ask again."

He knew the right thing to do. The decent thing.
The sane thing.

Instead, he gathered her into his arms and covered
her lips with his.

MATT'S KISS swamped her, inundated her, carried her
deep into an ocean of sensation. She lost her footing;
she couldn't breathe. She was drowning in his kiss,
and she didn't mind.

Once upon a time she could depend on Gary to keep
her afloat. She couldn't depend on him now, not anymore. Not ever again. Her parents were dead, her
lover dead, her brother crooked. She had no one.

But she didn't feel alone, not with Matt holding her, protecting her as she submerged herself in the splendor of his kiss. She didn't *have* him; he had come to Braxton for only one reason and he would be gone once he'd achieved his ends. But she had him for tonight, for this one precious moment in time. She had someone she could trust.

She felt him lifting her, cradling her in his arms and carrying her up the stairs. He didn't stop until he reached the open door to her bedroom. There he set her down carefully, as if she were breakable.

He gazed down at her with dark, unyielding eyes. His hand curled around the door frame, as if he were trying to prevent himself from entering the room. His other arm hung at his side, his fingers furling and straightening, searching restlessly for something to hold on to. She extended her own hand.

"Linda." It was a question, a lament, half groaned, half sighed.

"Please, Matt."

He didn't move. He was going to leave now, she knew. He'd gotten temporarily caught up in passion, but now he was going to be mature and sensible and gentlemanly. She had asked him to stay, and as she'd warned, she wouldn't ask him again. She knew as well as he did that they'd be wise to stop right now.

Still, asking had cost her a great deal. She'd done it only because she'd had to, because her soul had cried out for him. She'd spent the past few nights restless not because she was worried about her brother or angry with Matt, but because he was the rock, the idol of her girlhood dreams, the soldier with the virile chest and the seductive eyes who had starred in her very first romantic fantasies, and he was all alone at the Braxton Motor Inn and she was all alone here. She'd been restless because, right or wrong, they belonged together.

Matt belatedly had decided to care about right and wrong, and he was obviously going to do the right thing. She could accept that, but she couldn't bear to watch him reject what she had offered. Gritting her teeth to keep from imploring him to stay, she shut her eyes and waited for him to walk away.

The heat of his hand closing around hers shocked her eyes open. He crossed the threshold, enveloped her in his strong, strong arms and crushed his mouth to hers. There was nothing subtle in his kiss, nothing friendly or reassuring. His lips forced hers apart and his tongue lunged, filling her, taking, conquering her with ruthless surges and strokes.

She couldn't breathe, couldn't move. She could only yield to the brutal power of his mouth, the smothering possessiveness of his embrace. He splayed one of his hands at the back of her head, holding her steady. His other hand glided along the sleeve of her sweater to her shoulder and down her back, tracing the bones of her spine to her waist before he reached her hips and pressed her to himself, forcing her to acknowledge his hardness.

She reeled beneath the onslaught of sensations, emotions, a hunger she could scarcely identify. She felt too much. Matt was asking too much of her.

And she wanted to give it all and feel it all.

As abruptly as he'd kissed her he pulled away, sucking in a ragged breath. "Linda, I shouldn't . . ."

"I want you," she said, at last giving voice to the raging need inside her. She had made her decision, accepted it. There was a blessed inevitability to it.

"I'll go to the motel." His chest pumped against her as he struggled to control his breathing. "Right now."

"Don't run away."

A low, helpless groan coiled up from his throat. He steered his gaze back to her. His eyes were dancing with fire, only this time they reflected not a blaze in the fireplace, but the sensual heat burning inside him. "If I stay, Linda... It's just tonight. I can't promise you—"

"I don't want promises," she swore. If Matt made a promise he would only break it, and she wouldn't be able to bear that. "All I want is tonight."

He closed his arms around her again, now gentle and protective. His lips brushed hers, nipping, playing over hers with provocative tenderness. His last kiss had overwhelmed her, but this one lured, arousing her with merciful thoroughness, sending waves of melting warmth into her throat and down her back until her legs quivered and her hips swayed.

It had been so long, so very long since a man had loved her. So many years since she'd been kissed like this, since she'd wanted such kisses, since she'd dreamed of feeling such desire. Her lips mirrored his, moving with quiet resolution, skimming and slanting and parting enough for her tongue to slip out and touch his teeth.

He groaned again, lifting his hands back to her head and tilting it, pressing his mouth more firmly to hers, curling his tongue around hers. He twined his fingers into her hair, ran his thumbs over her cheekbones and temples, pulled back to kiss her brow, the bridge of her nose, her chin, her throat. He moved his hands to the decorative buttons below the neckline of her sweater and popped them open, one and then another and then the last. Spreading the fabric, he bowed to kiss her exposed collarbone.

Her legs continued to weaken as every drop of energy inside her flowed upward, inward, forming a nucleus of heat below her belly. It had been so long, she thought, too long. She might not remember what to do, how to please Matt. It had been too long since this core of heat had burned inside her, since her hips and breasts had ached with such excruciating pleasure, too long since she'd felt herself liquefying in the heat, growing damp and pliant and ripe for a man.

She ought to warn him about her lack of experience. "Matt—"

Taking her hand, he led her across to the bed. He nudged her to sit, then went to work on the buttons of his shirt, nearly tearing them in his eagerness. Linda reached out to undo the last one, and he caught his breath as her fingers grazed the warm skin of his abdomen.

He tossed the shirt onto the floor. In the dim moonlight that spilled through the window she saw his streamlined muscles, his sun-soaked skin and the mat of black curls that spanned his dark, flat nipples and wedged down to his abdomen. She saw his arms, moving sculptures of muscle and tendon, and the hand she'd mended, the bandage a pale stripe across his skin.

He lowered himself to sit next to her, and she ran her hands over the intriguing rises and hollows of his shoulders. A ragged sigh escaped him before he drew back and eased her sweater up over her head, snagging her arms in the sleeves, gently freeing them and then reaching for the clasp of her bra.

He gazed at her breasts for a moment, and she was certain he would touch them. Her nipples swelled and burned in anticipation. He thwarted her expectations, however, pushing her back against the pillows and stripping off her jeans, her socks, her panties.

His intense perusal of her body made her bashful. To keep him from staring at her she drew him down alongside her, then skimmed her hands over his firm shoulders, over the smooth contours of his back, the broad frame of his ribs. She felt the flexing and clenching of his muscles beneath his skin; she heard the unevenness of his breath as her hands roamed forward. Combing her fingernails through the dark swirls of his chest hair prompted yet another guttural groan from him, and when she scraped his nipples they tightened into points.

He pulled her hands away, easily circling both her wrists with one hand. ''Don't,'' he whispered.

A flush of embarrassment rippled through her. She was dreadfully out of practice, doing everything so ineptly Matt felt it necessary to stop her.

''I'm not very good at this,'' she confessed.

His smile seemed to outshine the moonlight. ''You're *too* good,'' he argued. ''Touch me like that again and I'll lose what little control I have.'' He kissed her lightly on the tip of her nose, then pulled back, his smile fading as he read anxiety in her expression. ''Second thoughts?''

''No,'' she swore, then bit her lip. She had to be honest with him. ''It's just that I haven't been with a man in...a long time.'' She wasn't about to admit how long.

He continued to peer down at her, his eyes so mysteriously, beautifully dark, his smile so poignant she wanted only to kiss it again and again until they both forgot she'd mentioned any of this. "Are you sure you don't want me to leave?"

"Yes."

He lifted her hand and pressed his lips to her palm. "Then don't worry. I'll go slow."

The husky affection in his voice rasped along her nerve endings, making her abdomen tighten and her mind cry out that she didn't want him to go slow at all. She didn't want him to stop her for being too good or too bad or anything else. She wanted him now, this instant.

Releasing her wrists, he shifted downward and cupped his palms around her breasts. His languorous massage caused her to rein herself in. She didn't want everything at once, after all. First she wanted this, she decided, and *then* she wanted everything.

Her back arched, pressing her breasts into his hands. Heat spread from his fingertips down to her womb as he caressed, kneaded, chafed his work-hardened fingers over her swollen nipples. Without thinking, she molded her hands to his head and drew him down. He rubbed his teeth over the inflamed red tip of one breast, then cooled it with his tongue, then sucked it into his mouth.

Her hips twisted, writhed, ached unbearably. His leisurely pace infuriated her—and aroused her in an incomprehensible way. She could beg him to go faster, but then . . . then she would miss this, the thrilling tension in her breasts and hips, the feverish pulse in her throat, the maddening longing that infiltrated every cell in her body.

She reached for him again, and this time he didn't stop her. Her hands roamed over his back, came to the edge of his jeans and snuck forward in search of the snap. He sucked in his stomach and sighed against her skin as she undid the fly.

Once he'd shucked his jeans, she took him in her hands. His hardness filled the hollow of her palm, and she closed her fingers around him.

A breathless laugh escaped him. "Linda, Linda..." He reluctantly peeled her hands from him. "You're impossible."

"I want you."

He groaned in assent. "I'm right here." He let his hand drift down her leg to her knee, to her shin, all the way to her ankle before he reversed direction. Taunting her, he traced the contours of her kneecap, the sensitive crease behind her knee, the satin skin of her inner thigh. His deliberate pace made her moan in frustration. By the time he reached the downy curls at the apex of her thighs she was writhing again, desperate.

Slowly, exasperatingly slowly, his fingers parted the damp folds, glided over her, dipped and glided again. Her body shook from the pressure inside her; her eyes squeezed shut. He slid deeper and her heart stopped.

"No," she gasped, too far gone. "No..."

A hot spasm seized her, undulating deep into her and igniting more spasms, an endless chain of them. It felt so good, indescribably good...but when her body finally grew quiescent, she was all alone.

She sank down into the quilt and opened her eyes. Matt's fingers continued to move against her, as light as air. He watched her face.

"I wanted *you*."

"You've got me." He glanced toward her night table, then back down at her. "Do you have protection?"

"Oh." The sensuous haze in her brain began to dissipate. Sitting up required some effort, but she managed to pull from her drawer the box of contraceptives Gary had given her. She fumbled with the plastic wrapping.

Matt eased the box out of her trembling hands and leaned down to kiss her. "I'll do it," he murmured.

While he opened the box she scrutinized his long, athletic body stretched out beside her on the bed, his hard chest, his taut stomach, his trim, muscular thighs with their manly dusting of hair. She gazed unashamedly at his arousal, then reached out and ran her fingers over the stiff, pulsing flesh. He flinched, dropped the box and caught his breath.

"Don't stop me this time," she said.

"I won't."

She curled her fingers around him, remembering, remembering how to please a man, how to make him wild with yearning. She tightened her grip and he responded with a low growl, moving with her, rising above her, settling between her legs and pulling her hand away. Lifting her legs higher, he braced himself and moved forward, easing into the tightness of her.

"Are you okay?" he asked. His hoarse voice betrayed the agony of his restraint, as did his eyes, half-closed and glazed with hunger, and the taut tendons in his neck, and the fisting of his hands in her hair.

The discomfort of his penetration was almost painful, but she would never tell him that. And then, gradually, the pain faded. Her body relaxed, relented, fluxed around him. She raised her hips, taking him deeper.

His control frayed, then snapped. He thrust again and again, in a hot, savage tempo, pressing, driving, forcing her to the edge of oblivion. She clutched his shoulders, hanging on, trusting him, trusting.

The spasms overtook her once more, consuming her, ravishing her soul. She heard herself cry out, and then heard Matt's deep groan as he erupted inside her. He sank down, clinging to her as she throbbed around him, sharing the final tremors of her pleasure long after his own body had become still.

She relished the weight of him, his breath harsh and erratic, his skin damp with perspiration and his lips weary as they browsed along the hinge of her jaw. She wanted him with her as they drifted through the sweet aftermath. She didn't want to let go of him, ever.

But eventually he propped himself up with his arms, and she loosened her hold on him. He peered down at her, examining her face as if committing every inch of it to memory. "Are you okay?" he asked again.

She smiled. "Yes."

"I was a little rough, I—"

"I'm fine," she murmured. "Better than fine."

A hesitant smile tugged at the corners of his mouth. He dropped a light kiss on her lips, then rolled away from her and groped for a pillow. Arranging the pillow against the brass headboard, he reclined against it and drew Linda into his arms. He kissed the top of her head.

She felt immeasurably peaceful. The turmoil of the past few days receded into the past; the travails that would confront her tomorrow had been fended off for the time being. She existed only in the present, in the shelter of Matt's arms.

Extending his legs next to hers, he encountered the package of condoms, which was half hidden by the rumpled quilt. Without jostling her, he reached down and scooped up the box. He studied it for a moment, then tossed it onto the night table. "For a woman who hasn't done this in a long time, you're well prepared."

"Are you complaining?"

"God, no," he drawled, smoothing her hair back from her face and planting a kiss on her temple. "I'm as thankful as can be."

She nestled closer, draping her arm across his chest and slinging one of her legs over his. "Save your thanks for Gary. He gave me those."

She felt Matt start. "Your brother?"

"It was a gag birthday present. He said I'd spent a long enough time in mourning. Even if I wasn't ready to fall in love again, he thought I needed some fun in my life."

Matt ran his fingers through her hair, stroking, soothing. "What do you think?"

When Gary had given her the contraceptives, he'd had in mind that she should fool around, party hearty, have a good time after her lengthy period of grief. What she and Matt had just shared was entirely different. It was too intimate, too intense, too emotional. "This wasn't fun, Matt," she said, then realized he might take her comment as an insult. "I mean—"

"I know what you mean," he assured her.

She nestled closer yet. He wedged his leg between her thighs and bent his knee, urging her hips against his.

She was sorry she couldn't see his expression—but maybe it was better that she couldn't. She understood a great deal merely from the feel of him, from the tensing and relaxing of his muscles, the steady rhythm of his breath as his chest rose and fell beneath her, the constant movement of his fingers through the hair behind her ear.

He could make her no promises, and she accepted that. But as her eyes slid shut, as her body molded to his and a shimmering wave of sleep washed over her, she found herself wishing things could have been different.

Letting go of Matt was going to break her heart. And sooner or later—sooner than she would like—she was going to have to let go.

CALL IT FOOLISH, he chastised himself. Call it irresponsible. Call it brainless. Call it whatever the hell he wanted—he shouldn't have done this.

He'd come to Braxton for revenge, not for sex.

What had happened between him and Linda Villard wasn't just sex, though. And he knew it. How had she put it? "This wasn't fun."

Indeed it wasn't.

Well, it *was,* he admitted with a roguish smile, gazing down at the woman dozing in his arms. The tranquillity of her deep, slumbrous breathing reminded him of a cat's contented purring.

Of course, cats didn't turn him on. Nothing turned him on the way Linda did.

But this wasn't about fun. Making love with Linda hadn't been the natural outcome of a long, evolving relationship, nor was it going to lead to anything real. It was just now, this one fleeting moment, and the transience of it saddened him in a deep, inexplicable way.

He could give her nothing more than what she'd asked for—nothing more than tonight. If only she'd demanded more of him, if only she'd trusted him less, if only she didn't harbor such profound faith in him and the magic of this night...

He wanted to give her everything. The moon, the stars, his soul.

But tomorrow his passion would redirect itself, transform back into rage and focus on Gary. Tomorrow the moon and the stars would be gone, and in the clear light of day he would remember why he'd come to Braxton.

Linda murmured something unintelligible, and her hand meandered over his ribs. Her touch was like a spark on dry tinder; he felt his body catch fire again.

She wasn't quite awake, but that didn't stop him. Encircling her tiny waist with his hands, he lifted her until her face was aligned with his, then guided her mouth down to his.

Her eyelids fluttered open, then shut again. A faint sigh escaped her as her breasts brushed his chest and her hair spilled down around them. She moved slowly, still more asleep than awake, but her lips parted in welcome and her tongue parried his. Her teeth closed around his lower lip in a playful challenge.

He moaned.

He couldn't get enough of her. She was too agile, too lovely, her skin too smooth, her hair too fragrant.

Her lips, her breasts, the roundness of her derriere...
He circled her bottom with his hands, squeezed and
caressed, stroked her thighs, and then took her again
by the waist and lifted her higher, until he could kiss
her breasts. He nuzzled them, nibbled, smiled at her
hushed whimpers of pleasure as his tongue moved over
her nipples, causing them to flush and swell, causing
her hips to twitch.

Wanting more of her, he lifted her higher. She
seemed confused at first, unsure, her fingers curling
around the brass bars of her headboard as he kissed
her belly and then lower, as he sipped the sweet honey
of her arousal, as he devoured her. She went rigid
above him, her cries now breathless in shock and
delight.

He wanted to please her this way, every way. He had
to give her everything tonight, before it was too late.

''Matt...oh, Matt.'' His name fell from her lips in
a sigh of exultation and despair. Trembling, she lowered her head to his shoulder and her body to his, her
eyes shiny with tears.

He would have been satisfied just to hold her, but
she had other ideas. One moment she seemed too exhausted to move, and the next she was snaking down
his body, touching the tip of her tongue to his nipples
with endearing awkwardness, tracing feathery lines
across his abdomen with her fingernails. She slid farther down, showering kisses across his stomach and
skimming her fingers lower, until the blaze she'd ignited threatened to incinerate him. Her lips followed
in the wake of her hands, exploring him shyly, ten-
derly. When she touched her tongue to the most sensitive spot on his body he had to gnash his teeth to
keep from crying out.

"Come here," he groaned, grabbing her arms and hauling her back up. He kissed her wildly, voraciously, forgetting her relative inexperience, forgetting to be gentle and go slow. He was in flames, out of control; he couldn't think.

She was the one who stopped him, who reached for the box.

For an insane instant he wished she hadn't. A fantasy flared inside his brain, an echo of something Linda had said earlier ... her guileless question about whether he'd had children.

He hadn't wanted children with Ellie. But with Linda, with this red-haired, jewel-eyed woman, all trust and goodness and love and kindness ...

God help him, if his life were everything it wasn't, if he were someone else, living another existence, he would plant his seed inside her. He would have his child with her. Right now. Tonight.

But she'd stopped him in time, and he tried to convince himself he was glad. When he pulled her down around him, his hands clamped tight on her hips as he arched up into her, he acknowledged that this was still much more than he had a right to hope for.

And when it was over, when his body had burned straight through to her soul, so deeply and powerfully that he'd needed to hear Linda's muffled sob of relief against his neck to know she had peaked, he told himself he was lucky to have as much as she'd given him.

He was lucky to have anything at all.

CHAPTER TEN

THE HOUSE ITSELF wasn't the problem. It was just a building on three acres of land, too far from town to be convenient to anything, but not far enough to be truly rural. Eighty years old, it had undoubtedly been built by someone looking to construct a practical dwelling for a minimum amount of money.

The sorry truth was, if Gary sold it, a minimum amount of money was all he was likely to get. The economy was not exactly booming in Braxton, Massachusetts.

He would get at least twenty thousand dollars for the place, of course. He might get three or four times that much. Even after paying brokerage fees and all the rest, he would wind up with enough money to cover his debt to Matt Calloway, pay off his credit cards and buy a more modest diamond ring for Debbie—one of those teeny tiny fifth-of-a-carat rings—if she still loved him.

Sure, he could sell the house. But what about Linda?

Between the taxes and utilities, she was paying somewhere around three or four hundred dollars a month in living expenses. There had to be someplace in town she could rent for that much money.

Yeah. A three-room flat above the liquor store, maybe.

How could Gary evict her? To him it was just a house, a chunk of property he could sell for desperately needed cash. But to her it was a home, *her* home. She had retreated to Braxton in a million pieces and put herself back together there. She had found a job there, serving the town's citizens for a pitifully low wage because she believed in what she was doing. She had created a quiet, tranquil, apparently fulfilling life for herself, and Gary couldn't bear the thought of taking it all away from her.

He was running out of options, though. If she couldn't lend him the money he needed, he would either have to sell the house or spend the rest of his life trying to elude Matt Calloway.

He was tired of hiding. He wanted to get things settled and go back to Debbie before he lost her for good. He kept thinking of her with another man. He couldn't stand to fill in the details; the general picture was awful enough. He had to get back to her.

He had to see Linda first.

The sun had just finished rising as he reached the entrance onto Route 2, heading west. He would have to go with whatever courage he had and whatever he could muster in the hour and a half it would take him to reach Braxton. He couldn't stall any longer. The time had come to straighten out his life.

He only hoped Linda wouldn't hate him for it.

FAR IN THE DISTANCE, she heard the click of a car door latching shut.

She opened her eyes. Sunlight spilled through the unshaded window above the front porch. She wanted to check the alarm clock on her nightstand, but to do so would mean extricating herself from Matt's snug embrace, and she was in no hurry to leave his arms. Instead, she used the sun's high angle to estimate that it was mid-morning. Given how little rest she and Matt had gotten last night, they deserved to sleep late.

His shoulder was firm beneath her head, his chest warm. She traced her fingers aimlessly across its surface, twirling through the wiry hair, admiring the lean layer of muscle that gave definition to his torso. He wasn't husky or brawny; he wasn't excessively hairy.

He was perfect. His body had done things to her that she could scarcely comprehend. His body, his hands, his mischievous tongue... His eyes. His heat and passion and soul.

And now—within hours or days—he was going to walk out of her life forever.

Closing her eyes, she snuggled closer to him and vowed to herself that she would never regret having spent a night with him. No matter if she never saw him again after today, if she never experienced anything this magnificent again, she vowed that she would always be grateful for having experienced it once, one sublime, miraculous night.

Her hand drifted lower and he stirred, clamping his larger hand over hers before she could reach her goal. He blinked his eyes open and gazed at her. "Don't tempt me," he murmured with a sleepy smile.

She mirrored his smile. "Why not?"

He conceded the point with a sigh, tilting her head to his, opening his mouth beneath hers. Before she lost herself fully in his kiss, she heard a deeper thump in the distance—not a car door this time, but a car's trunk.

She pulled back, struggling to clear her head. Her nearest neighbors lived far enough away that she wouldn't hear them opening and closing their car doors. The noises she heard, though muffled, were coming from nearby.

Someone was at her house.

Evidently Matt reached the same conclusion within seconds. Suddenly alert, his vision clear and sharp, he touched his fingers lightly to her lips to prevent her from speaking. Together they listened to the crunch of footsteps on her unpaved driveway, then silence as the visitor traipsed across the muddy grass to the porch, and then the hollow thuds of footfalls on the wooden porch steps.

"It's Gary," she whispered, her heartbeat accelerating and her skin prickling with apprehension.

While following the sounds Linda's visitor made on the porch below her window, Matt kept his gaze riveted to Linda. Sure enough, they soon heard the metallic rattle of a key sliding into the keyhole.

"Listen to me," Matt said in a low, intense voice. His fingers brushed her lips again, warning her not to interrupt.

She nodded.

"Get him inside and keep him with you. Take him into the kitchen, take his jacket, make him coffee, whatever you have to do. Just make sure he doesn't have a chance to get away."

She nodded again. From the entry, the familiar voice of her brother floated in stereo through the floor and up the stairs: "Linda? Rise and shine, lazybones! I'm here!"

"Whatever you do," Matt continued, his voice still low and even more intense, "don't let on that I'm here. Okay?"

Once more she nodded.

"If he finds out I'm here—"

"Hey, Linda?" Gary's voice soared upward to them. "Up and at 'em, kiddo! Come on down and give your loving brother a proper welcome!"

"I don't want him to get away from me," Matt continued. "Promise me you won't give him a chance to escape."

She nodded one final time, then sat up and swung her legs over the side of the bed.

Matt grabbed her shoulder and turned her toward him once more. "Can I count on you?" he whispered fiercely.

"Yes. I promise."

Satisfied, he released her with a slight nudge, as if sending her off on a mission.

Linda sensed that Matt's relationship to her had altered. She was no longer his lover, the woman who had shared her bed and her love with him throughout the night. She had reverted to being Gary Villard's sister, and Matt had reverted to being Gary Villard's foe.

A pang of sorrow seized her as she crossed to the closet for her bathrobe and pulled it on. It would have been so much nicer if she and Matt could have drifted back to reality gradually, lying together in the rectangle of morning sunlight and trading intimacies, affection, a few lingering touches. It would have been nice to pretend, at least for a few more minutes, that last night hadn't been an isolated moment, a flash of joyful madness bestowed upon them and then snatched away.

But even if she had wanted to savor the magic for a minute longer, Matt had obviously shaken it off with little effort, reverting to his role of wronged man in search of retribution. What had flared to beautiful life between them last night clearly hadn't left much of an impression on him. Austere and unbending, he exuded stone-cold resolution.

She shouldn't have wanted more. He had never promised more.

But couldn't he at least have given her a farewell kiss? A tender caress? A murmured assurance that no matter what happened next, he would always remember with affection the night he'd spent in her bed?

Evidently, his abandonment of her had begun the instant Gary opened the door.

"Linda!" Gary bellowed from the first floor. "If you don't come down, I'll come up!"

Matt sat up and waved her toward the door. She stepped into her slippers and tied the sash of her bathrobe around her waist. Opening the door, she cast a backward look at her rumpled bed, her misshapen pillows, the bars of her brass headboard, bars she'd clung to in her delirium last night, as if hanging on to them had been the only way she could remain earthbound instead of soaring straight into heaven.

Her memory of Matt's astonishing sensuality caused a wave of heat to rise from her hips to her heart. But glimpsing him as he chased her out of the room with a wave, his gaze implacable and his mouth set in a harsh, determined line, drained all the warmth out of her.

She mustn't hate him. She mustn't blame him. If anything, she ought to envy his ability to put last night out of his mind with so little effort.

With a sigh, she stalked down the hall to the stairs.

"Linda! There's my girl!" Gary stood at the foot of the stairway, grinning up at her, his face bright with morning cheer. Even after several years, Linda hadn't

grown used to his southern California coloring—his
golden skin, his dark freckles and his sun-bleached,
almost blond, hair. He wore a wool-lined denim
jacket, stone-washed jeans, leather sneakers and his
gold *D* earring. Linda hadn't got used to that yet, either.

"Come on, kiddo, wake up and smell the coffee.
Or, should I say, *make* the coffee. It's after nine, toots.
I've been up since six-thirty. What's with the car in the
driveway? You've got company?"

He was bursting with energy, overwhelming her with
his cheer. His barrage of questions made her head
ache. Only his smothering hug, as she reached the
bottom step, kept her from collapsing in a heap.

"The car has Connecticut plates on it. Who's
here?" he asked. "Anyone I know?"

Promise me you won't tell him I'm here, Matt's
voice resounded inside her throbbing skull. "It's . . . a
friend of mine from college," she lied, feeling sick
about it. Dishonesty didn't sit well with her. "She—
she's still resting, so . . ." *Get him into the kitchen.
Make sure he doesn't have a chance to leave.* "Why
don't we go into the kitchen and I'll make a pot of
coffee? And you can tell me all about Somerville."

"Somerville was good," Gary said, following her
into the kitchen, carrying a small duffel bag. "Steve's
still out of work. Any openings around here?"

"You know there aren't," she grumbled.

"Hey." Detecting her tension, Gary stepped back to
appraise her. "What's wrong?"

"Nothing." She'd already lied once; why not lie
twice? Fumbling with the coffee filters, she cursed
when she couldn't immediately separate a single filter
from the stack.

Gary scowled. "Don't tell me nothing, Linda. Language like that isn't your style. What's wrong?"

"Nothing's wrong. I'm half-asleep," she said petulantly. "You woke me up."

"About time, too. Well, hello there, Dinah." Gary bent down to greet the cat, who had wandered into the kitchen to investigate Linda's guest. Cupping his hand around her belly, he lifted Dinah to his eye level. "Dinah, what's wrong with my sister? She's swearing a blue streak."

One single oath, and he was calling it a blue streak. She fought off the urge to quibble with him, and the even greater urge to collapse under the weight of her raging emotions. How long was Matt planning to stay upstairs, anyway? When was the big confrontation going to occur?

"There's nothing wrong with me," she repeated, the strain of her secrets pulling at her, threatening to rip her in two. One half of her belonged to Matt, the man upstairs, her lover. The man who was about to demolish Gary and then leave, drive his rental car over the horizon and disappear.

The other half belonged to her brother.

The very fibers of her spirit were stretching and snapping. She was breaking, splintering, disintegrating.

Gary continued his interview with the cat. "Fill me in, Dinah. Linda's never this crabby in the morning. Has she got PMS?"

Dinah licked her lips and twitched her nose. Gary put her down by her water dish and crossed the room to the counter, where Linda hovered next to the coffeemaker. "Come on, Lin—what's eating you?"

"Nothing," she mumbled.

He reached around from behind her and gave her another hug. "This isn't a stranger you're talking to. This is me. I know when something's wrong. You can tell me."

"There's nothing to tell."

"You don't seem very happy to see me."

She turned in his arms and hid her face against his shoulder. He still had his jacket on. Matt had ordered her to take Gary's jacket so he couldn't escape.

But more important than Gary's jacket were his arms, his familiar brotherly love. This was Gary, her champion through thick and thin, through childhood and adolescence. This was the man who had liberated her from her parents' restrictive rules. This was the man who had continued to visit her and Andrew when most of their friends stayed away, no longer able to endure the sight of how ravaged Andrew was. This was the man who had come to her shortly after Andrew had passed away, and said, "He's no longer suffering, but you still are. Let's go home and make you well."

For her entire thirty-three years, Gary had been beside her, teasing her, hassling her, worrying about her, supporting her, loving her. Nothing she could do would ever make him love her less. Nothing he had done could make her love him less, either.

"You're in trouble, Gary," she murmured.

Loosening his hold on her, he took a step back and regarded her cautiously. "What do you mean?"

"I know what you did." The words tumbled out in a rush. "I know what you did to Matt Calloway. I don't know why you did it, but I'm sure you must have had a reason."

Gary's complexion lost some of its California burnish. His gaze met hers, and she might as well have been looking into a mirror. His eyes glittered with the same multitude of colors, the same kaleidoscope of emotions. "I did have a reason, Linda. I want to explain everything to you—"

"Not now," she said. "You've got to leave. Matt's here."

"Here?" Gary's voice was low, but he punctuated the word with a look of horrified shock. "He's here now?"

"Yes. It's his car in the driveway, Gary. Please—leave before he comes downstairs." She couldn't bear to see the two men go at each other. Matt was going to win, she knew he was. He had justice on his side, and he was stronger than Gary, both physically and morally. But she couldn't bear to see her brother lose. He and Matt would have to have their showdown somewhere else, far away from her. "Just go." She ushered him toward the doorway. "We'll talk later. Just get out of here, okay?"

"He's *here?* Calloway is *here?* He spent the night with you?"

Of all the times for Gary to turn into a doting big brother! She knew he was only being protective—too protective, but that was his way. He could give her a box of contraceptives as a gag present because he knew she wasn't the sort of woman who would use them casually.

Now wasn't the time for him to defend his little sister's honor. He had his own neck to worry about. "Gary, don't waste time. Just go."

He lunged into the hall, bellowing, "Calloway? Get down here, you bastard! So help me, if you touched my sister, I'll kill you!" He charged to the foot of the stairs. "If you so much as touched a hair on her head—"

"Gary!" She raced after her brother. "Stop it."

He clearly had no intention of stopping. At least he wasn't the coward Matt had predicted he would be when he'd instructed Linda to keep him from escaping. Quite the contrary, Gary was charging after Matt, thirsting for blood.

Matt seemed prepared to meet the challenge. He appeared at the top of the stairs, clothed and composed, his cheeks unshaven but his hair combed, his eyes as hard and black as onyx. He descended to the bottom step at his own leisurely pace, one hand on the railing and the other fisted against his thigh. His breathing was ominously deep and even.

He didn't even look at Gary. His gaze was riveted to Linda.

"Did you sleep with my sister?" Gary roared.

Matt ignored Gary. "You told him I was here," he said to her, his voice soft but steely.

"Matt—"

"Did you tell him?"

Swallowing, her spirit withering in the bitter anger of his stare, she nodded.

"And you told him to leave. You wanted him to flee before I could get to him. You tried to help him get away from me."

"Matt." She felt a sudden, unexpected surge of fury toward him. The promise he'd extracted from her upstairs hadn't been fair. "He's my brother, Matt."

"So you tried to help him escape."

"I love him, Matt. He's my brother. I never asked to be in the middle of this!"

Gary grabbed Matt's sleeve, determined to be heard. "What did you do to her?"

Something died in Matt's eyes, the last tiny flicker of light. They were barren as he turned to regard Gary. As if his stare had actually been pinning her to the wall, she felt her spine go slack the moment he glanced away.

"If you've messed with my sister, man—"

"I didn't mess with her," Matt asserted, his tone as muted as Gary's was incensed. "I slept with her."

Gary swore, and Linda acknowledged that the curse sounded much more natural coming from him than it did from her. "All right, then," he decided. "Step outside. We'll settle this, just the two of us. You mess with my sister, you answer to me."

"Gary," she protested. His chivalry was uncalled-for. This wasn't the Middle Ages, for heaven's sake. And if Matt had messed with her heart and her mind and her soul, there wasn't a damned thing Gary could do about it, inside or outside.

"What happened last night is irrelevant," Matt went on in an emotionless drone. "It's meaningless. Give my money back and stay out of my life, and I'll stay out of yours."

Irrelevant? Meaningless? Pain knotted inside Linda's chest, making her want to thrash him. She didn't need Gary to fight her battles; she would take Matt on herself. If he could do what he'd done with her last night and call it *meaningless*...

She wanted to kill him.

"Money," Gary snorted. "That's all that matters, right? That's what you came for, right?"

A muscle in Matt's jaw twitched. "That's what I came for," he said.

"So you slept with my sister in order to get to me. You came to her home, you weaseled your way into her life, you earned her trust and you slept with her. You used her—just to get your money. You're scum, man, the lowest of the low. A worm would have to look down to see you."

Linda's headache moved downward to the back of her neck, settling there like a clammy hand, cold and heavy. She knew Matt was angry, she knew what Gary had done to him, but why had he turned on *her?* What had *she* ever done to him?

She had trusted him, as Gary had said. She'd opened her life to him. She'd welcomed him into her home and her bed.

And when Gary had shown up, she'd tried to alert him, to save him. She'd been a loyal sister.

One impossible-to-keep promise wasn't enough to incur Matt's wrath, was it? One impossible-to-obey order that she deny any allegiance whatsoever to her brother—was that enough?

Or was it, as Gary charged, that Matt had simply been using her to get to Gary? Was it that he'd insinuated himself into her life and her heart only to reach her brother?

Was money, as he himself had just declared, all that mattered?

The clammy hand of despair stretched its fingers, circling her neck, squeezing a choked cry out of her. Matt and Gary scarcely seemed to notice, so engrossed were they in calling each other names. Linda slipped around them to the front door and out onto the porch, closing the door behind them and praying that neither of them would come after her.

The sun was high and bright, drying the last of the moisture from the front yard. Sinking onto the porch's top step, Linda leaned against an upright beam and gazed out at the pale brown expanse with its patchy hints of green. Despite those first shadings of spring, the air was nippy with a final taste of winter.

She hugged her robe more tightly around her and swallowed her tears.

She wasn't going to cry. Not for Matt, not for Gary. They would resolve their differences once they were done hurling profanities at each other. They would work it all out without any assistance from her. Maybe Gary would blacken Matt's eye in the name of Linda's honor, and maybe Matt would bloody Gary's nose on behalf of his precious money, and then they would forge a truce. Matt would go back to Oregon, Gary would go back to California, and Linda...

Well, she had Dinah.

Through the door she heard the distorted counterpoint of Matt's and Gary's voices, squabbling, shouting, swearing. She closed her eyes and tried to conjure up memories of last night, of the tenderness of Matt's hands on her, the boldness of his mouth, the hardness of him moving inside her, lifting her higher and higher until she had broken free from herself, until the world had seemed nothing more than pulses of energy, echoes of love.

Last night she'd felt as if she were a part of him, united with him. Now she felt more alone than ever.

Hearing the door open behind her, she hunched over, closing her arms even tighter around herself. She didn't want to know which of them it was. Matt or Gary, it didn't matter. She despised them both.

The footsteps neared her and she shut her eyes. Denim whispered against itself as he lowered himself to sit beside her on the step. Over the aromas of damp earth and tangy pine she smelled Matt. One night with him, and she would be doomed to remember his distinctive masculine scent forever.

He started to arch his arm around her shoulders, but when she recoiled he thought better and withdrew his hand. "You must be cold out here," he said quietly.

"Go away."

He remained seated beside her. She opened her eyes just enough to glimpse him and saw that his knees were bent sharply and his arms were resting on them. He had on the sweater he'd worn yesterday, with the sleeves pushed up. To distract herself from the virile shape of his forearms, she focused on the weathered planks beneath her feet.

"Look, Linda..." He sighed. "I'm sorry it ended up like this."

"One way or another it had to end up," she said, the sharp edge in her voice disguising the mournful quaver just below the surface. "It sounds like you and Gary cleared the air, at least."

"Are you kidding? The air is toxic in there."

"Well, you both had the chance to sound off."

"We yelled a lot. We called each other names. I told him he was a bastard for ripping me off, and he told me I was a bastard for sleeping with you. That's as far as it got."

"That sounds pretty accurate to me," Linda muttered. "You're both bastards. Thank God I'm related to only one of you."

"So you took his side."

"You had no right to ask me to take sides at all," she snapped.

He gazed out at the front yard, squinting against the morning sun. "I thought I could trust you. I thought last night counted for something."

She shivered, not from the frosty morning air or her attire, but from loss and betrayal, the recognition that nothing Gary might have done could hurt her as much as the understanding that Matt had used her.

"You were the one who said last night was irrelevant," she reminded him, unable to contain her bitterness. "How could you say those things to Gary? How could you make it sound so cheap?"

"Oh, Linda, Linda…" If she had any faith in him, she would have believed he was in anguish. "I was hurt. You had promised me—"

"You forced me to promise you. It wasn't fair of you, Matt. You forced me."

"You should have said something before you went down to Gary, then. You should have warned me you were going to tell him."

"I didn't know what I was going to do until I saw him."

Again Matt fell silent. His eyes were flinty, his lips curved downward at the corners, the bridge of his nose dented with a deep frown line. "Then you saw him," he said with quiet resignation. "And you did what you did." He sighed, then pulled himself to his feet and headed down the walk to the rental car.

Watching him drive away would be like watching her worst nightmare come true. Before he'd started the engine, she rose and went back into the house.

She found Gary seated at the table, slumped forward, his hands cupped around a full mug of coffee. He looked exhausted. As exhausted as Linda felt.

Without speaking, she pulled another mug from the cabinet, filled it with the freshly brewed coffee, and carried it to the table. She sat across from him and glared. "Well?"

"Well what?" he grunted.

"Why did you do it?"

He exhaled. All his life, people had always mistaken Gary for younger than his true age. Right now, however, he looked older than his forty-one years. Beneath his southern California tan his skin seemed pallid; his hair hung limp around his narrow face. His eyes looked flat and listless.

"It happened," he said.

"Things like this don't just happen, Gary. Robbing your war buddy doesn't just happen."

"All right, all right." He took a long sip of coffee, then straightened in his chair, extending his legs under the table and rolling his head back. His earring glinted in the sunlight from the window. "Back in January, I had this job. Some yahoo from out of town had flown in to do some business, and he rented a stretch limousine for the day. He was kind of quiet, kind of surly. He wasn't a show-off or anything."

Linda tapped her fingers impatiently against the handle of her mug.

"He did business in the back of the limo all day. He would ask me to take him to some address, someone would join him in the back seat, they'd ask me to drive them somewhere, and the guy who'd gotten in would get out. They kept the divider up. I had no idea what they were talking about. Anyway, at the end of the day, I dropped the client off at the airport and brought the stretch back to the garage. While I was cleaning out the back, I came across twenty-five thousand dollars."

"What?"

"I swear, Linda—it was just like on TV, these neat stacks wrapped in bands of paper. Five of them, five-thousand dollars apiece. They were lying on the floor under the drink tray. I figured they must have gotten overlooked."

"Twenty-five thousand dollars?"

"I deal with high rollers all the time, you know? Twenty-five thousand dollars is a day's pay for some actors."

"It's still a lot of money."

"Tell me about it." He drained his mug, then pushed back his chair and sauntered to the coffee-maker for a refill. Linda counted the seconds until he returned to the table and resumed his story. "I should have turned it in at the office, but . . . but it *was* a lot of money. I don't know what got into me, Linda, but I just . . . I wanted to hold on to that much money, just for a night. I wasn't going to keep it or anything. I just wanted to have it with me for a night, you know?"

Linda pursed her lips. She had had a great deal of experience in listening with compassion as her clients described their woeful life stories to her. She had learned in her years as a social worker never to lash out at her clients, to say, "You idiot! Why did you do something like that? Couldn't you see what it would lead to?"

She wasn't in her office, but she exercised professional control. "So you took the money home with you," she summed up.

"Yeah." Gary gave her a sheepish look. "I figured, the guy would phone my boss the next day and report the missing money, and I'd say I found it, and that would be that. Only thing was, the guy didn't phone. Day after day went by, and he didn't phone. And I got to thinking, maybe he hadn't even noticed the money was missing. Maybe he had so much loot, twenty-five thousand dollars could disappear and he wouldn't even notice."

"Gary." Compassion was one thing, but to hear her ostensibly intelligent brother rationalize his behavior so stupidly pushed her patience beyond its limits.

"All right, all right, so I blew it, okay? For once in my life, Linda—" his voice rose with emotion "—for once in my life, I wanted something. Okay? I'm forty-one years old, and what do I do? I drive important people around. I'm a limousine driver. I've worked all my life and gotten nowhere, and everybody else is getting theirs. I drive hotshots around Los Angeles for a lousy five hundred bucks a week, and nearly half of that goes for the rent. I've got a woman I love and I can't even afford to buy her an engagement ring."

"Debbie doesn't want an engagement ring," Linda said.

"But I want to give her one. Don't you see? I sat on that money for a whole month and nobody claimed it, and I said, that's it, I'm buying my woman a ring."

"You couldn't have spent twenty-five thousand dollars on a ring," Linda argued.

"No. I spent the rest on other stuff."

"Oh, Gary."

"For once in my life, I lived high. I told Debbie I had gotten a belated year-end bonus, and we ate out at fancy joints and bought a new TV and some other stuff. I don't know where it all went—nightclubs, a couple of days at the track, I don't know. But it went. And it was fun, Linda, it was fun having all that money to burn. I won't deny it."

"But it wasn't yours to burn."

"Don't turn moralistic on me. You asked what happened, and I'm telling you." He sighed, drank coffee, sighed again. "Yeah, it wasn't mine. Sure enough, the yahoo showed up in town with a friend, just before Valentine's Day, when I was planning to give Debbie this fantastic engagement ring. He contacted my boss and found out I was his driver. They found me after work one day. The yahoo said he had left the money in my limo and he wanted it back. It wasn't clean money, Linda, that much I'm sure of."

"How can you be sure?"

"If the guy's doing legitimate business, he isn't going to be handling stacks of cash in the back seat of a rented limo. Nobody does that kind of cash business unless it's illegal. Anyway, I pretended I didn't know what they were talking about, but then they threatened me. With a gun. Even worse than that—they threatened Debbie. They knew her name. Swear to me you'll never tell her, Lin."

Linda was too appalled to answer right away. The thought of Gary and his girlfriend being threatened by criminals with guns was too upsetting. After a minute she recovered enough to speak. "It's up to you what you want to tell Debbie."

"They told me I had to come up with the money right away. They wanted to give me only a day, but I convinced them to give me a week. I didn't have the money anymore. I needed time to raise that much cash."

"So, you ripped off the man who'd been your closest friend in Vietnam. Rob Peter to pay Paul, isn't that the way it goes?"

"Don't come down on me, Linda," he pleaded, sounding less defiant than defeated. "I didn't want to, but these men scared me. I don't have the kind of job where a bank's going to loan me that much money. The only property I have to borrow against is this house, but I couldn't get a bank in Los Angeles to accept a house in Massachusetts as collateral. I didn't know what to do."

She exerted herself to sound less judgmental. "What *did* you do?"

"I returned the ring and got five thousand back on that. I had a couple of thousand in the bank. I still needed a lot."

"So you went to Matt."

"I went to Matt. I knew he was doing well. Jimmy Green had told me he had his own construction firm up in Portland, he had a great house in the hills, no wife, no kids, no obligations. I figured I could borrow some money from him."

"Either that or you could doctor a check."

"I didn't start out with that in mind," Gary swore. His voice emerged tattered. "But as I drove up the coast, it just...I thought, well, if I could make it work... Linda, I was desperate. These men were threatening to hurt Debbie. I figured I could make things right with Matt later. First I had to pay off the men, then I had to clear out of town till the dust settled, and then I could work things out with Matt."

"How are you planning to make things right with him? How are you going to raise the money to pay him back?"

"The only thing I own of value is this house," Gary said slowly.

He was going to sell it. She knew without his having to say so. The house that she and he had grown up in, the house that was as much hers as his. But he'd been the older child, and her mother had assumed she would be marrying Andrew and remaining in Boston, and so Gary had inherited it.

And now he was going to sell it.

Linda stared into her mug. Her reflection shivered in the black surface. Only when she saw a teardrop hit the center of her ghostly image did she realize she was crying.

Not for herself. There were worse things than losing one's home. Surely there must be a rental somewhere, something within her small budget. She would have to get rid of some of the furniture, and an attic full of old report cards and moth-eaten blankets, but she'd deal with it.

She wasn't crying for Gary, either. He had done something inexcusable in keeping money that wasn't his, and then he'd compounded his folly by swindling Matt. Whatever pain he was suffering he deserved.

Matt was who her tears were for. He hadn't just been swindled, he'd been specifically and deliberately set up. Her own brother had found his target, plotted his approach and fired straight into Matt's heart.

No wonder he'd been enraged and bitter. No wonder he'd been hungry for revenge. Bad enough being burnt; far worse was being personally selected for burning by a trusted friend. Linda momentarily forgot the rancor of that morning as her heart swelled with sympathy for Matt.

"Why did you lie to him?" she asked, not bothering to conceal her disgust. "It wasn't just that you took him for money that hurt him so badly, but that you conned him. Why didn't you just come right out and ask him for the amount you needed?"

"Sure," Gary scoffed. "Do you think he would have given it to me? If I'd asked for that much I would have gone home empty-handed. And that would have been a death sentence, Linda, for me and maybe for Debbie. I had to play it this way. Actually, I only needed around eighteen thousand, but I couldn't figure out a way to doctor that number. Two could be changed to twenty much more easily."

"Oh, God." She shoved her mug away, too nauseated to drink. Gary's deviousness sickened her as much as Matt's coldness toward her. They deserved each other, two selfish, pitiless men.

"Work it out with him," she said, rising on unstable legs and clinging to the edge of the table until she was certain she wouldn't fall. "Work it out with Matt, however you want. I don't care anymore." *How's that for a lie?* she thought caustically. *I don't care anymore. The whopper of the century.*

Gary peered up at her, his face lined with worry. "What are you going to do?"

"I'm going to go upstairs to my bedroom and lock the door. I'm not going to come out again until you're gone. You and Matt both. So work it out fast, okay? Just do it fast, and get the hell out of here."

With that, she went upstairs to her bedroom and shut herself inside.

CHAPTER ELEVEN

BRAXTON HARDWARE reminded Matt of the hardware store that had graced the southeast corner of the town square in his hometown when he'd been a child. This store was a bit less spacious, its aisles narrower and its shelves more cluttered. But like so many small-town hardware stores, it carried an astounding variety of merchandise, everything from Pyrex cookware to penny nails, from bicycle locks to sewing needles, from garden hoses to garbage pails. The scuffed linoleum floor was coated with sawdust; above a cashier's counter hung a sign reading, Pay Gas Bills Here.

On this mild Saturday morning, the aisles were crowded with customers, just as they would have been in the town where Matt had grown up. Unlike in his hometown, though, the folks here moved faster and spoke with brisk Yankee accents—accents he would have mistakenly called Bostonian if Linda hadn't pointed out that there was a difference between the two.

Linda.

Gripping the edge of a metal shelf piled high with boxes of light bulbs, he closed his eyes and cursed under his breath.

Linda. Linda, with her velvety skin and her fiery hair, with her firm, round breasts and slim thighs, and the darkness of her, tight and damp and seething

around him ... Linda, with her fragile sighs and her
lusty moans, with her luminous eyes gazing up at him
or down at him, expressing love and passion and
abiding trust ...

Linda had betrayed him, and he had turned right
around and betrayed her.

It wasn't as if she'd caused irreparable harm by
telling Gary that Matt was in the house. Nor had it
made much difference that she'd urged Gary to leave,
since he hadn't listened to her. Sure, she'd broken a
promise. But in the long run, it didn't matter.

His anger had nothing to do with promises made
and broken. It had to do with choosing sides. She'd
told him he had no right to make her choose between
him and her brother, yet somehow he'd believed that
last night had given him certain rights.

Who was he kidding? He had no rights at all when
it came to Linda. He should never have slept with her.
That he had, that he'd surrendered to a hunger he'd
lost all control over, didn't mean he could make demands on her now. If anything, *she* ought to be the
one making demands on him.

Demand number one would probably be for him to
clear out of her life.

But she hadn't demanded that, so he'd gone into
town to buy what he needed to repair her porch. For
some reason, doing that favor for her seemed to take
precedence over everything else in Matt's life—getting his money back from Gary, flying back to Portland, resuming his normal routine.

Three-C was scheduled to begin renovation work
next week on the health club in southwest Portland.
He planned to be back in Oregon in time to direct the
project. If he spent all day on Linda's porch, drove

down to the airport in Hartford that night, and used
the remaining stub of his ticket on any plane that had
an open seat, he would be able to make an appearance at his office sometime Monday morning.

If he didn't fix her porch before leaving...he
wouldn't be able to live with himself.

A clerk approached him, wearing an affable smile.
"Can I help you find something?"

"Where do you keep your lumber?"

"Out back. Come on through."

The clerk led Matt to a small warehouse that extended into the parking lot behind the store. He selected the boards he needed and had the clerk run
them across a circular saw and lug them out to the car.
The boards protruded several feet beyond the edge of
the trunk. The clerk offered to tie them down and at-
tach a red rag to the ends.

Matt went back into the store to collect the other
items he needed: nails, a small tub of premixed cement for reinforcing the pilings under the porch, a
gallon can of water-repellent wood preservative for
Linda to apply once the weather grew more depend-
ably warm, a paintbrush, a hammer and a handsaw.
Matt hadn't thought to ask if she owned any tools.

Unloading his basket onto the counter, he tried to
picture her using the saw, the brush. He tried to
imagine her slender, sensitive fingers curled around the
rubberized handle of the hammer. Instead, his mind
conjured an image of her fingers curled around the
gleaming brass bars of her headboard as she arched
above him, as her body swayed and bowed and succumbed to his kisses.

A shudder of longing shot down to his groin and
remained there, aching.

He was grateful that the customer in front of him was taking his time, chatting with the cashier, discussing the superiority of one drill bit over another. By the time the purchase had been rung up Matt felt better.

The customer gathered his change and his parcel and turned to acknowledge Matt with a smile. Under his open jacket, he wore a white T-shirt with a bright yellow ribbon silk-screened onto it, along with the words Welcome Home, Desert Storm Soldiers.

Matt returned his smile, but a strange bitterness welled unexpectedly inside him. Nobody had ever worn a T-shirt welcoming him home twenty-odd years ago. Nobody had ever tied a ribbon for him. The few medals he'd earned had been mailed to him after he'd returned to the States, not pinned on his chest, and over the years he'd lost track of them. Maybe his mother had them. Maybe Ellie had kept them.

He told himself it didn't matter, he was beyond all that, he'd outgrown it, he didn't care. He told himself that that part of his life had ended long ago.

Still, the bitterness burgeoned inside him. Not just the remote bitterness of seeing a yellow ribbon but the acute bitterness of having been betrayed by one of the few men in the world who could understand this sort of resentment—who could share it.

Matt realized he shouldn't have come to Braxton. Twenty-thousand dollars wasn't worth having all the old wounds torn open, or opening a new one.

Linda. The most painful wound of all.

STEERING INTO the driveway, Matt spotted Gary on the front porch, lounging against one of the upright beams and sipping from a mug. The sun was high, and a glance at his watch informed Matt that it was nearly eleven-thirty. His lack of hunger surprised him.

His gaze moved from Gary to the front door, and then up to the second-floor window above the porch. Linda's bedroom window.

Was she in there? Had she banished Gary to the porch and locked him out? Or had she bolted the minute Matt left for the hardware store, choosing to make her escape the moment the driveway was unblocked?

Would he ever see her again? If he did, would there be any way for him to make things better?

The porch. Repair the porch and then get out of Braxton, he told himself as he swung open the car door and climbed out.

"What's going on?" Gary shouted to him.

There was no simple answer to that, but Matt provided one, anyway. "I'm going to fix the porch," he said.

"What are you, nuts?"

Compared to what Gary had called him earlier, "nuts" seemed tame—and pretty accurate. He pulled the bags containing his new purchases from the back seat of the car, closed the door and stalked across the yard to the porch. "I told Linda I'd do it."

"Hey, look, man," Gary said, his expression an uncanny mix of hope and contrition. "Let *me* fix the porch, okay? It should've been done a long time ago, but I'm just not around often enough to take care of these things for her."

"I'm doing it," Matt snapped. He wasn't going to let Gary steal this from him, too.

Gary said nothing as Matt slammed the bags onto the bottom step and then sauntered across the spongy brown lawn to the car for the lumber. When he turned back to the house, the boards balanced on his shoulder, he saw Gary poking through the bags, inspecting their contents.

The sight brought on a flare of anger. How dare Gary touch his things? He dropped the boards on the ground with a menacing thud.

The noise startled Gary enough to bring his snooping to a halt. "There's coffee in the kitchen if you want it," he offered.

Matt felt his rage pricking at him, needling him until his entire body was twinging from the effort not to explode. He glowered at Gary, then pulled the hammer from one of the sacks and used it to wrench out the nails in the loose board that had entrapped Dinah.

Gary observed him for a minute, then moved to the front door. "I'll get you some coffee," he said before vanishing inside.

Well, isn't he the proper host, Matt thought acerbically, funneling his fury into his attack on the nails in the splintering boards. It was surprisingly therapeutic labor. Each nail required exertion; yanking them out strained his arms and back in a cathartic way. Each nail was a problem to be solved, and with every successful extraction he felt a sense of accomplishment.

Not that he was accomplishing anything important, like getting his money back, beating Gary to a pulp or redeeming himself in Linda's eyes. But something was getting done, at least.

Ten minutes elapsed before Gary returned with a mug of coffee for Matt. He emerged from the driveway side of the house, carrying not just the coffee but a heavy steel tool chest. "I don't know if you need any of this stuff," he said, "but I brought it out, just in case."

Matt glanced briefly at Gary, then took the coffee and turned away. Merely looking at the man irritated him. Although he hadn't made the connection when he'd first met Linda, he could see her resemblance to her brother clearly now: the fair coloring, the fine-boned physiques, the straight, silky hair, the narrow faces and freckled noses. Gary was taller and lankier than Linda, and his features were coarser, but the likeness was there. Looking at Gary forced Matt to acknowledge the blood kinship between him and Linda.

"Where is she?" he asked, loath to speak to Gary but unable to bear not knowing.

"Inside," Gary answered. "Upstairs."

"How is she?"

"Not good." Gary cursed. "Why did you have to touch her, Matt? Why couldn't you keep your goddamn hands to yourself?"

Matt wrapped his fingers tightly around the mug, pretending it was Gary's neck. If he were the scoundrel Gary seemed to think he was, he would tell Gary that he'd wanted to keep his hands to himself, but Linda hadn't let him. That when he'd tried to leave she'd begged him to stay.

But he couldn't talk about her like that. He couldn't imply that she had seduced him. Last night wasn't about aggression and submission, one person leading and the other following. Matt and Linda had met someplace in the middle, in a shared instant of need and yearning. And they were both paying the price for it this morning.

Gary wasn't willing to leave the subject alone, though. "Money is one thing," he said, unbuttoning his jacket as the sun grew stronger. "You hate my guts? Fine. Come after *me*. Not my sister, man. Not her."

"Shut up." Matt set his coffee down on a level patch of dead grass and resumed his assault on the rusty nails. He and Gary had exchanged enough accusations and threats that morning. Matt didn't want to go through it again.

"I don't know what went on between you two," Gary persevered, "but she's hurting. She hates me for what I did, and I don't blame her. But she hates you, too, just as much as she hates me. So I've got to assume that whatever you did to her is just as bad as what I did."

"I didn't do anything," Matt retorted, then sucked in his breath at what a lie that was. He jerked another nail loose and tossed it into the growing pile of bent brown nails at the bottom of the steps. "We made love, all right? She wanted to, I wanted to, and that's what happened."

"And then you told me about it," Gary accused. "Like you thought it was a way to get back at me. Like that was all it meant to you—you slept with my sister and then rubbed my nose in it. The ultimate revenge, right?"

Matt threw down the hammer and spun around, his hands balling into fists. "It wasn't like that at all."

"So why did you tell me? Right in front of her! My God, I could see the pain in her face when you told me. I could feel it. My sister is more important to me than your money is to you, Calloway. And you stood there and hurt her, right in front of me."

"Because—" *Because she took your side,* he wanted to scream. *Because I was hurting, too.*

He let his arms drop, his hands unfurling, and expelled his breath. Damn. Gary was wrong in claiming that Matt had hurt Linda to get at her brother, but he was right that Matt had hurt her.

What a vain, selfish fool he was to think she would side with him rather than her own brother. Fixing her porch didn't begin to make up for his stupidity.

But what else was there? How else could he make amends?

If he went to her and dropped onto his knees and begged her forgiveness, what good would it do? Even if she were generous enough to forgive him, he was ultimately going to leave her. He could tell her that last night meant more to him than she could possibly imagine, and he would be speaking the truth. But when he was all done beating his chest and speechifying, he would only wind up kissing her goodbye.

What was the point?

He clamped his hands around the board he'd been working on and tugged upward with all his might. The board squeaked, then rattled free. Matt hurled it onto the grass and attacked the next plank, determined to work until he was sore and sweating, until he was too tired to think.

"I brought out a tape measure," Gary said.

Matt didn't bother to turn.

"Also a straight edge and a pencil. I could get started on the new boards, measuring and marking them."

"Don't do me any favors."

"It's not a favor, Calloway. I should've done this repair a year ago." When Matt didn't respond, he said,

"How about, *you* do the measuring and marking, and *I'll* tear off the old boards."

Tearing off the old boards was the harder part. Matt wanted it for himself. "I'll do the old boards," he grunted. "You mark the new ones." He would finish the job sooner with Gary's assistance, and the sooner he finished, the sooner he could leave New England and return to Portland.

The sooner he could run away from the damage he'd caused.

THROUGH THE PANES of her bedroom window she heard activity on the porch below: the rasp of a saw, the *bonk* of one board hitting another, the occasional sound of Matt's voice or Gary's, barking monosyllabic orders at each other.

If she looked out her window, she probably wouldn't see much; the porch's overhang would block her view. But that was all right—she didn't want to see Matt or Gary. She didn't care what they did, whether they made up or whacked each other with boards until they both fell unconscious to the ground.

She didn't care.

Lord help her, if there was one thing she truly abhorred, it was sulking. Every working day she met with clients whom she had to encourage to stop sulking, to cast off their emotional baggage, the burden of slights and affronts they had accumulated in their dealings with others, and get on with their lives. Sometimes she counseled them to throw themselves into their work, sometimes to take a vacation and get away from it all. Read a novel, she'd advise, and lose yourself in another world for a while.

She gazed at the family saga lying untouched on her nightstand. The last thing she felt like doing right now was losing herself in the world of European immigrants in New York at the turn of the century.

She had soaked for a while in a bath. She wanted to steam away the traces of Matt's lovemaking. She wanted to scour him from her skin, to scrub and scrub until she no longer remembered how he had felt against her, inside her.

After a while her fingertips had pruned and she'd climbed out of the tub, knowing that one bath—one thousand baths—wouldn't be enough to wash her memories of him away.

She'd donned her jeans and a sweater. When she heard Gary walk outside, she'd darted downstairs to the living room for her book. Dinah had been napping in the easy chair, but when she saw Linda she perked up and accompanied her mistress upstairs.

Now she was sprawled out on Linda's bed, grooming her paws and yawning. Linda prowled around the room, too edgy to sit. In truth, she was exhausted. She would like nothing more than to stretch out next to her cat and rest for a few minutes. But she'd lain down once and immediately smelled Matt's musky male scent on her pillow, in the linens. She had felt his heat closing in around her, the tranquilizing rhythm of his respiration as he slept, the gentle—and then not so gentle—friction of his hands, his lips, his tongue...

So now she was pacing, avoiding her bed as much as possible.

She would *not* sulk. He was a jerk, not worth brooding about. Sure, he had been bruised by Gary's betrayal. Sure, having a friend sever a long-standing bond of trust was a terrible thing. But did that give him the right to hurt her?

She was the victim of a betrayal. Matt had broken her trust. He had used her to get to Gary, or *at* Gary. He had exploited her, pure and simple. He'd gotten close to her, encouraged her friendship, helped himself to everything she had to give and then greeted Gary with the news that he'd scored with Gary's baby sister.

Well, damn it, she was glad she'd broken her promise to him. If he could use her to avenge himself on Gary, then the only promise she would give him was a vow of everlasting hatred.

She heard more sawing below, a wheezing, scratching sound that piqued Dinah's curiosity. The cat leaped gracefully from the bed to the nightstand and from there to the windowsill.

"It's just the porch," Linda whispered, sidling toward the window and running her fingertips through Dinah's soft black fur. "It's just men. Just fools."

Apparently convinced, Dinah turned from the window and used her nose to nudge Linda's hand. Understanding, Linda lifted the cat into her arms and strolled around the bed to the rocker. She sat and let Dinah curl up in her lap. Then she started to rock.

"It's just men," she murmured, scratching the cat gently between the ears. "Let's hope they go away soon."

Dinah purred in agreement.

THE PILINGS were in decent shape. Matt slapped a bit of quick-dry cement onto the cracks, then anchored a couple of fresh verticals into place. Gary finished cutting the final board to size and set down the saw.

Although it couldn't have been warmer than the mid-fifties, they were both sweating. Matt had removed his sweater a while ago; Gary's jacket hung over the front doorknob.

"Are you thirsty?" Gary asked. "I thought I saw a couple of beers in the fridge."

"Yeah," Matt grunted, not bothering to add that he'd been the one to buy the beer.

Gary ambled around the house to the mudroom door and inside. Matt kept his eye on the cement, testing it for hardness every so often. His stomach growled in hunger.

He was still too angry to think about fixing himself something to eat. Much too angry. At Gary, at Linda, but mostly at himself.

Gary soon returned carrying two bottles of beer and a bag of potato chips. He handed one bottle to Matt, then settled on the higher of the rebuilt steps and tore open the bag.

Matt abandoned the pilings to help himself to a handful of chips. He resisted sitting with Gary, then decided not to be so juvenile and lowered himself onto the step, leaving a no-man's-land of several inches between them.

"I appreciate your doing this repair," Gary said.

"I'm not doing it for you," Matt grumbled. "I'm doing it for Linda."

"Yeah, well . . . I should do more for her, but it's hard when I'm in Los Angeles. Besides, she likes to think she's independent."

"She is," Matt pointed out.

They drank their beer. A cool breeze dried the sweat on Matt's brow.

"Sometimes I forget how independent she is," Gary said. "I guess...she's always been my baby sister, and she always will be. That's something that's never going to change, no matter how old and independent she gets."

"You were babying her even in 'Nam," Matt recalled.

"Huh?"

"You brought home a doll for her. She wanted black stockings."

"She told you that?" Gary regarded Matt with skepticism, which gradually faded to grudging acceptance. "Black stockings. She was just a kid, for crissakes."

And now she was a woman, Matt thought. Younger than the two men drinking beer on her half-reconstructed porch, but infinitely more mature.

"I saw something at the hardware store this morning," he said, surprising himself. He had reached an emotional plateau that allowed him to respond to Gary's attempts at conversation, but he hadn't realized until that moment that he'd come far enough to initiate a conversation himself.

"Yeah? What?"

"A man was wearing a Desert Storm shirt with a big yellow ribbon on it. I haven't seen one in a couple of years. It kind of brought me up short."

Gary bristled. "Oh, man, don't I know it." He reflected on his words for a moment, then shook his head. "All right, maybe they went through their hard times, too. It wasn't like what we went through, and it wasn't fair that they got all the parades."

"I know."

Gary hesitated, then said, "Just too much coming down on me. I'm sorry it spilled over onto you. It shouldn't have happened. You were my buddy, Matt. My brother. You don't know how sorry I am."

"Yeah." Matt honestly believed him, but he wasn't ready to hand him a pardon. Not with twenty thousand dollars outstanding. Not with Linda upstairs, loathing him.

"It was bad enough turning forty and finding I was nowhere near what I wanted to be. I'm broke, I can't take care of my lady the way I want to... There's so much I want in life, and it just isn't happening. We risked our lives in Vietnam, Matt, day after day after day. And who ever cared what happened to us? Who ever worried about whether we'd make it home in one piece?"

"Some people did," Matt responded in a quiet drawl. He squinted into the sun, remembering everything Linda had told him about her youthful fixation on the war and her brother's friends, the fearless foursome. So many years later, she still remembered the letters she'd written and those she'd received from Gary. She remembered that Matt and Gary had saved each other's lives, that the trust that once flourished between them had kept them from going mad. "Linda was here," he reminded Gary. "She was here, waiting for you to come home, praying for you."

Gary issued a long, mournful sigh. "Now she's probably praying for me to die a painful death. She'll never forgive me for what I did."

"She's a good person," said Matt. "She'll forgive you."

"For fleecing you? Never. I've probably lost her forever."

I probably have, too, Matt thought, staring at the heap of contorted old nails without seeing them. He saw, instead, the hurt and anger in her lovely hazel-green eyes after he'd implied that getting his money meant more to him than she did.

He'd lost her forever, no doubt about it.

IT'S JUST AS WELL, he told himself as they resumed working.

Every now and then he would shout an instruction to Gary, who seemed quite willing to comply with Matt's commands. Perhaps it was because Gary knew Matt was the expert when it came to construction, or perhaps it was simply Gary's way of atoning for his sins.

When Matt wasn't shouting orders, however, they didn't speak at all. The silence gave him time to meditate. He wished he could empty his mind, but every time he tried it filled right back up again with thoughts of Linda.

He'd lost her, but maybe that wasn't such a terrible thing. What would have happened if he *hadn't* lost her? He would have had a pleasant day with her, and—if he were lucky—a pleasant night. And then he would have said goodbye. No matter what, this interlude had to end with his saying goodbye.

Braxton was her home. He lived three thousand miles away. Making love with her couldn't change that.

So perhaps it was just as well that she hated him. It might make his departure easier on them both.

"Listen, man," Gary called to him. "I was thinking—"

"Move your end over as close to the other board as you can. You don't want to leave gaps between the planks, okay? No, not touching it," he corrected as Gary moved his end of the board too close to the adjacent one. "About a quarter-inch, that's right."

Gary nudged the board into place and Matt fastened his end, hammering each nail flush in two clean hits. While Gary held his end steady, Matt moved along the board, fastening it at every cross beam. When he reached Gary's end, Gary stepped aside and Matt smashed the last two nails into place.

"Listen," Gary began again. "I need to make things right with you."

Matt gave him a cynical look. "Things are never going to be right between us, Villard."

He shook a handful of nails from the box and whacked them into place along the board, hoping Gary wouldn't pursue this line of discussion. Regardless of what he'd said that morning, money had never been his primary motivation in coming after Gary. Paying Matt back would replace only part of what Gary had stolen.

"Done," he said, straightening up and wiping his hands on the seat of his pants.

He and Gary stepped off the porch, avoiding the nails and scrap wood, and surveyed their work. The boards lay clean and level; they felt sturdy underfoot. In a couple of months Linda could slap on some wood preservative, and she'd have herself a fine porch.

Some things were easier to fix than others.

"I can't ever win back your friendship," Gary conceded. "That's beyond me. Okay. I'm sorry, but if that's the way it has to be . . ."

"Yeah."

"But I've got to pay you back."

Matt busied himself collecting the tools and stashing them in the toolbox.

Gary fingered his earring nervously. "It's like, these guys were threatening my life and Debbie's. I had to give them twenty-five thousand dollars, and—"

"Spare me the gory details," Matt silenced him. He supposed he was remotely curious about why Gary had ripped him off, but he wasn't in the mood to hear about it now.

"I was desperate, Matt. I don't have many rich friends I can turn to."

"You didn't turn to me. You robbed me."

"Well...because I thought you'd say no. I was scared. I wasn't thinking straight."

"That's for sure."

"I'm trying to think straight now, Matt. I'm trying to figure out how to pay you back."

"I'm listening," Matt grunted, trying to stir up some enthusiasm.

"The house," said Gary, gesturing toward it with a generous wave of his arm. "I own it. It's in my name."

Matt's attention sharpened. He knew Gary owned the house. What he didn't know was whether he was going to like what Gary said next.

"If I sell it, I'm sure I could get more than enough to cover my debt to you."

"Sell it? Why can't you just borrow against it?"

"I don't have the income," Gary explained. "I don't have the credit rating. And if I'm dealing with banks in California, they aren't going to give a hoot that I own property three thousand miles away."

Matt took a deep breath. "What about Linda? She lives here."

"I know."

"So what are you planning to do?" Matt asked with barely tempered anger. "Put her out on the street?"

"I'll help her find another place to stay. It's the only way I can raise the money, Matt. I've tried to think of some other way to do it, and I can't."

"You're not going to sell her home," Matt said, an ominous undertone in his voice. "I won't let you do that to her."

"Oh, right. After what you've done to her—"

"She was loyal to you," Matt reminded Gary, trying not to choke on the words. "I'm not going to let you stab her in the back after she stood by you."

Gary raised his hands in a plea. "I can't get the money any other way."

"There are other ways," Matt said.

"Tell me what you want me to do."

Matt didn't answer at once. Instead, he lifted the toolbox and some of the lumber trimmings and headed for the garage barn. Taking his cue, Gary gathered the rest of the leftover lumber and joined Matt in the barn, showing him where everything went. Then they returned to the house through the mud-room. They took turns washing up at the sink, and then Gary fixed a fresh pot of coffee.

While Gary bustled around the kitchen Matt wandered into the living room. Sun flowed through windows where once he'd watched the snow accumulating. The thick burgundy cushions of the easy chair and sofa held indentations where he and Linda had sat last night. The fireplace grate contained the charred remains of their fire.

He felt as if his soul lay in the hearth, burnt out, black and cold.

Returning to the kitchen, he found Gary filling two mugs with coffee. They sat facing each other at the table. Matt took a sip.

"Tell me what you want," Gary demanded.

Matt issued a short, mirthless laugh. What he wanted was Linda in his arms, loving him.

Wrong answer. What he was supposed to want was reimbursement and a chance to go about his daily business without being angry all the time. "We could work out a repayment schedule," he said. "Or at least we could if I trusted you. Which I don't."

"What other choice do you have?" Gary asked. "I'd like to pay you back any way we can work it. Selling the house—"

"No." Matt eyed the cat's food and water dishes, the houseplants on the windowsill, the homey drapes. Linda lived here. Her life was here. Right this very minute, she was ensconced in her room, her refuge. Gary couldn't deprive her of this. Matt wouldn't let him.

Gary crossed the room and opened a drawer—the drawer Matt had rifled through the morning after he'd first spent a night here—and produced a pen and a pad. "Look," he said, returning to the table. "I don't earn much."

"That's not my problem."

"I'll pay you whatever I can manage. What do you want, once a week? Once a month? You name it. We'll put it in writing."

Matt snorted. "Guess what I think your signature is worth."

Gary plowed valiantly ahead. "Fifty bucks a week, for a start. Would you accept that?"

"Fifty dollars a week," Matt repeated. "To pay back twenty thousand dollars..." He did a quick mental calculation. "Not counting interest, it's going to take you almost eight years to retire the debt."

"You want interest, too?" Gary asked, cringing at the prospect.

"Do you think I don't deserve it?"

Gary threw up his hands. "Look, figure it out. I can pay you fifty bucks a week for as long as it takes—assuming I don't lose my job and disaster doesn't strike. Fifty bucks a week. You want interest? I'll pay it for nine years. Ten. I don't care."

"What do you mean, you don't care?"

"Your money may be important to you, man. What's important to me is making things right. If it takes ten years, I'll pay for ten years. Just tell me what you want, and I'll put it down right here." He jabbed his index finger at the pad.

Matt stared at the blank sheet of paper, at the pen, at their mugs of coffee. Pain gnawed at him, a deep, fierce agony at the knowledge that no amount of money, no amount of time, could make anything right.

He closed his eyes and familiarized himself with the pain. He had a feeling he was going to be living with it for a long, long time. "Nine years," he said, not caring how the interest rate would compute. "Write it out—fifty dollars a week for nine years. Write it out twice and sign it. God knows whether it's going to be worth the paper it's written on."

While Gary wrote, Matt drank his coffee. He watched with detached curiosity as Gary dated two pages, copied the terms onto each, signed his name at the bottom of each and then nudged the papers across the table to Matt.

He stared at them, read them, and the pain in his gut increased.

Where was his anger? Where was his self-righteous indignation? Where was his satisfaction at having achieved his purpose in coming to Braxton?

Why was he here, hammering out this stupid agreement the way he'd been hammering nails just a half hour ago, when he wanted to be upstairs, in Linda's arms, receiving her sweet love one more time?

He set down his mug and scraped back his chair. "I'll sign it later," he said.

His long strides carried him out of the kitchen, up the stairs and along the hall. At Linda's closed door he hesitated.

He shouldn't do this. He should just clear out. Seeing her before he left was only going to make leaving that much harder.

But he had to tell her that he was willing to go much, much farther than Gary to gain her forgiveness. He would go to the ends of the earth to make things right with her.

He had to make sure she knew that.

Drawing in a deep breath, he knocked on the door.

CHAPTER TWELVE

SHE HAD BEEN LISTENING to them for hours. She'd heard the continuous noises of construction on the porch, the sawing and hammering and shouted directions, the whine and thump of the mudroom door opening and closing, the rare exchange of dialogue. Then she'd heard them enter the house and go into the kitchen. She'd heard the rush of water running in the sink, the tread of footsteps into the living room and back, the shuffle of chairs around the kitchen table.

She couldn't make out their words as they conversed in the kitchen, but neither of them seemed to be shouting. Their voices were low and even, if not exactly peaceful at least not belligerent.

Great. They were working out their differences. How happy she was for them.

The knock on her bedroom door didn't surprise her, since she had traced the sound of footsteps up the stairs and through the hall. She knew who was on the other side of her door. Gary would have bounded up the stairs; these footsteps had been slow and deliberate, like those of a prisoner marching to the gallows.

"Come in," she said, unconsciously rocking more vigorously in the chair and tightening her hands around Dinah, who rested in her lap.

The door swung open and her vision filled with Matt. He appeared tired, grim, his jaw scruffy with a day's growth of beard, his hair mussed, his sweater gone and his shirt wrinkled, a beige smear of sawdust adorning the left knee of his jeans.

Her body tensed with suppressed emotions—anger and grief prominent among them. A fluid heat billowed up inside her, surging out to her extremities and then back again, condensing into something fierce and tight deep inside her.

Not just anger and grief, she acknowledged dolefully. She was also being buffeted by desire, yearning...love.

Dinah let out a yelp as Linda's fingers reflexively dug into the poor creature's sides, and she gently deposited the cat onto the floor. Then she drew in a deep breath and gazed toward the window, trying her damnedest to erase any affection she felt toward him by summoning memories of that morning.

But every time she plumbed outrage from the depths of her heart, it slid out of her grasp and sank back down, leaving in its place other memories of his gentleness, his sensitivity, the sweeping passion of his kisses, the intimacy of his touch. The sublime pleasure he'd taken in her pleasure and then his own, his complete, excruciating surrender to something much bigger and grander than mere sex.

She wanted so badly to hate him. But as her gaze journeyed back to him, as she observed his weary posture, his lanky physique and strong hands, his streamlined torso and his face, his eyes still aglow with longing and despair...

Lacking the cat, she gripped the arms of her chair and rocked harder, her toes shoving against the rug as if she could push herself away from him.

He stepped across the threshold. She opened her mouth and then shut it, realizing that if she tried to speak, the wrong words would come out. Pressing her lips together, she watched him uneasily as he ventured farther into the room, around the foot of the bed toward the rocker. As he lowered himself to sit on the edge of the mattress, she stifled the urge to skid her chair backward into the bathroom.

She was going to be brave. She hadn't run away from her love for him last night. She wasn't going to run away today.

"Your brother and I worked out an arrangement," he said.

His voice affected her the way his body did. It was dark and potent, arousing in its intensity.

She rocked in a steady rhythm, refusing to let him know how much his nearness disturbed her. "Did you," she said dryly. "I'm so pleased."

"Linda." He extended his hand toward her, but evidently sensed her alarm and pulled back. "I want to work things out with you, too."

"We have nothing to work out."

"We have everything to work out."

Tears pricked her eyes and she attempted to blink them away. There would be plenty of time for crying once Matt was gone. But not now, not in front of him. She couldn't let him know how badly he'd hurt her, how badly she had hurt herself by trusting him.

"This morning I said some things I shouldn't have," he admitted.

"Forget it," she said with forced flippancy. "I know I already have."

He gave her a bittersweet smile. "You're the worst liar in the world. I guess your brother got all the genes for dishonesty in the family. You just can't pull it off."

"I'm not lying," she snapped, aware that that, too, was a lie. "You've solved your problem with Gary. He's going to sell this house and pay you back. It seems like a fine solution all around."

"I won't have Gary selling this house," Matt told her. "That would leave you with nowhere to live."

"Don't worry about me," she said grandly. "You boys take care of your money problems. I'll take care of myself."

"Linda. He's not going to sell the house. He's going to pay off his debt out of his salary, one week at a time."

She shrugged, as if none of it mattered to her. "However you and he have worked it out, you'll get paid back. Money was what it was all about, right? You're going to get your money. You must be absolutely thrilled. I know I'm just tickled pink about it."

He reached for her again, this time ignoring her unspoken protest, and took her hand in his. The hard surface of his palm closed over her knuckles and sent a searing tremor up her arm. For a brief, insane moment she ached for his touch, for his powerful, talented hands to pull her to him, to trail their magic over her skin, to tease and tantalize and open her to him, to bring her again to the crest of sensation, to join himself to her and carry her with him beyond everything she'd ever known before he had come into her life.

As if he could read her mind, he shifted his hand slightly, curling his fingers around her wrist and running his thumb over the delicate ridge of her knuckles, teasing, tantalizing, trailing magic.

A tiny sigh escaped her before she could smother it.

"The money was never that important to me," he murmured. "You know that, Linda. You know it."

She resented him for continuing to move his thumb in lazy figure eights across the back of her hand. She hated him for being able to arouse her so easily. She hated herself for responding, for being so vulnerable to even this aimless caress.

"You must be awfully rich, if twenty thousand dollars isn't important to you," she remarked, reassured by the firmness of her voice even as her heartbeat grew faster and wilder, as her flesh continued to melt in the pulsing heat that spread from his fingertips up her arm and through her body.

"The money was never as important as the fact that Gary was the one who stole it," he reminded her. "And it was never as important as you were."

His use of the past tense reverberated shrilly inside her. Rationally she knew that whatever had happened between her and Matt was over and done with. But the minute he'd invaded her bedroom, the moment he'd taken her hand in his, she'd lost the ability to think rationally.

"I don't believe you," she said, sounding appallingly weak.

"You're lying again, Linda. You do believe me. You know money had nothing to do with us. And you know that last night was incredible. It was too special for words."

"Then please stop talking about it," she implored. "You've got to go back to Oregon, don't you? So go."

"I can't go until . . ." He faltered.

For the first time since he'd entered her room, he seemed unsure of himself. She took advantage of his hesitancy. "It doesn't matter what we say to each other now, does it, Matt. You're going to leave. You're going to fly back to Portland, and I'm going to stay here in Braxton, and that'll be the end of it. So why don't you just go?"

"Linda—"

"Have a good trip," she said, tearing her hand from his and lurching out of the rocking chair. "Have a good life. It's been nice knowing you."

Before she could catch her breath he was upon her, forcing her around to face him and binding her to himself in a smothering hug. His lips crushed down upon hers, savage and coercive, forcing hers apart. His tongue pushed deep, fought hers and won.

Her tears returned, not in anger or pain this time, but in recognition of her utter helplessness when it came to him. He had lashed out at her that morning, and he was going to leave her that afternoon, and yet she couldn't stop loving him.

Her tongue answered his. Her fingertips dug into the taut muscles of his upper arms, either pushing him away or holding him closer, she didn't know and she didn't care. She felt him swell against her, his body as inflamed as hers, his hips searching, pressing, surging against her.

Her hands clung tighter to him. Her mouth angled, fused with his, drew him deeper. Her entire consciousness had been reduced to this one explosive, devastating kiss.

It was a kiss goodbye, and she couldn't bear for it to end.

But it had to end, and to her dismay, Matt was the one to end it.

His arms remained closed around her, his breath quick and harsh. He pressed her head to his shoulder and ran his trembling fingers through her hair. His hips continued to move against hers, gently now, subsiding, letting the fire burn itself out.

"I'm sorry," he whispered. "God, Linda, I'm so sorry."

Was she supposed to forgive him? Was she supposed to reassure him that she harbored no ill will, that she wished him a long and healthy life, and perhaps true love in his future?

"I'm sorry" would never be enough. She would never give him absolution for having broken her heart.

The most she could give him would be a promise not to hate him forever. And that would be just one more promise she wouldn't be able to keep.

Gradually his arms relaxed and he took a step back. Linda spun toward the window and pressed her forehead against the cool glass. Somewhere below her, obscured by the overhang, was her porch, rehabilitated thanks to Matt's skilled labor. She imagined the fresh boards with their piny fragrance, the sparkling silver nails, the level, solid surface.

Maybe after he drove off she would take an ax to it.

"I have to go," he said.

She refused to turn.

A moment passed, an eternity, and then he left, shutting her door with a final, melancholy click.

"WHAT DO YOU MEAN, you're at Steve's?" Debbie asked, rubbing the towel through her wet black hair. She'd swum laps for an hour in the apartment complex pool, then gone inside to shower. It was a little after one o'clock. She'd been planning on meeting

Rosie down in Santa Monica at two. Overlooking the beach there was a bar built on a wharf where they served potent fruit daiquiris and men and women could look each other over.

Going to the bar had been Rosie's idea. Rosie knew how irritated Debbie was with Gary, and she wanted to prove to Debbie that he wasn't the only fish in the sea. "So that other guy turned out to be a jerk," Rosie had blithely remarked when Debbie described her disappointing outing with the octopus. "They aren't all jerks."

The problem wasn't the ratio of jerks to nonjerks among the male populace of southern California. The problem was that Debbie didn't want anyone else. She wanted Gary Villard: a new, improved Gary Villard. One who didn't conceal things from her, didn't disappear on her, didn't run off and leave her in the dark. One whose commitment to her didn't begin and end with his earlobe.

"I'll have a drink with you," Debbie had promised, "but I'm not looking for another man."

Now she stood in the kitchen, one towel wrapped around her body while she worked on her hair with another towel, and listened to the only man she really wanted telling her he wasn't where she thought he would be. "Why are you in Somerville? Didn't you visit your sister?"

"Yeah, I visited her," he said. "I'm coming home tomorrow, okay? I'm taking an early flight out. I'll be home mid-afternoon."

Debbie ought to have been happy, but she was too bewildered. "Why didn't you stay longer with your sister? You wasted all that time up in New Hampshire when you could have been visiting her. What's going on?''

He sighed. ''It's a long story. I thought I might have to sell the house in Braxton. But I'm not going to.''

''Sell the house?'' That was a mighty big develop-ment not to have discussed with her. She wondered what else Gary hadn't bothered to tell her. ''Does Linda want to move?''

''No. I'm not selling. She'll stay where she is. I don't want to talk about it over the phone, Debbie. I just want you to know I love you.''

''Yeah, sure,'' she said. Words were easy. ''Why didn't you tell me about the house, Gary? Is there a problem with your sister?''

''No. I mean, there wasn't. She's ticked off at me, but . . . she gets to stay at the house, so . . .''

''So, what? Why would you want to sell it? Do you need money?''

''We'll talk when I see you.''

Money? After that big bonus he'd gotten? After the high living and the partying and the new TV? ''Why didn't you tell me?''

''I *will* tell you,'' he swore. ''I've run up a debt, but I'm going to be able to pay it off without selling the house. Okay? That's all that matters.''

That wasn't all that mattered, not by a long shot. What mattered was that Gary had come into a money problem and he hadn't discussed it with her. He'd been in trouble, and he hadn't turned to her for help. Whatever his intentions, he'd hidden something vi-tally important from her. He hadn't trusted her.

''You should have told me,'' she said, sounding less angry than mournful.

''It's just a little debt, Debbie. No big deal.''

"A big enough deal that you flew across the country and thought about selling the house."

"There were personal issues involved, okay? Can't we talk about this when I get back?"

"What personal issues?" She knew she was coming across shrewish, full of suspicion, but she couldn't help it. "What personal issues that you couldn't tell me?"

"I don't like to lay my money problems on you, Debbie. It was a debt to an old friend. We worked it out. I'm going to pay him back. I'll be home tomorrow."

"You should have spent more time with your sister," Debbie reproached.

He mumbled something under his breath. "She wasn't in the mood for company," he said aloud. "I've got to go, Debbie. I'll see you tomorrow."

"Yeah, maybe," she muttered. "You should have told me your problems, Gary."

"I'm sorry," he said. "No more lies between us. I promise."

She said she'd see him tomorrow and wished him a safe flight home. Hanging up the phone, she tossed her towel over the back of a chair and sighed.

No more lies? More than anything, she wanted to believe that. She wanted to know everything about Gary, every hurdle he was facing, every snag he encountered. If he owed the guy at the newsstand a quarter for the newspaper, she wanted to know about it.

Rosie's husband used to run around with other women, and Rosie had gotten a divorce. When it came to that sort of dishonesty, Debbie trusted Gary with all her heart. He didn't play games, he didn't flirt, he didn't even look at anyone else. She trusted him so much.

But even if he wasn't hiding a secret affair with another woman from her, he was hiding something else. A little debt. A little debt that had driven him to consider selling the family home.

No more lies, she thought, shaking her head. If only she could believe it.

MATT HEARD wisecracks and laughter. He shoved himself out of his swivel chair and moved to the louvered window at the rear of the trailer that served as his on-site office. Three crew members had taken their lunch break and were seated on the steps leading into the concrete-and-girder skeleton of the health club addition. The men wore flannel shirts, jeans and hard hats; they guzzled soda from cans, wolfed down their sandwiches and reveled in the glints of sunlight that winked through breaks in the clouds.

If Matt were in a better mood, he would have gone outside and had his lunch with them. He too had on a flannel shirt and jeans, and his hard hat was within reach on a chair near the door. He was the sort of manager who felt comfortable with his crew, who enjoyed working side by side with them and unwinding with them during their breaks.

But given his current disposition, he knew he would probably be as welcome among his crew as the dense clouds rolling in off the ocean, blotting out the sun.

Turning away from the window, he stared down the length of the trailer. It held a steel desk, several steel file cabinets, a bottled-water machine and a coffee-maker, a few chairs with vinyl upholstery and a combination telephone/answering machine. A blueprint was tacked to one wall; inventory lists, a production schedule and a shift roster were tacked to another. The color scheme of the trailer's interior was gray.

Too often in the past couple of weeks, Matt had found himself thinking about wallpaper. Cream-colored wallpaper, with wide vertical stripes and rows of tiny flowers. Braided rugs. A sofa and an easy chair with burgundy cushions that enveloped a person when he sank into them. A fireplace, a fire burning low. A bed with a colorful quilt and a headboard composed of bars of gleaming brass.

He stalked back to his desk, lifted his barely touched submarine sandwich and tossed it into the metal trash can in the corner. Certain thoughts had a way of destroying his appetite.

He heard footsteps on the stepladder leading to the trailer door, and then a light rap. By the time he yelled, "Come on in," the door was already open and Jean bounced inside, lugging a bulky canvas tote.

"Hi, Matt," she said, hoisting the tote onto his desk. "How's it going?"

While Matt was stationed at a construction site, Jean remained at the Three-C office across the Ross Island Bridge on the other side of the Willamette. She took care of most of the paperwork there, receiving calls, running through the mail, overseeing the various demands on Matt's time and energy, and contacting him by telephone when necessary. But around noon every Friday, she drove to the site to deliver the paychecks for his crew so they wouldn't have to detour to the office to receive their wages.

"Everything's going fine," he answered, reaching for the tote.

"Keep your hands to yourself," she chided. "I've got important stuff in here." She poked through the bag and pulled out a stack of uniform gray envelopes held together with a rubber band. "On my way over I stopped at the five-and-ten to buy goodies for my son's birthday party. Don't start messing with it—everything's organized just the way I want it."

Matt gave her a long-suffering smile. Jean's idea of organization differed vastly from his. But he never complained; although he could make no sense of her filing system, and her desk was invariably strewn with scraps of paper and open envelopes, she never lost anything, never fouled up a contract, never neglected an invoice or a payment. Only once in the four years she'd worked for Matt had the clutter and confusion of her desk resulted in her making a mistake.

An eighteen-thousand-dollar mistake.

"Okay," she said, handing him the envelopes. "Paychecks. And here's a few letters that came in this morning..." She continued to rummage through the tote. "Also, you got a call from Dick Lennert. He wants to talk to you about that complex he's designing out in Beaverton."

"Fine. Set up a meeting." Matt thumbed absently through the mail.

"Looks like you're ahead of schedule on this job," she said, gesturing in the direction of the building addition. "You're ready to start doing the duct work, aren't you?"

"The weather's been kind."

"And meanwhile, Matthew, you look like hell."

Matt smiled at the elfin blond woman, who was appraising him with the same critical eye she no doubt used on her eight-year-old son. "Jet lag," he said with a shrug.

She curled her lip. "It's been two weeks since you were on a jet."

"Delayed reaction."

Her lip curled higher, distorting the shape of her nostrils. "How long a delay are we looking at here? I'm getting a little tired of your sourpuss act."

"Don't be a mother, Jean, all right?" He dropped into his chair, rolled it to his desk and counted the envelopes to make sure none of the paychecks were missing.

Jean hovered over his desk for a moment. He avoided looking at her, but he could feel her bearing down on him, preparing to pounce. "Matt. It's my fault, and I still feel guilty about it."

He sent her a smile. "I repeat. Don't be a mother. Let go of the guilt, Jean. It's over."

"I started the whole thing with my carelessness—"

"You didn't start anything. At worst, you failed to stop it. It was already well under way by the time the bank called you to confirm the check. Please, Jean—it's over. Let's just put the entire episode behind us."

"I will if you will," she challenged him.

He met her cagey gaze. "I've put it behind me."

"And that's why you look like hell."

He sighed and turned away. Closing his eyes, he pictured a freestanding, oak-framed mirror, and then a starburst quilt, and then Linda, her hair splayed across a pillow in an even more breathtaking starburst. Linda, her skin as soft and golden as the skin of a peach, beckoning him, welcoming him into her arms, into her heart.

He blinked and saw her again, seated across a luncheonette table from him, telling him in a modest, no-regrets tone of voice that she'd sacrificed three years of her life so a man she loved would be able to die in his own bed. Another blink, and there she was again, her expression brimming with serenity as she answered his question about why she had trusted him so completely: "You're Matt Calloway."

Another blink, and he saw her in her rocking chair, bitter, desolate, despising him.

He shuddered.

"Matt?"

Dragging himself back to the present, he swiveled his chair to face Jean. "Jet lag," he said curtly, his tone warning her away from further probing.

"Whatever you say." She straightened and lifted the tote from the desk, sliding it up onto her shoulder. "I'm going to go say hi to the guys, and then I'll head back to the office and set something up with Dick Lennert."

"Thanks," he said, referring not to her scheduling his appointments, but to her tactfully steering clear of his personal problems.

He waited until she had left the trailer, then flipped through the small stack of letters she'd brought him. She must have removed all the bills and junk mail; what remained was a letter from his attorney, some informational pamphlets on new group-health plans from his insurance company, a fund-raising letter from a museum looking for corporate donors, and a mysterious white envelope with a Los Angeles postmark and no return address.

He tore open the white envelope. Inside he found a check for fifty dollars from Gary Villard, along with a folded rectangle of stationery. "Payment number one," was inked across the paper. "I'm doing my best. Gary."

Through the window he heard an outburst of boisterous laughter—Jean joking with the guys.

"I'm doing my best," he reread, then lifted the check.

Gary's first payment might turn out to be his last. Matt wouldn't trust the man to replace a burned-out light bulb, let alone pay back a twenty-thousand-dollar loan. But...

I'm doing my best.

And what was Matt doing? Feeling glum and ornery? Raging at fate and his well-meaning secretary? Hating the spacious emptiness of his house on its hill overlooking the city, hating the lonely expanse of his bed, hating the void at the center of his life? Closing his eyes and seeing Linda everywhere, seeing her sometimes joyful, sometimes angry, sometimes attentive and sometimes moaning in the throes of the rapture he'd shared with her, an ecstasy physical and spiritual, a joy he'd been too thoughtless to hang on to.

What he was doing was torturing himself, missing her, castigating himself for every damn fool thing he'd done to her. And he was calling his malady jet lag.

It was about as far from doing his best as he could get.

He pushed away from his desk, stood and strode to the window. "Jean!" he shouted. "Come here! I've got to talk to you!"

"Just a sec," she shouted back. She chatted with the crew for a moment longer, then jogged across the lot to the trailer. She raced up the stairs, threw open the door and hurried inside. "What's up?"

"Would you do me a big favor?"

"Depends on what it is."

"Book me on a flight to Hartford."

Planting her hands on her hips, she regarded him with bemusement. Matt met her stare, saying nothing, clarifying nothing.

"I thought the louse was in California," she muttered when Matt didn't elaborate on his request.

Actually, he almost said, *the louse is in Portland.* "This has nothing to do with him. There's someone else I've got to see."

"In Hartford?"

"In Braxton, Massachusetts. Just get me a ticket, okay? For tonight, if you can."

"What about Dick Lennert?"

"This is more important. I'll see him when I get back."

Jean tilted her head slightly, looking dubious. "If you fly across the country, you're going to be giving yourself more jet lag."

"I'm thinking maybe another trip will cure me," he said. "Do whatever it takes, Jean. Don't worry about how much it costs. Reserve me a rental car in Hartford, too. I've got to go back."

She sized him up for a moment more, then shrugged, pivoted on her sneakered heel and left the trailer.

His gaze wandered from the door to the rosters, to the blueprint, to Gary's check and then his brief note.

Matt's best might not be good enough, but it was all he could do.

CHAPTER THIRTEEN

EARLIER THAT MORNING, as the sun broke over the horizon with the promise of an out-like-a-lamb day, Linda had lugged her rocker down the stairs from her bedroom and outside onto the porch. Maybe later in the weekend she would coat the fresh-smelling pine boards with that wood preservative Matt had left for her. Gary had informed her that she was supposed to wait until the weather was reliably warm and the wood had a chance to season itself, or some such thing, and then just brush the stuff on.

Maybe next week. Linda didn't have the energy for it today.

She sat on the porch, clad in her oldest, most faded jeans and her baggiest sweatshirt, her hair tied back from her face in a loose ponytail, her bare feet propped up on the railing. She looked like a rag doll, and she didn't care.

The coffee in her mug—her fourth cup since rising, and the only breakfast she'd consumed so far—was cooling off. She didn't care about that, either, or about getting something nutritious into her stomach.

Gazing out at her front yard, she admired the tiny green spikes that cut through the dense mesh of last season's dead grass to stake their claim on the earth. Lawns were always dying and being reborn, she thought. Out of the strawlike thatch emerged new life.

Two weeks, she thought. Two weeks of inexcusable lethargy. Two weeks feeling as drab as the stiff brown remnants of last year's lawn, and just as dead inside. When was she going to be reborn?

She had managed to drag herself to her office each weekday morning, where she spent eight hours duping her clients into thinking she knew how to overcome human hardship and sorrow, dishing out advice for them that she couldn't seem to apply to herself. And then she had returned home each night and sighed and brooded and felt sorry for herself.

Why should she? Because she had fallen for a man and he'd left her? Because she had given her heart to someone who didn't want it? Because Matt Calloway had come to Braxton with one goal in mind, and when he'd achieved what he'd come for he could think of no good reason to stay?

She had known what would happen from the start. She'd had fair warning; her eyes had been open. But like an idiot, she'd closed them. She'd pretended. She'd fallen in love.

She wasn't the first woman who had ever been abandoned by a man. She would recover. Eventually.

Maybe.

"Enough with the black crepe," Gary used to cajole her when she claimed she was still in mourning for Andrew. There was a certain sensibility in his attitude. Soon, she promised herself, she would decide she was tired of expending all her emotional energy on Matt Calloway. She would get busy fertilizing her lawn, weeding and mulching her flower beds, coating her porch with that wood preservative—

The porch Matt had constructed. The preservative he'd bought.

As if he'd felt obligated to pay her back for sleeping with her. As if he were compensating her for services rendered. As if she were nothing but a . . .

The distant peal of her telephone worked its way out to her, sparing her from her wretched thoughts.

She had long ago given up expecting a phone call from Matt. Those first few days of flinching whenever the phone rang and plummeting into a funk when she answered and heard someone else's voice on the other end of the line had worn her to a frazzle. She had forced herself to stop riding the hope-and-despair roller coaster, and in the past few days she had actually been able to greet the ring of her telephone with something akin to indifference.

She swung her feet down and headed into the house. On the third ring, she reached the kitchen and lifted the receiver. "Hello?"

"Linda? It's Debbie."

"Debbie." Linda took a sip of the tepid coffee in her mug and rested her hips against the counter, unsure of what to say. She hadn't talked to Debbie—or Gary, for that matter—since Gary had left Braxton just hours after Matt. "How are you?"

"Linda . . ." Debbie sounded breathless, her voice low and jittery. "Linda, I have to talk to you. Last night, Gary asked me to marry him."

"Oh. *Oh!*" Linda exclaimed, forcing jubilation into her tone. "Congratulations! Wow, you must be excited, calling me so early. It's not even seven o'clock your time."

"I know. Gary's still asleep. Do you know about the ring he got me?"

Linda scowled and gnawed her lower lip. What she knew about the ring was that Gary had bought it with money that wasn't his, and that he'd returned it to the store. At least that was what he'd told her.

She also knew he was supposed to be paying off his debt to Matt. Where on earth would he get enough spare cash to buy a ring for Debbie? Didn't Gary have the brains he was born with?

She drained her mug and set it on the counter. "A ring," she said noncommittally.

"A two-and-a-half-carat stone," Debbie reported. "An emerald cut—my favorite—set in eighteen-karat gold. Oh, Linda..." She sighed.

"It sounds beautiful," Linda managed, trying not to let her exasperation with her profligate brother enter her voice.

"He was going to give it to me on Valentine's Day," Debbie continued, her words hushed and rapid. "But he couldn't. He had to take it back to the store. He told me, Linda. When he got home two weeks ago, he told me about the debt he'd run up. He didn't tell me everything, though. I knew he was holding back. We've been fighting, Linda. Arguing. He promised to be honest with me, and I knew he wasn't telling me everything."

"If he told you about the ring—"

"He finally did, last night. I'd gone to spend a couple of days at my friend Rosie's place. I told Gary that when he was ready to come clean he could find me there. And he finally came, last night."

"And he told you the truth?"

"Everything," Debbie said. "He told me where he'd gotten the money for that ring, and he told me why he couldn't give it to me. He told me about the thugs who came after him. They had a gun, Linda. He could have died. He said . . ." Her voice cracked. "He said they even threatened me."

Linda let out a long breath. "What did you think?" The same thing she herself had thought? That Gary was a fool and a thief, that he'd been blinded by greed, that he'd broken the trust of too many people?

"The thing with the thugs, Linda . . . Well, it was stupid, you know? But it's like, when I find a quarter on the sidewalk, I keep it. Don't you?"

"Twenty-five thousand dollars isn't the same thing as twenty-five cents."

"I know, but . . . I could understand the impulse. What really upset me was when he told me what he did to his war buddy in Oregon. That was the worst. Ripping off a friend like that . . ." She concluded with a low sob.

Linda stood straighter. She was pleased that Gary had found the guts to tell the whole truth to Debbie, but she was concerned about where that left the couple.

"You knew all about this, didn't you?" Debbie's voice held an accusation.

"I found out when he was in Braxton."

"Why didn't you tell me?"

"If anyone was going to tell you, Debbie, it had to be him. You know that."

"I guess so," Debbie conceded with a sigh. "I wish I had known earlier, but . . . I suppose it doesn't matter anymore."

"What are you going to do?"

"I don't know." Another sigh. "You're a social worker, Linda. I was hoping you could tell me what to do."

"I can't," Linda protested. "I'm too involved. I have no objectivity when it comes to you two. Gary's my brother, and I'd like to think you're my friend. I care for you both."

"I know," Debbie agreed, her voice losing its edge and thickening with sorrow. "I'm so mad at him. He's lucky he's not in jail right now, or dead. I can't believe how stupid he was, risking his life for a pile of money."

Linda couldn't implore Debbie to stand by Gary in his time of trouble. But she wished with all her heart that Debbie wouldn't walk away from her brother, not now, not when he needed her.

"He said he wanted to be able to support me. He wanted to be able to buy me nice things. He said it wasn't fair that I spent my working hours selling all these luxurious things to rich people and he couldn't even buy me a diamond ring. This is going to sound weird, Linda, but it wasn't like he spent the money on himself. He spent it on us. I know it wasn't his to spend, but he spent it on stuff we did together, and on a ring for me."

"Does that make a difference?" Linda asked.

"I think it does. He made a mistake, but he was so generous. He wasn't doing it for himself. And when he went to Portland and swindled his buddy—he was doing that for me, too, to protect me." She paused. "Am I rationalizing?"

Perhaps, but so what? Debbie was looking for a way to make the best of things, to come out of it happy. "It isn't a simple situation. There are many ways to look at it."

Debbie laughed sadly. "He blew it, he made a terrible mistake, but I love him. To err is human, right?"

She sounded solemn when she continued, "I want to make a life with him. When you love someone, you've got to forgive him. You've got to give him a chance to earn back your trust." She hesitated. "Tell me I'm not crazy."

"You're not crazy."

"Because I don't care about a ridiculous diamond ring." Debbie was laughing again, but her laughter sounded suspiciously like weeping to Linda. "I told him yes, I'm going to marry him."

"I've always wanted a sister," Linda assured her, her vision blurring as her eyes filled with tears.

"Me, too." Debbie's voice wavered, then resumed, stronger than before. "We'll get through this, Gary and I. We'll pay back his friend in Oregon and make things right. Nobody ever said love was easy, you know?"

Linda felt dampness on her cheeks. She mopped her tears with the sleeve of her sweatshirt and managed a crooked smile. "It sure as hell isn't. Go wake up my brother and tell him he doesn't deserve a woman as good as you."

"I tell him that all the time," Debbie said with a watery laugh. "Take care of yourself, Linda. I'll talk to you soon."

Linda said goodbye and hung up. She stood over the sink for a minute, squeezing her eyes shut until the urge to cry had passed. She ought to be thrilled for Debbie—and especially for her brother, who truly didn't deserve a woman as loving and devoted as the one he'd found. Linda ought to be happy for them both. They were going to survive this crisis intact, find strength in it, grow from it.

She would survive her own crisis, too, she vowed, emptying the coffee decanter into her mug and padding across the kitchen floor. Dinah was pacing the entry, and when Linda opened the front door, the cat vaulted outside ahead of her. Linda once again settled into the rocker, sipped the fresh, hot coffee and watched Dinah scamper across the yard, reveling in the unseasonably warm sunlight.

Linda would survive. She would find her own strength. Maybe, someday, she would even learn to forgive Matt for having betrayed her that horrible morning, when he'd revealed his true thoughts, his real feelings, his icy soul. Maybe someday she would forgive Matt for telling her brother that all he wanted was his money and that once he had it he would gladly walk out of their lives forever.

When you loved someone, as Debbie said, you had to forgive him. You had to let him earn back your trust. But Linda didn't want to love Matt, and he certainly didn't give a damn about earning back her trust.

She rocked harder, rejuvenated by a fresh surge of bitterness. She wasn't ready to forgive or trust anybody yet. Least of all herself for falling in love with the wrong man.

The truth was, she had probably fallen in love with Matt Calloway twenty-two years ago, when he'd been one of the fearless foursome. Matt had always been her favorite of Gary's pals. The rock, Gary had claimed. The kind of man you could depend on through thick and thin...

Yeah, sure.

She pushed her toes against the smooth, clean planks of the porch and set the rocking chair in motion. Far away she heard a bleat. The Crockets' sheep must have wandered down the slope to the stone wall to graze. The benign bleating of sheep was a distinctive spring sound, and she tried to get into the spirit of it. She tried to count the pointed daggers of green poking through the soil where she'd planted daffodil bulbs last summer, tried to locate the blue jays chirping garrulously among the trees across the road from her house. Tried to pretend the glorious weather cheered her.

She heard another bleat, and then the low hum of a car engine off to her right—at the fork, she estimated, and then straining up the hill toward her house. Within a minute, the vehicle loomed into view.

It was a nondescript blue hatchback. Shielding her eyes, she noted that the driver was the only person in the car. As it cruised closer, she saw that the driver was a man. A dark-haired man. A dark-haired man with a hawklike nose and...as he slowed at the foot of her driveway she noticed the overnight growth of beard shadowing his rugged jaw. She recognized the blunt, strong fingers on the steering wheel. She recognized the onyx-hard eyes.

The car turned in at her driveway and rambled to a stop on the loose gravel.

She stared at him through the windshield. He returned her stare. It took all her willpower not to scream at him to go away.

Maybe someday she would be ready to forgive him. But not yet. Not when she was still hurting so much.

HE HAD MANAGED to snatch some sleep during the overnight flight east. Even if he hadn't, though, the sheer abundance of adrenaline pumping through his body would have kept him alert and wired.

Hartford was unexpectedly hot. Before driving out of the parking lot at the airport, he'd shed his leather jacket and crew-neck sweater and given serious consideration to digging his sneakers out of his suitcase and donning them in place of the heavy waterproof boots he had on. But Braxton was a good hour and a half north and in the mountains. Maybe it would be colder there.

Into Massachusetts, and the interior of the car began to bake. North along the interstate, exiting west, winding into the Berkshires, and the sun rose higher, grew hotter. He pegged the air temperature at close to seventy degrees. Of course, if he hadn't dressed for winter, he probably would have found another snowstorm in progress when he'd arrived.

He opened the window and let his hair blow in the balmy gusts of wind. The air carried the fragrance of spring, a complex perfume of moist earth, budding leaves and sunshine. He was too realistic to interpret the magnificent weather as an auspicious sign, however. His inability to dress for the season proved he was in the wrong place at the wrong time, reaching for something he could never recapture.

The drive seemed to take forever. Yet when the Villard house loomed into view beyond the familiar curve in the road, he wasn't sure he was ready to face her. He hadn't thought through his approach, hadn't rehearsed what to say. In truth, he wasn't quite certain what he felt. His only hope was that seeing her would enlighten him as to what to do.

She was seated on the clean pine porch, dressed like a waif in faded jeans and an oversize sweatshirt. Her hair was tied off her face with a limp pink ribbon, but a few strands had escaped the ribbon and drizzled softly around her face. The sunlight snagged on them, turning them into filaments of copper.

He had wanted to experience only happiness when he finally saw her, but in fact the sight of her brought on a stabbing pain in the pit of his stomach. If his apology hadn't been enough two weeks ago, why the hell did he think it would be enough now?

As the car neared the mailbox at the end of her driveway, he braked and turned the wheel. There was a flash of black—her cat darting across the lawn. The beast leaped up onto the porch and into Linda's lap, as if positioning itself to defend its mistress against a hostile invasion.

Which might well be how Linda viewed Matt's visit.

After turning off the engine, he remained in the car, studying her through the windshield. Her feet were bare, he noticed, her hands curled around a coffee mug. Not a trace of makeup spoiled the exquisite beauty of her face.

She returned his scrutiny, her mouth set in a straight line, her eyes wide, glinting with facets of green and gold. He felt grungy and rumpled after his overnight flight and his long drive in the stifling morning warmth, and he felt even more grungy and rumpled when he compared himself to her. She was the essence of purity, clarity, truth—everything that mattered.

He recalled the time, more than twenty years ago, when all he had known was mud and blood and terror, when his life had been defined by the agony of shooting at people and being shot at, watching his friends die, trudging through alien forests and villages, skirmishing, trudging back to camp and aching for a way to forget all the horrors he'd seen and done.

And then he would get a letter from a woman. His mother, his sisters, Ellie, even his high school English teacher.... He would cling to that letter, which was more powerful than any drink or drug. He would immerse himself in the words, devouring news of things that had happened to people whose names he didn't know, of yam harvests and hog prices, of presidential politics and the election of the homecoming queen, of peace and prayers and all the goodness that still existed in the universe.

Somewhere in that haven, that heaven on the other side of the world, a girl had been writing letters and dreaming her innocent dreams of hope and family and black stockings.

Now she was a woman, gentle and generous and good in all its meanings. And he was a man who had hurt her.

He gazed at her, rocking slowly on her porch, her cat in her lap and her hair streaming down her back, and wondered how in God's name he would be able to go on living without her.

Throwing back his shoulders, he shoved open the car door and climbed out. She continued rocking, continued watching him, her expression forbidding. She made no move to elude him as he strolled across the lawn toward her, no move to chase him off her property. She only rocked, glowered at him and scratched the fur behind the ears of her cat, who bared its sharp, nasty teeth at him.

He got as far as the bottom step of the porch without saying anything. He searched her face for a clue of how to begin. But her eyes offered no hints, no openings, and her lips curled slightly in distaste. She petted her cat and glared at him.

"The porch looks good," he said.

She lowered her gaze to the fresh boards. "Yes, it does," she agreed. Her honey-sweet voice was enough to stir his body to keen awareness. The sound of it soaked into him, caressed his nerve endings, filled him with an understanding of the kindness and decency she had inside her. He watched the patterns her fingers traced into the cat's scruff and his nervous system quivered, no longer satisfied by thoughts of her goodness. He wanted her fingers on him, moving, touching, unpracticed but blessed with magnificent instincts, her love overcoming her limited experience.

Oh, God, he wanted her. And here they were, on a bright and shiny Saturday morning, discussing her porch.

"I never thanked you properly for fixing it," she was saying. "You did a very nice job."

"Gary helped me."

"According to him, you did most of it."

An awkward silence stretched between them. He eyed the second step, then screwed up his courage and moved that much closer to her. He might have just imagined it, but she seemed to shrink deeper into her chair.

He cleared his throat and said, "I got my first payment from him." Damn. He didn't want to talk about Gary any more than he wanted to talk about the porch.

"He's trying to do the right thing," Linda confirmed, her tone impassive.

"I'm trying to do the right thing, too," Matt said, daring to conquer the last step.

She continued rocking, craning her neck slightly to view him, although she didn't quite meet his eyes. She maintained a steady rhythm with her toes against the boards, but he felt her tension. It emanated from her in palpable waves. It tightened the tendons in her wrists and throat, chased the blood from her knuckles, caused her breath to rasp between her pale lips. He read her tension in the severe green of her eyes, in their glassy coldness.

How different this was from the first time he'd come to her door, when he had identified himself and her eyes had lit up in awe at the discovery that one of the fearless foursome was standing before her. He remembered the way her eyes had softened with reluctant acceptance when he'd produced convincing proof of what her brother had done.

He remembered the way they had grown golden in the moonlight that slanted across her bed, the way they had glowed with desire as he had taken her, with a love as pure and good as everything about this woman. She had known that he was only passing through, that he would have to leave her. She had made no demands, asked nothing of him but the passion of that one night—because she'd loved him.

He hadn't understood that until this moment. He had known that she'd wanted him, and he had satisfied her. But until he'd walked away from her and realized how unbearably empty his life was without her, he hadn't understood that this was about love, real love, the kind of love that kept a man alive long enough to find it, if he was lucky enough to have the chance.

"I love you," he said, the words suddenly coming easily.

"Oh, please," she snapped. "You don't care anything about me. I don't even know why you're here, unless it's to admire your carpentry."

Her scathing tone took him aback. "How can you say that?"

"You walked away and never looked back, Matt. You never even called. You put me out of your mind. That's not love."

"It's fear," he said.

"What were you afraid of?"

"Admitting that I loved you," he said as it all became clear to him. He had started to call her dozens of times, but he'd never gotten more than halfway through her number before hanging up. Why torture them both? he had asked himself each time. He and Linda had their own lives on opposite ends of the country. And anyway, she hated him. Why bother?

He'd been afraid, afraid of hearing her say, "No. Don't come. Stay out of my life. I can't forgive you."

But he'd come, anyway. The fear expanded inside him that she would say those things to his face.

She averted her gaze, focusing on something in the distance. "The money was the important thing," she said bleakly. "All you wanted was to settle a score with Gary. You wanted your money."

"I told you," he argued, clinging to what little composure he had left, "the money was never the main issue. It was trust. Your brother broke my trust. That was all that ever mattered to me, Linda. He broke my trust. And then *you* broke it. And so I broke yours."

"Well, everything is broken now."

"Then we've got to fix it," he said, risking attack by Dinah's lethal teeth and lifting her from Linda's knees.

"A porch starts sagging, and you can either let it collapse or you can fix it. Your brother rips off an old friend, and the only way he can save himself is to fix it." He plucked the mug from Linda's hand and set it on the railing, then gripped her wrists and pulled her out of her chair. "We're both broken, Linda. Can't we at least try to fix it?"

His touch sparked something inside her. She peered up at him, her eyes now damp as the ice in them melted into tears. A faint moan of protest slipped past her lips, and then, refusing her the opportunity to stop him, he covered her mouth with his.

DON'T DO THIS, she thought as her mouth molded to his. She wasn't sure if she was warning herself or him. All she knew was that if she kissed him she would be his forever—and then he would leave.

Don't, she cried silently, her lips softening, parting to admit his tongue, opening wider and luring him deeper. *Don't give in. Don't love him.*

But it was as pointless as telling the ocean not to crash upon the shore, telling a flower not to turn its face to the sun, telling a woman not to listen to her reckless heart. She already loved Matt. It was too late.

She didn't remember walking to the door, but somehow she found herself inside the entry with Matt, kissing him again. He bound her to him with his arms, brought one hand up to the ribbon that held her hair and undid the bow with an efficient tug. As her hair came loose around her face everything came loose inside her—two weeks of pent-up longing, two weeks of anger and sorrow and rage and love.

"Linda...God, so sweet..." His lips browsed up to her forehead, to her temple, to each damp, lowered

eyelid, along her cheekbones and down to her chin.
She turned her head this way and that, wanting his
kisses everywhere. His stubbled jaw scraped the sensitive skin below her ear and she whimpered, not from
pain but from frustration, from fury at her inability
to stop loving him, wanting him.

"I'm sorry," he murmured, pulling back. "I'll
shave. Do you want me to shave?"

The last time he'd said he was sorry, it was because
he had smashed her heart into bits. Perhaps he would
do the same thing this time. Perhaps he would engage
in another sexual romp with her and then desert her
again. Of course, most men didn't fly three thousand
miles for a sexual romp, but then, Matt wasn't most
men.

And he *was* going to desert her. Those three thousand miles separated her life from his, and they
wouldn't simply disappear because she wanted them
to.

Matt had come to Braxton to "fix" things, as he'd
said. A few nails, a little cement, a couple of boards,
and then he'd be on his way.

Too late to stop. She loved him; she would take
whatever he could give and deal with the conse-
quences later.

"Don't shave," she whispered, scraping her fingernails lightly over the dark bristle and savoring his swift
intake of breath.

His lips bore down on hers, hard and demanding,
his tongue sliding deep, stealing her sigh and then re-
treating. "I want you," he groaned, each word re-
shaping his mouth against hers. "In your bed. Or
here." His hands slid down to her hips and drew her
against him, angling her, thrusting against her with an

almost pagan disregard for the fact that they were standing in a bright, sunny foyer, fully clothed. "Right here, right now," he whispered, reaching for the snap of her jeans and yanking it open. "I don't care."

"We should go upstairs," she said, not out of any concern for propriety but simply because her legs were feeling rubbery, swaying beneath her, pressing her to him but doing little in the way of supporting her. She couldn't possibly make love standing up.

"Okay," he agreed, although he made no move toward the stairs. He slid his hands under the loosened waistband of her jeans, under her panties, and cupped her bottom. He rocked her to himself once more, his hardness straining against her, then groaned at the delicious agony he was causing them both.

Slowly, he withdrew his hands and raised them to her waist. "I don't want to let go of you," he said, sounding as helpless as she felt.

She gathered his hands in hers and lifted them to her lips. He groaned again. It dawned on her that he was as helpless as she was. They were both going to wind up with broken hearts from this.

Climbing the stairs seemed too arduous. She ushered him into the living room.

He grabbed a cushion from the sofa, then led her to the thick rug in front of the fireplace. The warm spring sunlight contradicted the stereotypical romantic setting of nighttime, a blazing fire in the hearth, quiet talk and snifters of brandy—but Linda and Matt didn't need that scene. They could make their own setting and weave their own atmosphere of romance.

He dropped the cushion onto the rug, then helped her down until her head was pillowed comfortably against it. He lowered himself into her arms, propping himself up so as not to smother her, and scattered light kisses across her face, nipping and teasing, pretending not to notice the impatient motions of her body beneath his.

She slid her hands between their chests and began to undo the buttons of his shirt.

He stopped kissing her and rose higher, granting her access to the lower buttons. She pulled the shirttails free of his trousers and rolled the cloth over his shoulders. Unable to resist, she let her hands linger there, refamiliarizing herself with the craggy contours of his upper back, the hollows and angles, the hard bones and resilient muscle. With his arms ensnared in his sleeves, he could do little but let her have her way.

"I've never been like this before," she confessed as her hands roved forward into the delectable triangle of hair covering his chest.

"Like what?"

"Aggressive."

He laughed and worked at freeing his arms from his tangled shirt. "Be my guest," he offered, leaning back so she could reach his fly. "I like your kind of aggression."

Encouraged, she managed to work the button free despite the fact that her hands were trembling with excitement. The zipper was more difficult to unfasten, given his aroused state, but other than to shift his hips, he refused to assist her. At last she had it open.

"Don't stop there," he whispered.

She glanced at his cotton briefs, stretched taut over his swollen length, and then raised her eyes to his face. Inhaling deeply, she wedged her fingers inside the elastic and filled her hands with him.

He gasped.

"You make me feel fearless," she said, with a bit of pride and also resignation. If only she had the good sense to fear what was happening, she could defend herself against it. She could spare herself the inevitable heartache.

"You make me feel good." He gasped again as she ran a fingernail lightly over his rigid flesh. "Oh, God, Linda...much too good." He shed his slacks and briefs, then attacked her clothes, pulling off her jeans and panties in one economical motion, then drawing back from her and lifting her off the cushion to rid her of her sweatshirt. That she wore no bra seemed to astound him, and then a slow smile spread across his face. "You're so beautiful," he breathed, sliding downward and taking one flushed nipple into his mouth.

Her body responded to his kiss all over, her muscles clenching, her flesh becoming feverish, burning with expectation. He teased her nipple to a ruby point with his lips and tongue, then turned to the other breast, massaging it with his hand, circling it, chafing it with his fingers, bringing his mouth to the inflamed tip.

Much too good, she thought, agreeing with his assessment. She raked her fingers through his hair, down to his back, along his ribs and forward, able to reach only the upper part of his chest. She wanted to hold him again, to stroke and mold him, to touch him in a way that made him gasp and groan the way he had just moments ago.

But before she could, he moved lower down her body, nibbling a path to her navel and dipping his tongue inside.

She recalled the astonishing way he had made love to her last time, when she'd been warm and drowsy and, afterward, afraid that perhaps she'd dreamed the entire thing. She wasn't dreaming now. After five mugs of coffee, she was thoroughly awake.

He let his fingers float from the bony corners of her pelvis to the softness of the flesh below, caressing her bottom, her outer thighs, the firm muscles along the fronts of her thighs and then the trembling surface of her inner thighs. The quiet persistence of his touch seemed to sap her legs of what little strength they had; she was unable to resist as he moved them apart, as he settled between her knees.

His fingers found her, then his lips, then his tongue, gliding with almost painful precision over her heated flesh and then probing deeper, penetrating, claiming and controlling and wringing every extreme of sensation from her.

Her back arched off the rug and her head sank deep into the cushion, her hands fisting and groping for something to hang on to. She found Matt's upper arms and held tight, grateful for the masculine solidity of them. She clung to him as he conquered her with deft, demoralizing kisses.

"I can't—" she moaned, meaning that she couldn't bear the excruciating pleasure of this, the incinerating blaze, the powerlessness she felt in the grip of his sensual assault. "I can't—" and then her voice dissolved in a breathless cry as her body released itself, sensation washing through her, surging and ebbing in a tidal pulse that left her too weary to move.

Matt drew in a shaky breath and slid up onto her until he could plant his hands on either side of her head and gaze down at her. "I love you," he whispered.

Hearing him utter those precious words revived her. She shifted her tired legs under him, aligning herself with him, and was surprised to discover that he was even more aroused than before. "I love you," she echoed, then wrapped her legs around his waist and drew him in.

She was so ready for him, after what he'd done to her, so damp and open and needing. His thrusts were hard, deep, his passion as urgent as hers. They moved together, in one rhythm, in the same direction, breathing in unison, striving with a seamlessness that couldn't be possible—and yet it was. Matt was a part of her, an extension of her, as she was of him. He was her mythical hero, her friend, a warrior whose wounds she could heal, whose soul she could set free as he set hers free.

He was her lover, and when his body ought to have reached its limit he defied it and continued moving, bringing her along with him, refusing to enter paradise without her.

She was too drained, too exhausted, but he kept thrusting, kept trying, finally reaching down with his hand and igniting her with his touch. And then, at last, he let go.

His hoarse groan registered vaguely on her. She was dazed, utterly spent, her mind a blur of ecstasy and her body blessedly sore and sluggish. She lacked the will to move out from under him.

She remained where she was, her hands wandering tentatively over his sweaty, damp back, down to his hard buttocks and up to his waist again. She didn't want to think. She just wanted to hug him to her while her mind drifted, while rainbows of hope arced between one white cloud of consciousness and the next.

But eventually the clouds burned away, leaving a clear blue stretch of comprehension.

Now they had "fixed" things. Now they had hammered together a peace of sorts.

Now Matt would think things were settled between them, and he would feel all better, and he would go back to Portland.

And she would remain behind. Alone.

CHAPTER FOURTEEN

HE MUST HAVE SENSED the change in her mood. He freed himself from the cradle of her arms, and his departure left her chilled, but she was already cold inside, cold with the knowledge of how much she was about to lose . . . how much she'd already lost.

He peered down at her. "What's wrong?" he whispered.

"Nothing."

He perused her face, unconvinced. "Didn't I tell you you were the worst liar in the world?" he teased, although he sounded solemn. "Something's bothering you."

"No. Really."

"Linda."

She sighed and lowered her eyes. "Nothing you can fix, Matt."

He hooked his finger under her chin and forced her face back to his. "Try me."

She did her best to meet his penetrating gaze. If she was fearless enough to open his shirt, fearless enough to give herself over to his love, then she would be fearless enough to face him now. "You live in Oregon," she said, feeling one tear and then another filter through her lashes and skitter down her temple into her hair.

He ran his finger gently over the delicate arch of her collarbone, traced the downward curve of her lower lip, then stroked her tear-stained cheeks. "Marry me," he said.

She stared at him in disbelief. He couldn't be serious. It was the sort of thing a man was supposed to say afterward, when the woman was upset. He didn't really mean it.

Her silence prompted him to repeat himself. "Come to Portland with me. Marry me."

Her heart began to pound. She thought about Portland, about Braxton, about everything her life had been and what it could be if—

If she married him. If she married the man she'd had a crush on since she was eleven years old. If she turned her back on her home, on her life, and just ran off with him, erased those three thousand miles and married him. If she married the man who had saved her brother's life, and who had wished her brother dead.

If she married Matt Calloway, who had once told her he could promise her nothing more than a night...

"We need social workers in Oregon as much as folks in Massachusetts do," he went on when her silence extended past a minute. "I'm sure you could find work there, if that's worrying you. You wouldn't have to work, of course—I earn enough. But if you wanted to, you'd have plenty of opportunity."

If she married the man who had broken her heart...

"Maybe you'd like to fly out for a while and have a look around," he suggested, his practicality at odds with the fierce darkness of his eyes, the imploring undertone in his voice. "I've got a nice house, but if you don't like it, we can find something else. And you can get a feel for the city."

If she married Matt, whom she loved more than she'd ever thought possible . . .

"I know you're attached to Braxton—"

She laughed.

He looked startled, then mildly insulted.

"I am *not* attached to Braxton," she explained. "I grew up here. I rebelled against my parents here. I spent three years in mourning here." She shook her head, still grinning. "This isn't even my house. It's Gary's."

"It's your home," he reminded her. "Damn it, Linda—I fought hard to make sure Gary wouldn't sell the place as long as you were living in it."

She laughed again, knowing she shouldn't—but after all the suffering he'd put her through, he deserved to suffer a little as well. "Well, gee, Matt—if you fought all that hard, maybe I'd better stay here."

"Linda—"

She'd teased him long enough. "Home is where you make it," she said, all traces of humor gone. "Let Gary sell the house and pay you back what he owes you. Let him get it over with so he can get on with his life."

"You'll come to Portland?"

"If Portland's your home, I'll make it my home, too," she vowed, brushing her fingers lightly over his lips to rub away his frown. "I love you, Matt."

"Then you'll marry me?"

"Yes."

He pulled her to himself and placed an eloquent kiss on her lips. Although it wasn't passionate, the mere warmth of her mouth on his caused him to revive. She

brushed her hand down his side and forward to caress
his swollen flesh. He groaned, then smiled against her
lips. "Don't," he pleaded, drawing her hand away and
settling on the rug beside her, curving his arm around
her. "We're not done talking yet."

Linda didn't think they'd be done talking for at least
the next fifty years. She wove her fingers through his
and let him guide her hand to the relative safety of his
chest, then listened to what he had to say, to what
could possibly be as important as what he'd already
said.

"I need to apologize," he said. "I'm sorry about
what happened."

"Just now?"

"Last time."

She brushed her fingers over his lips to silence him.
"A smart woman taught me something this morning—that when you love someone you've got to give
him a chance to earn back your trust."

"Have I earned it back?"

"I trust you," she swore. "With all my heart."

He tightened his arm around her until she was close
enough to kiss, close enough so he could weave his legs
around hers.

"How do you feel about children?" she asked.

"I'd like some."

"I'm thirty-three," she reminded him.

"And I'm forty-one. We'll have to get started
soon."

She stroked her thumb along the beard-roughened
edge of his jaw. "Remember that birthday present
Gary gave me? That box? It's upstairs." She ran her
finger under his chin, to his throat, to the wiry tangle

of dark hair adorning his chest. "We may have already gotten started."

"Fine with me," he said. She detected no hesitancy in him, no regret, no panic. Just plain, simple pleasure at the prospect of making a baby with her.

"I love you," she said again. It felt so wonderful to speak the words out loud, to admit the truth.

"I love you, too." He leaned toward her as if about to kiss her, then flinched and let out a yelp. Rising to sit, he twisted to look behind him.

Linda propped herself up to see what had made him jump. Dinah was prodding the back of his knee with her cold pink nose. "There's Dinah, too," she remarked.

"What about her?"

"If you want to marry me, she's part of the package."

"You're one of those love-me-love-my-cat types," he grumbled.

"Where I go, she goes."

"She's not going into my bed," he warned.

"Actually, we're in her territory right now," Linda pointed out. "She has every right to barge in on us."

"Then let's get out of her territory."

Linda smiled. "We can go upstairs," she said.

"Yes," Matt agreed. "I've been dreaming about that big brass bed of yours ever since I left Braxton."

"My bed, huh?"

"With you in it. You and me and the door locked."

"Come." Linda stood, slipped her hands into his and pulled him to his feet. "Let's go make your dreams come true."

"You already have," he murmured, lifting her into his arms and carrying her up the stairs.

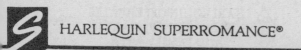

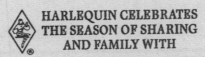

HARLEQUIN CELEBRATES
THE SEASON OF SHARING
AND FAMILY WITH

Harlequin introduces the latest member in its family of
seasonal collections. Following in the footsteps of the popular
My Valentine, Just Married and *Harlequin Historical Christmas
Stories*, we are proud to present FRIENDS, FAMILIES,
LOVERS. A collection of three new contemporary romance
stories about America at its best, about welcoming others into
the circle of love.... Stories to warm your heart ...

By three leading romance authors:

KATHLEEN EAGLE
SANDRA KITT
RUTH JEAN DALE

Available in October, wherever
Harlequin books are sold.

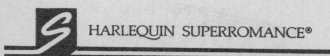
HARLEQUIN SUPERROMANCE®

THE MONTH OF LIVING DANGEROUSLY

**LIVE ON THE EDGE WITH SUPERROMANCE
AS OUR HEROINES BATTLE
THE ELEMENTS AND THE ENEMY**

Windstorm by Connie Bennett pits woman against nature as
Teddi O'Brian sets her sights on a tornado chaser.

In Sara Orwig's *The Mad, the Bad & the Dangerous,* Jennifer
Ruark outruns a flood in the San Saba Valley.

Wildfire by Lynn Erickson is a real trial by fire as Piper Hillyard
learns to tell the good guys from the bad.

In Marisa Carroll's *Hawk's Lair,* Sara Riley tracks
subterranean treasure—and a pirate—in the Costa Rican
rain forest.

Learn why Superromance heroines are more than just the
women next door, and join us for some adventurous reading
this September!

HSMLD

Fifty red-blooded, white-hot, true-blue hunks from every
State in the Union!

Beginning in May, look for MEN MADE IN AMERICA!
Written by some of our most popular authors, these
stories feature fifty of the strongest, sexiest men, each
from a different state in the union!

Two titles available every other month at your favorite
retail outlet.

In September, look for:

DECEPTIONS by Annette Broadrick (California)
STORMWALKER by Dallas Schulze (Colorado)

In November, look for:

STRAIGHT FROM THE HEART by Barbara Delinsky
(Connecticut)
AUTHOR'S CHOICE by Elizabeth August (Delaware)

You won't be able to resist MEN MADE IN AMERICA!

Relive the romance...
Harlequin and Silhouette
are proud to present

by Request

A program of collections of three complete novels by the most
requested authors with the most requested themes. Be sure to
look for one volume each month with three complete novels by
top name authors.

In June: **NINE MONTHS** Penny Jordan
                            Stella Cameron
                            Janice Kaiser

**Three women pregnant and alone. But a lot can
happen in nine months!**

In July: **DADDY'S**   Kristin James
           HOME   Naomi Horton
                            Mary Lynn Baxter

**Daddy's Home... and his presence is long
overdue!**

In August: **FORGOTTEN**   Barbara Kaye
           PAST   Pamela Browning
                            Nancy Martin

**Do you dare to create a future if you've forgotten
the past?**

Available at your favorite retail outlet.

Calloway Corners

In September, Harlequin is proud to bring readers four involving, romantic stories about the Calloway sisters, set in Calloway Corners, Louisiana. Written by four of Harlequin's most popular and award-winning authors, you'll be enchanted by these sisters and the men they love!

MARIAH by Sandra Canfield
JO by Tracy Hughes
TESS by Katherine Burton
EDEN by Penny Richards

As an added bonus, you can enter a sweepstakes contest to win a trip to Calloway Corners, and meet all four authors. Watch for details in all Calloway Corners books in September.